# THE BURNING CHASE

# Also by Cap Daniels

**The Chase Fulton Novels Series**
Book One: *The Opening Chase*
Book Two: *The Broken Chase*
Book Three: *The Stronger Chase*
Book Four: *The Unending Chase*
Book Five: *The Distant Chase*
Book Six: *The Entangled Chase*
Book Seven: *The Devil's Chase*
Book Eight: *The Angel's Chase*
Book Nine: *The Forgotten Chase*
Book Ten: *The Emerald Chase*
Book Eleven: *The Polar Chase*
Book Twelve: *The Burning Chase*
Book Thirteen: *The Poison Chase*
Book Fourteen: *The Bitter Chase*
Book Fifteen: *The Blind Chase*
Book Sixteen: *The Smuggler's Chase* (Winter 2021)

**The Avenging Angel – Seven Deadly Sins Series**
Book One: *The Russian's Pride*
Book Two: *The Russian's Greed*
Book Three: *The Russian's Gluttony* (Fall 2021)

**Stand-alone Novels**
*We Were Brave*

**Novellas**
*The Chase Is On*
*I Am Gypsy*

# THE
# BURNING CHASE
**CHASE FULTON NOVEL #12**

## CAP DANIELS

ANCHOR WATCH
PUBLISHING
** USA **

The Burning Chase
Chase Fulton Novel #12
Cap Daniels

Published by:

ANCHOR WATCH
PUBLISHING
** USA **

13 Digit ISBN: 978-1-951021-04-7
Library of Congress Control Number: 2020945826
Copyright © 2020 Cap Daniels – All Rights Reserved

Cover Design: German Creative

Printed in the United States of America

# Dedication

*This book is dedicated to...*

*Pat Wood aka "My Favorite"*

*Sometimes it seems like I've been writing for a hundred years, and other times, it feels as though I started only yesterday. When this magic carpet ride began, I spent a great deal of energy building my mailing list so I could stay in touch with readers who enjoy my work. I put out a cry for attention on Facebook and offered some silly prize for the 100th person who signed up for my massive mailing list. (I think I had around forty people on the list back then.)*

*Pat Wood, a wonderfully whimsical, delightful young lady from one of the grooviest-named cities in America, Punta Gorda, Florida, was that 100th sign-up I so desperately wanted. We've added a few thousand names to the list since then, but I'll always treasure hitting that century mark. Little did I know just how important Pat would become to my writing career and in my personal life.*

*Not only was Pat the 100th sign-up, she quickly volunteered to become a member of the tiny team of beta readers who read my manuscripts before anyone else on Earth. That small group of amazing people has had more influence on this wild adventure than most readers could ever imagine. I playfully began to refer to Pat as "My*

*Favorite Reader."* This spawned more than a little good-hearted banter within the beta team and has become an inside joke all of us enjoy dearly.

*Aside from being an incredibly valuable member of the beta team, I've come to love Pat as if she were my crazy aunt. (You know . . . the one you love the most and will let you eat all the cookies you want.) The friendship we've built is treasured beyond measure, and I'll never be able to adequately thank her for being honest when it stung, kind when I needed it, and always a beautiful addition to my already blessed life.*

*I hope we get to create a thousand more books together, but more than that, I hope we get to spend a thousand more days together celebrating our mutual love of being alive. I love you, my dear friend.*

# Special Thanks To:

*My Remarkable Editor:*
*Sarah Flores—Write Down the Line, LLC*
*www.WriteDowntheLine.com*

*This little section has become tired and redundant, so I thought I'd mix it up a little and tell the truth about Sarah this time. Here's how it really is: Sarah is loud, stubborn, and she hurts my feelings. I've stomped around my office saying bad words and calling her terrible names more times than I can remember. She makes me think things like: Why does she hate my writing so much? Why does she always make me change the parts I love the most? Why is she so mean to me?*

*Through thirteen novels and two novellas, I've learned the answer to all of those questions. The answer isn't simple, but it's important. Sarah saw a writer inside me when there was no evidence on the surface to support her vision. She believed I was always capable of better prose, better narration, better dialogue, and better truth in what I write. She hurt my feelings because they needed to be hurt. She redlined the garbage I wrote because it was garbage. She devoted countless hours dragging the writer, who lived deep inside of me, to the surface. She cared enough about my career to be loud and hurtful and aggressive when those were exactly the tools necessary to make me better. But that's not all she is. She's also kind, supportive, en-*

*couraging, and the perfect editor for a stubborn, arrogant, grouchy writer like me. (Just don't tell her I said anything nice about her.)*

*I'll forever be grateful for everything she is and for every tool she uses to make every line I write a little better than the last one. If you enjoy my work, thank Sarah for pushing me so hard to live up to the high standards she—and you—expect.*

*The Burning Chase*
**CAP DANIELS**

# Chapter 1

## *Answers*

My amphibious Cessna Caravan had her limits; of these, speed was her greatest. She would fly with almost anything I could shove through the doors. She could land in seas that would unnerve most powerboaters, but when I demanded that she be a time machine, she failed miserably. Pushing her as hard as I was willing, she made 192 knots with the help of a fifteen-knot tailwind from Saint Augustine to my home in Saint Marys, Georgia.

As I approached Bonaventure Plantation from the south, the black smoke rising into the sky sickened me beyond description. Bonaventure had been the home of my mother's family for two hundred years. I had inherited the antebellum mansion and accompanying acreage from my great uncle, Judge Bernard Henry Huntsinger, when he claimed his great reward after nine decades on Earth. The manor and the two centuries of life that still creaked inside its woodwork and walls were succumbing to the flames lapping into the afternoon sky in defiance of the deluge of water the Saint Marys Fire Department poured onto the inferno.

The North River bounded the plantation to the east, and in less than five minutes, would be my runway. The billowing smoke roared the deafening proclamation of wind speed and direction and forced me to run the before-landing-checklist—the blue one, since this would be a water landing.

Landing gear . . . up.

Propeller . . . high RPM.

Area . . . clear of obstructions.

Water rudders . . . up.

The irresistible need to focus on the fire consuming my home made it all but impossible to fly the approach as I'd been taught and practiced hundreds of times. I hit the water with far too much speed and skipped like a flat stone. Spooling the turbine up in time to arrest my hop was mechanically impossible. All that remained was doing everything in my power to keep the bows of the pontoons from submarining when the airplane finally settled back to the water's surface.

When the contact came, it was jarring for both plane and pilot, but the pontoons, bows and all, stayed on the surface. The excess energy I'd carried into the landing was absorbed by the collision with the surface, and the Caravan settled into the water just as she'd been designed to do.

*Aegis*, my fifty-foot sailing catamaran, as well as the eighty-foot Mark V patrol boat, should've been moored at the Bonaventure dock, but they were missing. Normally, their absence would've left me consumed by both questions and immeasurable concern for where my boats had gone; however, the collection of fire engines, men clad in bunker gear, and suction hoses trailing into the river held my attention and made the material possessions of my boats nearly meaningless.

I hit the dock with my portside pontoon almost as aggressively as I'd struck the surface of the North River. The outgoing tide powered a current of at least two knots, and my anxiety to get my feet on the ground provided far more than adequate energy to stick the float to the dock. My headset was lying on the floor beside my foot, my harness was thrown across my shoulder, and my hatch was open long before the collision. When I hit the floating dock some three hundred feet from what remained of my home, the scorching heat lapped at my skin and left me shielding my face against the onslaught.

Exposing my airplane to such ravages was irrational and cruel, so I shoved the portside pontoon with all my strength to unpin her from the dock against the relentless current. I finally wrestled the seaplane around the end of the dock and set her free in the outgoing current. She would come to rest in the marsh, and if she didn't, she'd drift into Cumberland Sound and find her way aground.

Instead of watching my beloved airplane disappear downstream, I sprinted from the dock toward the agonizing sight of my home as the ravaging flames devoured the structure. As if he were a linebacker, a fireman in full regalia hit me from my blind side. Instinct, training, and adrenaline combined to prepare my body for the coming collision with the ground. I emptied my lungs, lowered my chin, and embraced my attacker. When our motion stopped, I was on top, swinging an angry fist toward my assailant's head. His mask and helmet took the blow, but in doing so, left his head and went tumbling across the yard. I recoiled to send a second blow to his now unprotected head, but before I could unleash the fist, the man yelled, "Sir! You can't be here! It's not safe."

I retained enough logical thought in my panicked mind to reconcile his warning with his uniform. "This is my home!" I bellowed.

He threw his arms up in front of his face like a battered boxer. "Yeah, I know, but it's not safe. Let me take you around front to see the chief."

I stumbled to my feet and offered him a hand. He ignored me and crawled upright in his heavy rubber boots. With a look of disgust, he swung a hand to reclaim his helmet. "Come with me, and stay on my left. The chief is out by the road."

Everything inside of me wanted to run into the house and save anything I could grab, but doing so would not only result in my death, it could also potentially endanger the firefighters who would, undoubtedly, come in after me.

At the fireman's insistence, we gave the flaming house a wide berth to the south. The front yard had been obscured by smoke on my approach, but as the scene unfolded in front of me, it looked like chaos of the highest order. Four ambulances rested on the crushed shell drive, and a team of paramedics administered oxygen to an exhausted fireman.

One man sat on the bumper of an ambulance while two medics treated his wounds. He was covered with soot, and his clothes were badly burned.

The fire chief grabbed my sleeve. "Are you Chase Fulton?"

"Yeah. This is my house. What happened?" I split my attention between the burnt man and my home.

The chief shook me. "Look at me. There's no one else in the house."

"What do you mean, no one *else*? There shouldn't have been anyone in there at all."

He motioned with his chin toward the man on the bumper of the ambulance. "Just him. We pulled him out."

"Who is he? And what was he doing in my house?"

"That remains to be seen, but he's hurt. . . ."

I jerked away from the chief, drew my pistol, and charged the ambulance. Whoever the man was, he was going to answer my questions, regardless of how badly he was hurt.

A bevy of police cars lined the driveway beyond the ambulances, so putting a bullet in the man's skull wouldn't end well for me. However, every cop in the state of Georgia couldn't stop me from getting to the man. If he was inside my house, he probably started the fire, and that was enough to justify anything I needed to do to get answers.

The closer I got to the ambulance, the more damaged the man appeared to be. The medics had an oxygen mask over his face and an IV in each arm. The flesh of his upper body, face, and arms was scorched black, and his hair was burnt to the skin.

When I was five steps from the man, I watched his gaze flash to the pistol in my right hand and then to meet my eyes. There was no doubt my expression said I was coming for answers and that I wouldn't tolerate anything less than the absolute truth.

As I covered the remaining ten feet to the ambulance, the world moved in slow motion. The burnt man shoved one of the medics away and grasped the oxygen mask. The medic looked over his shoulder at me, and terror filled his eyes at the sight of my raised pistol. The remaining medic spun on his heel and fell to the ground in disbelief at my threatening approach.

As I opened my mouth to demand the first answer, Singer's voice emerged from beneath the burnt flesh of the wounded man. "Chase, I saved your family Bible."

## Chapter 2
### *Everything Else*

The dichotomy that was Jimmy "Singer" Grossmann was almost impossible to describe. On the outside, he was the deadliest sniper I've ever known. I've seen him make over a hundred life-or-death shots that most snipers would've never attempted. Escaping his crosshairs alive is not done. Beneath that lethal exterior, however, lives the soul of the most faithful man of God on Earth today. His nickname, Singer, was earned on the battlefield, as he never failed to sing Southern Baptist hymns as he squeezed the trigger of his deadly implement. He was the choir director and the greatest financial benefactor of his church, supporting more charities than everyone else I knew.

To see my friend and brother-in-arms burned so badly left me sickened to my core, and suddenly, the raging fire behind me meant nothing. I fell to my knees in front of the man who risked his life to save the Bible that had been handed down through two hundred fifty years of my family and finally entrusted to me.

Realizing I still held my pistol, I holstered the weapon and reached to find an unburned spot on his arms to rest my hands. "I'm sorry I drew on you. I didn't know it was you. I would've never . . ."

He shook his head and took another breath from the oxygen mask. "Do I look that bad?"

I bit my lip. "You're burnt badly, my friend, but these guys are going to take good care of you."

I turned to the paramedics. "I'm sorry I scared you. I thought he might be the arsonist."

"It's okay," said the shorter of the two medics. "I didn't know what was happening, but I'm glad you didn't start shooting. There's a bunch of cops out there who are still a little jumpy from the sniper thing a couple weeks ago."

I pointed toward Singer. "You may not realize it, but you're working on the man who silenced those shooters."

The second medic looked down at Singer. "*You're* the sniper?"

Singer shrugged and took another breath. "I just got off a couple lucky shots. That's all."

"Two shots in less than two seconds from half a mile away ain't exactly what I'd call lucky," the medic said. "You're not burned as bad as it looks. Most of this is soot and smoke, but we're taking you to the hospital. The doc will make the call whether to send you to the burns center, but I'm betting most of it's limited to first degree."

"I'm having a little trouble breathing," Singer said, "but it doesn't really hurt. I think I'll be fine once I cough up the smoke."

I shook my head. "I don't think that's how it works, but I'm glad you're not in pain."

He tried to smile. "I'll just rub some dirt on it and soldier on. Is Hunter back yet?"

"Back from where?" I asked.

"He was moving the boats."

"That explains why they're not at the dock."

Singer grimaced and let out a muffled groan.

The older paramedic reached for an orange pouch. "I knew it was coming. I'm going to give you a little something to help mask that pain. Are you ready to get on the gurney now so we can get you to the ER?"

He squeezed his eyes closed and nodded his wordless submission.

"Are you allergic to morphine, sir?"

Singer didn't answer, so the paramedic looked at me.

I said, "No known allergies. He's not taking any prescription medication. He's in perfect health, and his blood type is A positive."

"How do you know all of that, sir?"

"He and I were in the service together . . . sort of."

"Sort of? What does that mean?"

"It's a long story," I said, "but I have a medical power of attorney." I glanced over my shoulder at the flames. "At least, I *did* have one. It was in my safe."

The paramedic's eyes lit up. "Oh, your buddy told the firemen about the vault. They've been pouring water on it constantly since they got here. They don't want the ammo to cook off in there, so they're keeping it as cool as possible."

"I guess he took care of everything," I mumbled under my breath.

The medic reached inside the ambulance, pulled my family Bible from the floor, and handed it to me. "Yeah, he did. Now, if you'll excuse us, we need to get him to the ER. Are you okay?"

I stood and stepped back. "Yeah . . . yeah, I'm fine. Just take care of him, and tell the doctors to do whatever is necessary. I'll be there soon to sign whatever they need."

Without another word, the medics strapped Singer to the gurney, closed the ambulance doors, and sped off with lights blazing and sirens screeching.

I turned to watch the antebellum mansion succumb to the ravages of the fire. Watching it burn drove daggers through my heart and left me empty and broken.

The fire chief approached with a radio in his hand. "Mr. Fulton, at this point, it's going to be a total loss. Everyone is out of the house, and there's no danger to surrounding structures. You have to make the decision. Do you want us to keep fighting the fire, or should we let it burn to the foundation?"

I alternated staring between the fire and the chief, thoroughly incapable of answering his question.

"Do you want us to keep fighting the fire, Mr. Fulton?"

The longer the firemen fought the blaze, the more likely it was that more of them would end up in the back of an ambulance like Singer, so I set my eyes on the ground between my feet. "Let it burn."

He keyed his microphone and gave the order. "Keep the water on the vault, but pull off the main house."

My knees felt like useless bags of wet sand, and I surrendered. Sitting on the grass and watching my home collapse beneath the ravages of the heat left me feeling exactly as I'd felt when I learned my parents and sister had been killed. I was plummeting into a pit of unadulterated loneliness and utter disbelief.

"What happens next?" I whispered to myself.

"When it cools enough, the arson investigation team will pore over the remains for evidence of foul play. Do you know of anyone who would want to harm you, Mr. Fulton?"

I found his questions absurd and broke into uncontrollable laughter. When I finally caught my breath, I said, "You might start with Vladimir Putin. I piss him off on a regular basis, but he's not the only name on the list."

The chief pulled a small, spiral-bound pad from his pocket and scratched a note inside. I hoped he hadn't written Putin's name on the pad, but something told me he'd taken down every word I'd said.

Before I could make a bigger fool of myself, Hunter knelt beside me. "Hey. Are you okay?"

I looked up at my partner. "My house is burning to the ground. Singer is on his way to the hospital. I'm everything but okay."

He laid his hand on my shoulder. "I'm sure Singer will be fine, and we can replace the house. Have you called Penny?"

"What am I going to tell her?"

"She has to know, Chase. I'll call her if you want me to do it."

"No, I'll call her. I just need a minute to gather my wits. This is not how I expected my day to go."

He didn't say another word; instead, he sat on the grass beside me in silent support as my heart broke a little more with every piece of falling debris.

It may have taken an hour, or perhaps a thousand years, for the fire to reduce my home to a smoldering pile of history. Hunter and I sat through every agonizing second of the ordeal. He's seen me at my best, lying in the dirt with bullets flying over our heads, and after the time spent on my front yard with the flames scorching our flesh, he'd seen me at my worst. Something I had done, some action—or inaction—I'd taken resulted in the home that my ancestors built, loved, and protected for centuries succumbing to destruction. All that remained were the two stone chimneys, the foundation walls, and the vault. Everything else had turned to ash.

Finally, Hunter said, "You have to call Penny. It's only right."

"I can't."

He lowered his head. "I understand. I'll make the call."

I caught his forearm. "No. I'll go find her. I need to tell her in person. Can you manage this for me until I can get back from L.A.?"

He nodded. "Of course. I'll take care of everything."

* * *

At the information desk, a candy striper said, "Mr. Grossmann has been moved up to room four-fifteen. You can take the elevator just down this—"

Without listening to the remainder of her speech, I bounded up the stairs quicker than any elevator could've carried me. Singer's room was three doors past the nurses' station, and I didn't take the time to ask permission or to knock.

The second stride inside the room brought relief I never expected to feel. My friend, sniper, and priest sat relatively upright in the hospital bed with sporadic bandages on his upper body, but he was clean, bright-eyed, and even smiling.

The first words out of his mouth made the smile make perfect sense. He held up a gray, cylindrical device with a small red button on top. "It's a magic morphine button."

I'd never seen him take a drink of alcohol, and I'd certainly never seen him stoned on narcotics, but the scene made me smile for the first time in hours.

*We should all be so lucky.*

I pulled up a chair beside his bed and took a seat. "So, if you're sober enough, I'd love to hear what the doctor had to say."

He grinned a childish expression of pharmaceutical delight. "First dah-dah-degree on twenty-five cents of my body, and seconds on tens."

I tried to hide my laughter. "Oh, really? Twenty-five cents, and seconds on tens, huh? That sounds . . . perfectly reasonable."

He nodded in an exaggerated demonstration of agreement. "Yep, that me too."

I gave up and let the laughter come. It felt good and made Singer lose himself in uproarious laughter of his own.

When I could speak, I said, "Does that mean you don't have to go to the burns hospital?"

He shrugged. "Sure."

I pulled a pad from the bedside table and wrote, *I've gone to see Penny in California and tell her about the fire. If you need anything, I'm just a phone call away, and Hunter is always available.*

I slid the pad back onto the table. "I left you a note right here so you'll remember, but I'm going to L.A. to tell Penny about the fire. I'll be back in a couple of days. Keep pressing that button, my friend. I'm glad you're going to be all right."

The smile left his face. "It's good Penny wasn't here."

I took his hand. "Yes, it's very good. I know you're a little goofy on the pain meds right now, but I want you to know how much it means to me that you'd risk your life to save my family's Bible."

He smiled. "Everything else is just stuff, and I've gots somes money if you need it to buy more stuffs."

"Thank you, Singer. I don't need stuff when I have friends like you. Get some rest, and read the note when you wake up."

I left the hospital with every intention of flying my Mustang to L.A., but passing the mirrored glass of the front of the hospital changed my mind. I looked like a man who'd been dragged through Hell backward.

I dialed my phone, and Mongo answered on the first ring. "Chase, are you all right? I just got off the phone with Hunter."

I sighed. "Yeah, I'm okay, but I need to get to L.A. Is that charter service of yours still available?"

"I'll give them a call for you," he said. "If they're not available, I'll find someone who is. When do you want to leave?"

I took one more glance at the man in the mirrored glass. "I need a shower, but I want to be in California tonight."

# Chapter 3
## *Comfortably and Confidently*

I found Hunter back at Bonaventure Plantation. "Thank you for staying. I don't really know what to do next."

He motioned toward the vault that was still standing, relatively unharmed on the exterior. "One of the first things we have to do is get that gear into another lockup. I've got a big safe at my place, but it'll never hold all that stuff."

"That's why I need you," I said. "I'm in no condition to make decisions like that. Can you make some arrangements with the armory on the Navy base or maybe the vault at the police department?"

He nodded. "Of course. I'll take care of it."

"Thank you. I appreciate that. Singer said you moved the boats. Are they safe?"

He motioned for me to follow him. "They're fine. The Mark V is up at the base, and *Aegis* is moored down at the waterfront. I also pulled the Caravan out of the weeds and anchored her in the sound."

I patted him on the shoulder. "What would I do without you?"

"Chase down your own boats and airplanes, I guess. Speaking of airplanes, we should probably go get the Caravan before the sun goes down."

"Let's do that," I said. "If you'll drop me off, I'll fly it back to the airport and put it in the hangar. I wish I could put *Aegis* in the hangar with her."

We mounted the rigid hull inflatable boat and motored downstream. The Caravan lay at anchor behind Cumberland Island, protected from the wind and major marine traffic. I stepped from the RHIB onto the plane's pontoon and pulled up the anchor.

Hunter backed the RHIB away from the pontoon. "I'll get *Aegis* and bring her back up to the Bonaventure dock and then meet you at the airport."

The Pratt & Whitney PT6 turbine whistled to life as I introduced the fuel and the temperatures came up. After checking for vessel traffic, I set takeoff power and pulled the yoke into my lap. With the airplane nearly empty except for my two hundred twenty pounds, the floats came out of the water quickly and accelerated across the smooth surface of Cumberland Sound. I lifted the starboard float first to break the grip of the glassy water, and seconds later, the portside float was airborne. I climbed over the sound to five hundred feet and made a pass across the smoldering remains of my home.

Perhaps the house had never truly been my home. It was the home of generations before me, but those families weren't what I am. They were tobacco farmers and pecan producers. The men fought when their country called on them to do so, but when the wars ended, they returned to the plantation and continued life as they'd known for decades.

As I studied the ruins of the grand old structure, I realized, perhaps, the blackened, scorched earth beneath me may not have been ruins at all. It may have been the end of an era and the beginning of another two-hundred-year tradition of honor. Perhaps what I would build on the foundations laid by my ancestors would be the core of my service to my country. What I would build would not be a plantation-style home at the center of agricultural production, but a place from which generations of warriors could train, operate, and defend the freedoms my family and millions of other families had fought and died to build for me. Bonaventure—or *Good Fortune*—would become The Preserve.

With my mind clearer than it had been in hours, I kissed the runway with precision and taxied to my hangar. Hunter hadn't arrived yet, so I towed the Caravan inside and took advantage of the shower to wash away the grime, dread, and anxiety I'd worn since Singer called to tell me my home was ablaze. By the time I'd finished and dressed, Hunter was securing the enormous hangar doors.

When he saw me emerge from the head, he said, "Where's your phone?"

I patted the pockets of my clean clothes and found nothing. "I don't know. Maybe it's in my dirty pants. Why?"

"Mongo's been trying to call you. He said the charter is on its way."

I rummaged through my dirty clothes and found my wallet, phone, and keys. Four of the keys on the ring were no longer of any value. The locks they'd opened lay in ashes, so I pulled them from the ring and watched them fall into the oversized metal trash can.

"Here it is," I said. "Mongo was arranging a charter flight to L.A. so I could talk to Penny."

"Yeah, he told me. I still think you should call her, though, just to let her know you're coming. You don't even know where she is, do you?"

I studied the polished concrete floor of the hangar. "I just know she went to L.A., but if I call to say I'm coming out, she'll know something's wrong. I'll call her once I get on the ground in California."

He scratched his chin. "I'm not suggesting this is a good idea, but I'm sure Skipper could find her, no matter where she is."

"Has anyone called Skipper about the fire?"

"I don't think so," he said. "I haven't called her, and I don't re-member Singer doing it."

I took a seat on the couch in the corner of the hangar and dialed Skipper's number in Silver Spring, Maryland.

She answered with her usual cheery demeanor. "Hey, Chase. How did Earl take the news about being the guardian of eight million dollars' worth of gold?"

Less than eight hours earlier, I had been in Saint Augustine explaining the success of my most recent mission to Earl at the End. My team and I recovered almost two thousand pounds of gold bars Earl's husband stashed in the mountains of East Tennessee before he died in a plane crash in Central America. Singer had cut my meeting short with the shocking news of the fire, and I'd immediately flown home.

"She was a little shocked, but pleased," I said. "But that's not the reason I'm calling. Something terrible has happened. . . ."

"Is everyone all right?"

"Yes, we're all okay, except for Singer. There was a fire at Bonaventure. We lost the house, and Singer got burned retrieving our family Bible."

She gasped. "Chase, I'm so sorry. What caused the fire?"

"I don't know yet, but the arson investigator will get to work as soon as it cools enough to touch."

"Does Clark know?" she asked.

"No, not yet, but I guess I should call him next."

She grunted. "I hate to say this, but if it was arson, and if it has something to do with our work, Clark definitely needs to know right away. He'll probably send an investigator of his own."

"I hadn't thought of that," I admitted. "I'll call him now. In the meantime, I need a favor."

"Anything. Just name it."

"I need you to find Penny. I'm flying to L.A. in a few minutes. I don't want to tell her on the phone, and I need to know where she is. Can you do that?"

"Sure I can. I'll send her location to your phone with updates when she's on the move. Does she know you're coming?"

THE BURNING CHASE · 27

"No, I want to tell her about the house in person, so I haven't called her."

"I guess that makes sense. Again, I'm sorry about the house, but I'm glad you're all right. Before you go, tell me about Singer."

"He's in the hospital here in Saint Marys. It's mostly first-degree burns, apparently over twenty-five percent of his body. He was a little messed up on pain killers when I went to see him, but he looks good."

"Okay," she said, "I'll keep checking on things. Let me know if you need anything from me."

"I will. Thanks, Skipper."

Clark answered quickly. "Yeah, I know, and I'm on it. There's an FBI arson team en route from Quantico. They'll be boots-on-the-ground when the sun comes up tomorrow. I've already spoken with the fire marshal and instructed him to stay off the property until the FBI boys are finished."

"You must've spoken with Hunter," I said.

"Yeah, he did the right thing and called me as soon as things started settling down. I'm sorry about the house, Chase. Have you talked to Penny?"

"No, I'm waiting for a charter to pick me up now. I'm headed to L.A. to tell her in person."

"That's a good plan," he said, "but you should've called me for the charter. I would've taken care of it."

"Mongo set it up, but thanks."

He cleared his throat. "I know this isn't the best time, but speaking of Mongo . . . where do you think Anya is?"

Anya Burinkova, the former Russian SVR officer turned American defector, had vanished immediately after completing our mission in Saint Augustine. Her weapons of choice—custom-made fighting knives and pistols—and some of her clothes had vanished, along with her. She and Mongo, our resident giant, shared the house in Athens, Georgia, that had once belonged to my mentor and Anya's father, Dr. Robert "Rocket" Richter.

"I don't know," I said, "but I don't have time to think about that right now. I've got enough on my plate."

He groaned. "Yeah, I know, but she's going to turn up, and when she does, God only knows how many dead bodies are going to be in her wake."

I shook him off. "Again, I can't think about that right now."

His tone exuded anxiety. "Anyway, keep me posted and let me know if you need anything. I'll brief you on what the FBI boys learn."

"I will. And hey, one more thing. Do you think we'll need security on the property until all this calms down?"

"That's probably a good idea. I'll take care of it. Let me know how it goes in L.A."

I heard the whine of twin jet engines taxi to the ramp outside my hangar.

"I think your ride's here," Hunter said.

I shoved two pairs of cargo pants and a couple of shirts from the hangar locker into a bag and hit the door.

The fuel truck was parked beside the Citation before the engines had spun to a stop. A uniformed pilot with three stripes on his epaulets opened the door and deployed the stairs.

I bounded up the steps and took the pilot's offered hand. "I'm Chase. I take it you're my ride to L.A."

"Yes, sir, but we can't make it nonstop. We'll get fuel in Santa Fe, unless you'd prefer someplace else."

"No, Santa Fe is fine. Whatever's fastest."

We blasted into the western sky and leveled off at forty thousand feet. I was a terrible passenger and insisted the pilots keep the cockpit door open so I could see everything that was happening. I would've rather been sitting in one of their seats up front than my plush leather throne in the back.

The fuel stop in Santa Fe was a *quick turn* by any definition of the phrase. The captain never left the cockpit, but the first officer came back and said, "We have to make a decision on where you want to land."

I pulled out my phone and checked Skipper's latest update on my wife's location. I held up the phone for the pilot. "I don't know anything about Southern California, but that's where I want to be as soon as possible."

He took the phone from my hand and studied the display. "We'll go to Bob Hope Airport in Burbank."

I didn't time the stop, but we were back at cruising altitude before I finished the drink the flight attendant insisted I have. The extravagance of two pilots, a flight attendant, and a twenty-million-dollar jet for one person was more than I could rationalize, but it was worth the expense to get to Penny as quickly as possible.

The main landing gear chirped, and the thrust reversers roared. When the first officer opened the cabin door, I saw a black Range Rover at the tip of the wing with the right rear door standing open.

I took the stairs two at a time and then looked back up at the pilot. "You'll bill me for this, right?"

He waved. "It's all taken care of, Mr. Fulton. We'll be waiting here when you return, and we'll take you and Mrs. Fulton back to the East Coast."

I nodded and turned for the Range Rover. A young man who looked like he'd been sent over from central casting held the door for me. "Where to, sir?"

I fumbled for my phone again and pointed at the message from Skipper. "I need to go there."

He took the phone from my hand and studied it carefully. "No problem, sir. I'll have you there in twenty minutes."

I couldn't see the speedometer, but unless the speed limits in California are twice what they are in Georgia, he was in danger of a ticket every minute of the trip. His estimate wasn't even close. We pulled into the driveway of a three-story glass behemoth of a house in fourteen minutes.

I shoved a hundred-dollar bill into the driver's hand. "Wait here. We'll probably be leaving soon."

Without looking at the bill, he said, "Yes, sir."

I rang the doorbell at the top of a winding stone staircase, and an elegantly dressed young lady opened the door. "Good evening, sir. May I help you?"

I pushed past her and across a marble foyer that was bigger than most houses in Saint Marys. The assembly of people in the sunken area off the foyer was a collection of elitist-looking characters I detested on sight. I believed finding my six-foot-tall beautiful wife would be easy, but every woman in the room met that description.

When I finally spotted her hair, unruly and windblown, I tunneled through the throngs of people holding champagne flutes and hors d'oeuvres. I was out of my element and determined to get my wife alone so I could break the most horrific news imaginable.

What I didn't expect to see was the hand of a man twice my age resting comfortably and confidently on Penny's butt.

# Chapter 4
## *Party Pooper*

Subconsciously, I measured the distance between myself and the hand resting on my wife. It was four and a half strides. I took the half stride first and accelerated through the next three. As my foot landed between the man's heels, I grasped his wrist and drove my left knee into the back of his leg. His highball glass crashed to the floor an instant after he did.

"I suppose no one ever took the time to teach you any manners, asshole, but this is lesson number one. Don't ever put your hands on my wife, even when you think I'm three thousand miles away."

Gasps of shock and disbelief filled the room, and Penny spun to see me pinning her aggressor to the floor. "My God, Chase! What are you doing here?"

Applying a little more pressure to the offending wrist than necessary, I looked up at her. "I'm teaching etiquette class at the moment, but that's not why I'm here. We need to talk."

She scowled. "Take your hands off him, and stop acting like a barbarian."

The toe of my boot reminded him which part of his anatomy he wouldn't be using that night as I returned to my feet and reached for my wife's hand.

She yanked her hand away from mine as if I were a pit viper. "Don't touch me. Why did you have to come in here and embarrass me like this?"

I shot a glance at the whimpering jackass at my feet. "Penny, he was groping you."

She narrowed her eyes. "Yes, and he was a second away from getting a drink thrown in his face. I didn't need you to race in here to protect me."

We'd become the center of attention, and I didn't like it. I closed my eyes and swallowed the bile in my throat. "Let's go somewhere and talk. Something terrible has happened."

She shook her head. "No, Chase. A jerk got a little handsy, and I was going to take care of it. That doesn't qualify as something terrible."

I leaned in to within inches of her ear. "No, Penny, not him. Something terrible has happened at Bonaventure."

Her eyes turned from anger-filled slits to orbs of concern. She grabbed my hand, gathered her dress around her thighs, and turned for an alcove, leading me through a doorway and into the room beyond. It was decorated in some sort of ultra-modern fashion with chrome and glass everything. The space looked like something from a low-budget movie set.

I pressed the door closed behind us. "You'll want to sit down for this."

Instead of sitting, she planted both hands on her hips and stared at me. "What is it? What is this terrible thing that you had to come all the way out here just to embarrass me for, huh? What is it?"

"Penny, I didn't come here to embarrass you, but that guy—"

"Forget about that guy," she demanded. "I already told you I had it under control. Clearly, you can't see how important this is to me. I've waited for this moment for half my life, Chase. Now, you've made me look like your property . . . like a woman with a jealous, violent asshole for a husband. Do you have any idea what—"

"Penny, our house burned to the ground today."

For a long moment, she lost all expression. I'd never seen her beautiful face completely devoid of life. She tilted her head in confusion. "Bonaventure?"

I held out my hands, and she placed her palms in mine. "Yes, it's a total loss."

"But how?"

Her hands were cold and clammy as I pulled her toward me. "We don't know yet, but we'll probably have some answers tomorrow."

Tears fell one-by-one. "And you came all the way out here to tell me instead of calling?"

She let me pull her body against mine and laid her head against my chest. As she sobbed, she whispered, "And everything is gone . . . everything?"

I stroked her hair. "Yes, everything except our family Bible. Singer saved it from the fire."

She leaned back abruptly and stared up at me. "The Bible? Singer? Is he all right?"

"He suffered some burns and smoke inhalation. He's in the hospital, but he's going to be fine."

"What about *Aegis*?" she said.

"The boats are fine. Hunter got them away from the dock before the heat got bad enough to hurt them."

She frowned. "So, Hunter saved the boats, and Singer saved the Bible? Where were you?"

"I was in Saint Augustine telling Earl about the gold when Singer called me. I flew back to Bonaventure, but by the time I got there, it was too late to save the house."

The tears kept coming. "What about the horses?"

I shrugged. "I'm sorry, I didn't check on them. But the barn wasn't damaged. I'm sure they're okay."

"I'm sure they're scared," she breathed.

I pulled her back against my chest and held her.

Without pulling away, she said, "So, what do we do now?"

I leaned back and pushed her hair out of her face with my fingertips. "I'm going back to Saint Marys. The plane is waiting at the airport. What you do is up to you. If you want to come back with me, that's great, but if you need to be here, I think I understand."

She looked across my shoulder, back toward the party beyond the closed door. "Come with me. There's a side door out of here."

She led me down a corridor lined with framed pictures of movie stars, musicians, and a whole host of people I couldn't identify. When we reached the nondescript side door, she grasped the knob. "Which plane?"

I thought she must've meant to ask which airport, so I said, "Bob Hope, Burbank Airport."

"No," she said, "which airplane did you bring, and are you sure you're okay to fly all the way back home tonight?"

"It's a charter. Mongo arranged it. I was just a passenger."

Still clenching the doorknob, she said, "Is Anya there?"

"Is Anya where?"

"At Bonaventure."

"No, she's not at Bonaventure. I don't know where she is. No one does."

"Then I'm coming with you. Let's go."

The driver and the Range Rover were waiting exactly where I'd left them. He hopped from the front seat and opened the door for Penny. She slid inside the backseat, and as I lowered my head to follow her inside, the driver winked. "Nice. When you go to a party to pick up a woman, you don't mess around."

I took my seat and yanked the door closed. "Just get us back to the airport."

It took only slightly longer to make our way back to the general aviation terminal and through the security gate, but when the back door opened, we were thirty feet from the waiting stairs of the Citation.

We'd been silent in the Range Rover, but as soon as the door closed on the jet, Penny said, "You know how you felt when you saw that man with his hands on me?"

"Yeah. I felt like I wanted to rip his arm off and beat him to death with it."

She rolled her eyes. "Yeah, well, that's exactly how I feel every time I think about you on a mission with Anya."

"You don't understand," I argued. "I'm not going to let anything happen with Anya. Those days are long gone, and I don't want to go back there."

She huffed. "Yeah? Is that so? Well, I wasn't going to let anything happen with that guy at the party, either, but that didn't stop him from trying, now, did it?"

"No, it didn't but—"

She held up one finger. "No buts. It's exactly the same. I have no way to know what Anya might try, just like you don't have a clue what some of these Hollywood creeps might do when you're not around. It's the same thing, psychologist. Don't you get that?"

I pulled at my shirt collar and let her words sink into my skull.

She said, "You go off into your world of bullets and knives and bad guys. I'll never understand that world, and sometimes you take her with you. This world out here in L.A. is the same for me. It's dangerous, too. It's just fewer guns and knives and a lot more creeps. I'll learn how to navigate it, just like you learned how to stay alive in yours. You have to trust me and let me go, just like I let you go every time the phone rings."

"Maybe—"

"No, Chase. No maybes, and no buts. I'm a screenwriter, and this is where screenplays become movies. This is where I'm going to realize my dreams. You're a spy or operative or something, and the battlefield is where you live up to your 'calling' or whatever it is. Since I've been out here in Hollywood, I've realized it's the same."

The flight attendant peered down the aisle with inquisitive eyes as we leveled off in cruise. I mouthed, "Bourbon," and held up two fingers. Seconds later, she materialized beside us with a tumbler in each hand. Penny and I took the cocktails, and the attendant placed a pair of napkins on the bird's-eye maple table between us.

As quickly as she'd arrived, she vanished, and Penny asked, "Do you understand what I'm saying?"

"I do, and I'm truly sorry."

"Don't be sorry. Be better."

I wanted to chuckle at the adage she'd stolen from Clark, but instead, I swirled my bourbon, took my first sip, and placed the glass back on the napkin.

Penny peered down into my drink, lifted my glass, and let the golden whiskey glide across her lips, onto her tongue, and down her throat. She licked her lips and smiled. "I like that you liked watching me do that."

"That's exactly what you said after tasting my old-fashioned on our first date at the Peninsula Grill in Charleston."

She raised her eyebrows. "I know." Her foot slid seductively up my leg and came to rest on the inside of my thigh.

I bit my lip as the whirlwind of memories and emotions stirred inside my head. Perhaps I should've understood what sort of milestone we'd just passed in our relationship, but men with the foot of a beautiful woman in their lap tend to lose all capacity for rational thought.

She wiggled her toes. "I was really mad at you back at that party, you know."

"Yeah, I know."

She bit her bottom lip and sucked in a sharp breath. "But you coming to my rescue like that was kinda hot. Just don't make a habit of it, okay?"

I stopped listening after "kinda hot."

Two hours into the flight, the first officer came into the cabin and took a seat across the aisle from us. "Is there anything I can do for either of you?"

Penny said, "Yeah, you can let us keep this airplane."

He smiled. "Everything is for sale, but I'm just the driver. I came back to tell you that we've picked up a really nice tailwind, and if it continues, we'll be able to make Saint Marys nonstop."

"That's great," I said. "We really appreciate you taking such good care of us."

He shrugged. "That's our job." He looked around the cabin, admiring the interior. "If you decide you want one, they're only about six million bucks with an annual operating cost of seven fifty to nine hundred thousand."

Penny held up a pair of fingers. "In that case, we'll take two."

The pilot stood and turned back for the cockpit. "Let us know if you need a crew."

The tailwind held, and we landed in Saint Marys without an additional fuel stop. Eastbound high-altitude travel is always faster than the other direction.

Penny and I spent the time on the plane intentionally avoiding conversation about the fire, but the instant we walked off the plane, she inhaled through her nose. "That's a terrible smell."

I took her hand. "Yes, it is, but thankfully, we can replace what we've lost, and we'll always have the memories of Bonaventure."

We stood in the backyard by the gazebo that was blackened with ash, soot, and smoke. The old cannon still stood in the center of the gazebo, proud and defiant against the devastation only a few hundred feet away. It wasn't the first, nor the worst destruction the cannon had beheld, but I prayed it would be the last.

Penny squeezed my hand and pointed toward the ruins of our home. "That's where you knelt in front of me the day the Judge married us. Remember?"

The scene exploded in my memory. Neither Penny nor I imagined we would be married the day we climbed the steps to the back gallery of Bonaventure where the Judge was drinking lemonade. He didn't ask if we wanted him to conduct the ceremony. He simply ordered me to take a knee, asked if we pledged ourselves to each other, then had us hold hands. He'd placed his hand on top of ours. "May God bless and keep you both, and may you both live a life of service to each other and to Him as faithfully as you are able. By the power vested in me by the great state of Georgia, you are now, by both the blessing of God and by my lawful pronouncement, man and wife. You may, of course, kiss your bride."

His words rang in my ears like a mighty gong, and I turned to my wife. "Even with the world falling down around us, I still do."

# Chapter 5
## *Classified*

We spent the night aboard *Aegis*, anchored behind Cumberland Island, and upwind of what had been Bonaventure Plantation. The smell of a fire is unmistakable, and the emotion left in the wake of a destructive inferno is absolutely inescapable.

While we should've been falling asleep, Penny and I instead lay in each other's arms, trying to imagine what the other was thinking.

She kissed my cheek with little more than a touch. "Who started the fire?"

"I don't know if anyone started it. It could've been an electrical issue. We won't know until the arson investigation team does their work. Clark says the FBI team will be here in the morning."

She ran her fingers through my hair. "Who do you *think* started the fire?"

I sighed in resignation. "I don't know, but I have a few possible theories."

"Before you give me your list, where do you think Anya is?"

I didn't like where the conversation was headed, but I wasn't going to rule out anything. "Honestly, I haven't thought about that since Mongo said she was missing. Predicting what a former Russian SVR assassin is going to do is not in my bag of tricks. Why do you ask?"

She traced my jawline with her fingertips. "I know you don't want to consider this, but could she have started the fire?"

"I've given that some thought," I admitted, "but I can't come up with any motivation for her to do it. She has no reason to have any animosity toward us. And she's never mentioned arson as being one of the skills she has tucked away in her belt. I have every reason to believe she's behind the slicing up of the two guys in Saint Augustine. That's her style. But fires . . . I don't see it."

Someone had sliced two men to ribbons after they'd escaped custody in Saint Augustine for attacking Earl and sinking her boat. Anya Burinkova was instrumental in putting the men behind bars in the first place, so making them pay for their sins after they escaped sounded exactly like her modus operandi.

Penny leaned back, pulling her face away from mine. "What if it *was* her?"

I closed my eyes. "If it turns out to be arson, I'll turn the person who did it inside out, and no one will ever find their body."

She snuggled against me again. "Let's hear your short list."

"The first thought I had was someone connected with the mass shooting attempt. Singer and I quashed that pretty fast and cost those guys their fifteen minutes of fame."

"Didn't you tell me the third guy involved in that started singing like a bird when the cops questioned him?"

"Yeah, that's what I heard, but stool pigeons don't always sing the truth, and almost never do they sing the whole truth."

"Okay, so that's a viable possibility. Who else?"

"The Russians are always near the top of my list when bad things happen around us."

"Which Russians?" she asked.

I sighed. "All of them."

"Including Anya?"

"Maybe."

We lay in silence for several minutes, my brain roiling inside my head.

Penny whispered, "Anyone else come to mind?"

"There's one more, and I think he may be the best suspect of the bunch."

She leaned back again. "I can't wait to hear this one."

"Jerald Davis's little brother."

She wrinkled her forehead. "Who's Jerald Davis?"

"Jerald Davis is the man who pretended to be Gary Weathers. He and Eustis Carmichael are the two guys who attacked Earl and sank her boat."

"Oh, yeah. Sorry, I'm not thinking as clearly as I should be right now."

"I know exactly how that feels. I'm a little screwed up, too, but we'll get through this together."

"Yes, we will," she said. "So, continue about Jerald Davis's brother."

"Davis and Carmichael are the two who escaped in Saint Augustine and got themselves diced up . . . most likely by Anya. Davis's younger brother was wrapped up in the scheme on some level, but he wasn't directly involved with the sinking of Earl's boat, so the authorities probably couldn't hold him long without more evidence than we gave them. I'll have to check with the cops in Saint Augustine, but I'd bet he's out of jail and pretty pissed about his brother."

To my surprise, Penny started to giggle like a child and couldn't seem to stop.

"What are you laughing about? None of this is funny."

She pawed at the air as if she wanted me to stop talking but kept giggling like a teenage girl at a slumber party. After several minutes, she regained her composure and caught her breath. "I'm sorry. I don't know why I'm laughing."

As much as I didn't want to join her, I felt an involuntary chuckle rising in my chest, but I suppressed it . . . mostly. "It's okay. We sometimes do that when we're overwhelmed. Our crazy brains release all sorts of endorphins we don't expect when we're fatigued and flooded with stress."

She laid her hand across my chest. "Yeah, you may be able to explain it, psychology boy, but it still makes me feel guilty."

I held her hand in mine. "Don't feel guilty. It's perfectly natural."

"No, it's not natural to think what I was thinking."

"Now, I'm intrigued. What were you thinking?"

She looked away. "It's terrible. I can't say it."

"You can always say anything to me. You know that."

She rolled over and put her head on my shoulder. "I was just thinking that no one would ever believe it wasn't fiction if I wrote a screenplay about your life."

It was my turn to laugh. "As they say, sometimes truth is stranger than fiction."

We drifted off to restless sleep and woke to a pair of dolphins playing off the starboard bow. They'd apparently found a buffet and wanted to celebrate. I made coffee while Penny lay on the trampoline, wrapped in her favorite blanket. Coastal Georgia October mornings aren't always particularly warm for people who prefer three-digit temperatures, and Penny and I fell into that group.

She took the mug from my hand as I settled in beside her.

"May I share your blanket?"

She untucked a corner about the size of a handkerchief and offered it. "You can have this much."

"You're in a good mood this morning. Did you sleep well?"

"When I finally *went* to sleep, it wasn't bad, but I couldn't stop thinking about everything."

I watched the bottlenose dolphins frolic in the shallow water. "Yeah, me, too. I guess the FBI arson team should be here soon."

"Are we allowed to be there while they're doing their work?"

"It's our house," I said. "Or at least it *was* our house."

"If they determine it was arson, will it become a crime scene?"

"I don't know. I guess it's possible."

"That might be important to know. You've got a lot of . . . tools in the vault. If the FBI declares it a crime scene, they'll probably confiscate all of it as evidence."

I patted my pockets in search of my phone and leapt to my feet. "I've got to call Hunter."

He answered with, "Hey, where are you?"

"We're on the boat out behind Cumberland Island. We couldn't stay at the dock last night. The smell and all. . . ."

"Sure. That makes sense. Do you know the feds are here?"

I said, "I thought they would be. That's why I was calling. Did you get our gear out of the vault?"

"Yeah, of course. I left you a message. Didn't you get it?"

I pulled my phone from my ear and saw the icon indicating a missed call and a voicemail. "I see it now, but I didn't check my messages. It was a long flight, and . . ."

"I get it," he said. "No need to worry. The heavy stuff is in the armory at the base, and Singer and I split up the rest in our safes at home. I've got a bunch of files and paperwork in my truck. I didn't know what you wanted to do with that stuff."

"Thanks, man. I really appreciate you taking care of all of that. I'm sorry I've been out of it."

"Stop it. I understand, and I'm here to help. So, relax."

"We'll pull the hook and be there in fifteen minutes."

Penny had the engines running and the windlass hauling the anchor aboard before I hung up. I sprayed the mud from the Danforth anchor as it found its way into its pocket.

The dolphins apparently didn't like the engines. They vanished and were replaced by a pair of pelicans diving on whatever the dolphins had abandoned.

Penny shut down the engines as I tied us off at Bonaventure dock. Hunter was sitting in the gazebo, carefully watching every move the FBI team was making.

I poured a third cup of coffee and met him by the old cannon. "Have you had your coffee yet?"

He looked up and took the cup from my hand. "I have, but I never turn down a cup of boat coffee."

Penny and I joined Hunter in a pair of Adirondack chairs that were always far more comfortable than they looked.

"What are they doing?" Penny whispered.

"I don't know. I don't know anything about arson investigation. How about you, Hunter?"

"Oh, sure. I know it all. They're looking for the point of origin, evidence of an accelerant like gasoline or lighter fluid, obviously missing items of furniture or valuables from the house, lightning strikes, wall heaters, and old wiring."

I stared at my partner. "How do you know all of that?"

"I saw it on *Law and Order*."

I kicked the arm of his chair. "You're an idiot."

He laughed. "I have no idea what they're doing, but maybe they're doing some of those things."

Penny, still whispering, said, "Why would they look for missing furniture and valuables?"

Hunter joined her in the conspiratorial whisper. "People who burn their own houses usually take stuff out they don't want to lose."

Penny's eyes turned to saucers, and the whispering ceased. "You mean, they think *we* set the fire?"

I put my hand on her arm. "No, I'm sure they don't think that. You were three thousand miles away, and I was in Saint Augustine. I'm sure they're just doing their jobs. If it was arson, they'll figure it out."

Penny never took her eyes off the team as they worked for hours, raking through every inch of the house. "Why are they taking so many pictures?"

I turned to Hunter, our resident *Law and Order*–trained arson investigator.

"Don't look at me," he said. "They didn't do that on the show."

Morning turned into afternoon, and Singer showed up with a bag of sandwiches and a jug of lemonade. His arms were bandaged, and he wore a cap covering the burns on his head. "How long have they been at it?"

I leapt to my feet. "Hey! I didn't know you'd be out of the hospital so quickly. How are you feeling?"

"The doctors didn't know either," he said. "I decided I'd stayed long enough. I've got stuff to do."

Questioning Singer when he's made up his mind is like arguing with a stump, so I reached for his bag and pulled out a sandwich. "No mayo, right? You know how I feel about mayo."

He yanked the sandwich from my hand. "You don't want that one." He handed over a second sandwich. "This one is yours, mayo hater."

I took a peek inside the wrapper. "You better not be sneaking even a drop of mayonnaise onto anything you expect me to eat."

"Why do you hate it so bad?" he asked, and Penny giggled.

She had everyone's attention, but I gave her "the look."

She made a locking motion across her lips and shook her head.

Hunter eyed Singer. "You mean, you don't know the story?"

Singer shook his head, and Hunter chuckled. "Oh, you have to get Chase to tell the story. It's the nastiest story I've ever heard, but it cracks me up every time."

Singer held up his palms. "So . . . do I get the story?"

I shook my head. "No, you don't get the story. I'm trying to eat."

"I'd love to tell you," Hunter said, "but it's so much better coming straight from the horse's mouth, so to speak."

I pulled a pickle from my sandwich and hurled it at Hunter's head. His effort to catch it in his mouth left him with a pickle firmly affixed to his chin.

"To answer your question," I said, "they've been here since about eight this morning."

"How long does it usually take?"

I shot a thumb toward Hunter. "Ask Detective Lennie Briscoe over here."

Hunter piped up. "Oh, they'll have the case solved and the conviction in forty-two minutes, not counting commercial breaks."

Singer shot looks back and forth between Hunter and me until I said, "It's a *Law and Order* joke. We have no idea how long it'll take."

The FBI agents appeared to ignore the four spectators until the sun was well into the western sky. An older, wiry agent stepped from the debris, removed his booties, and approached the gazebo.

"Mr. and Mrs. Fulton, Mr. Hunter, Mr. Grossmann, I'm Special Agent Norman Briscoe."

Penny stifled a chuckle, but Hunter couldn't. "Briscoe? Really?" he said.

The agent looked perturbed. "Yes, Special Agent Norman Briscoe with the FBI arson investigation unit."

"How did you know our names?" I asked.

His perturbed look continued. "It's my job to know your names. I don't typically speak with the victims directly, but this isn't the typical case. Mr. Johnson in Miami asked specifically for me and my team, so, naturally, I had a few questions about who Mr. Johnson in Miami is. I was told to cooperate with him and with you, Mr. Fulton. Although that wasn't a direct answer to my question, I'm cooperating."

"And we appreciate that, Agent Briscoe." I motioned toward the ruins with my chin. "What can you tell us about what you saw in there?"

He glanced over his shoulder and cleared his throat. "Whoever did this should've just hung up a flashing neon sign that said 'Arson.' They made no effort to cover their tracks. It's like they wanted us to know the fire was intentional."

He paused, dusted off his pants, and pulled a pad from his pocket. "No one was home when the fire started. Is that correct?"

"It is," I said. "I was in Saint Augustine, and Penny was in California."

Agent Briscoe eyed Singer's bandages.

The sniper said, "I live in that house out there past the horse barn. When something didn't sound right, I came outside and saw the house already fully involved." He held up his arms. "Chase's family Bible was upstairs in his bedroom. It came across the ocean over two hundred years ago. I couldn't let it burn."

Agent Briscoe wrote furiously in has pad and then turned to Hunter. "How about you? Where were you when the fire started?"

"I was at my house fifteen minutes away. Singer called me, and I came down and moved the boats off the dock and told the firefighters to keep the vault as cool as possible. There was ammo in there."

Briscoe raised his eyebrows. "Ammunition?"

I nodded. "Yes, ammunition, and some weapons. If the ammo had cooked off, it would've destroyed everything in the vault."

Briscoe said, "And no one has been in the vault since the fire, right?"

Hunter glanced at me, and I nodded for him to answer. "I went in last night and got the ammo and weapons out," he said. "They're locked up in the armory at the Navy base."

Briscoe's pen hovered over his pad. "I'm going to need a complete inventory of that vault."

I smiled. "Mr. Johnson in Miami will provide that for you if he feels it's necessary for your investigation."

Briscoe put his pad and pen away. "Yes, well, I suppose that means cooperation is a one-way street."

"No, not at all," I said. "We're completely cooperative, but you said it was blatantly obvious it was arson. That means nothing in my vault could've played a role in starting the fire. Therefore, the contents of my vault are irrelevant to your investigation. They're also classified."

He glared at me over the rim of his glasses. "Classified?"

"Yes," I said. "Classified. That means you must possess the level of clearance necessary to view the list, have a need to know, and have signed an NDA."

"NDA?"

"Yes, a nondisclosure agreement," I said.

Briscoe huffed. "I know what an NDA is, but I'm investigating an arson, and the site was tampered with prior to my arrival."

I motioned toward the debris with my chin. "Agent Briscoe, where did you say the fire's point of origin was?"

He put his hands on his hips. "There were four points of origin."

"And which ones were near my vault?"

"None were near the vault, but that doesn't—"

I held up my hand. "I'll get Mr. Johnson on the phone if you'd like to speak with him, but it might be a good idea for you to check in with your supervisor first. We're on the same team, and we're not trying to be difficult."

He closed his eyes, took a long breath, and let it out. "Okay. It's been a long day, and we still have a lot of work to do."

I poured him a plastic cup of lemonade. "We'll stay out of your way, but I have one more question before we go. Do you believe you'll find any evidence in the remains of my house that will lead you to the arsonist?"

"That's rarely how arsonists are caught," he said. "Even if they left behind fingerprints, articles of clothing, or DNA, it would've been destroyed by the fire."

"That's what I thought. Now that you've determined it was definitely arson and that you have no definite way of catching the perp"—I shot a look to the people in the gazebo—"how my team and I will find him is also classified."

# Chapter 6
## *You're Welcome*

"Starting a pissing match with an FBI agent isn't the best way to make friends, Chase."

I didn't have to check the caller ID to know who'd dialed my number. "Hello to you, too, Clark. Would it matter if I said he started it?"

Clark grunted. "No, it wouldn't, but I have no doubt he did. How's Penny?"

I winked at my wife sitting across from me. "She's good. None of this is easy, but she's married to me, so easy isn't what she signed up for anyway."

"Putting up with you makes her a saint. We've got plenty of room here in South Beach if you want to spend a little time with us. Maebelle is tied up at the restaurant most of the time, but you know you're always welcome."

"Thanks. We may take you up on that at some point, but we're fine on the boat for now. Did that big-time crime buster of an arson investigator tell you anything other than it was definitely arson?"

Clark riffled through some papers. "Yeah, he sent me a copy of the preliminary report, but it doesn't say much more than that." He continued shuffling. "Oh, yeah, here it is. It says multiple point-of-origin determinations . . . blah, blah, blah . . . unknown accelerant, identification pending laboratory results . . .

yada, yada, yada . . . likely multiple arsonists due to . . . some big words I can't pronounce . . . directional burn rates."

I scratched down a few notes. "I didn't know the part about multiple arsonists, but that's a handy piece of information. I love it when there's more than one perp. When that happens, I get to have a lot of fun interrogating everyone until they turn on each other like vipers."

Clark sighed. "Would it make any difference if I told you to let the cops catch the guys who did this?"

I laughed. "Sure, it would if you could look me in the eye and genuinely tell me you believe the cops are *going* to catch the guys who burned my house to the ground. Can you do that?"

"No, you know I can't do that. They're not going to catch them, so let's hear your short list."

"That's what I thought. My short list is really short. Number one is Jerald Davis's little brother. Number two is someone associated with the mass shooting attempt here in Saint Marys. Number three is someone associated with the Kremlin. If it's not one of those three, I may not do any better than the cops at finding the guys."

"All of those are good possibilities," he said, "but remember, when you hear approaching hoofbeats, don't think about crocodiles."

"You have no idea how that saying goes or what it means, do you?"

"Ah, you know what I mean."

"No, I have no idea what you mean. I don't think hooved crocodiles burned my house down."

He laughed. "I meant, don't make it complicated. It could've been completely unrelated to work. It could've been some lowlife scum who gets off on burning down two-hundred-year-old houses."

"I think the fire-starting crocodile is more likely, but whoever it was, I'm going to find them."

Clark let out a long breath. "That's what I thought. What can I do to help?"

"I thought you'd never ask," I said. "You can start by putting out some feelers for Russians mucking about in the Georgia low country, especially some smelling like smoke from an antebellum plantation."

"I'm way ahead of you, College Boy. There are two suspected SVR operatives who are a couple weeks overdue for checking in with Mother Russia, but we've had them under watch for a while now. They do most of their mucking about—as you put it—inside the Beltway, but they occasionally take little field trips. I'll see what I can do to have someone sniff them for any hint of pecan smoke."

"I should've known you'd already be on it. Thanks."

The ice cubes inside his glass tinkled through the phone. "That's why I'm the boss and you're still a worker bee."

"You're the boss because you're old and broke your back on the Khyber Pass and I had to come rescue your sorry butt. If you were young and in shape like me, you'd still be kicking down doors instead of drinking whatever's in that glass with your feet up on a desk in Miami."

"Hey," he protested, "only one of my feet is on the desk. The other is on the Herman Miller footstool, so you can kiss my sorry butt."

"You're welcome," I said.

"Welcome for what?"

"That whole saving-your-butt thing. You sure are a lot of trouble, but I guess you're worth it . . . most of the time. I have to go. I've got an arsonist to catch."

"Before you go," he said. "Thank you for that whole saving-my-butt thing."

I hung up and briefed the team on what I learned from Clark. Penny was the first to speak. "You left Anya off the list."

"No, I didn't. I said, someone associated with the Kremlin."

She rolled her eyes. "That's a little vague, don't you think?"

"Maybe," I admitted, "but the report said there were likely multiple participants in setting the fire. Do you think Anya picked up a couple of sidekicks with a penchant for starting fires?"

She held up both hands. "Maybe."

"Okay, moving on. The next item is finding out Davis's brother's status. I'd originally planned to go to Saint Augustine to visit with my old friend, Officer O'Malley, but I'm having second thoughts about that."

Hunter frowned. "What's wrong with hitting O'Malley up for the inside dope? He's always been more than willing to help. He's one of the good guys down there."

"Oh, I agree," I said. "He's definitely on our side. But if I start asking questions about a guy they cut loose, and then that guy ends up with his head on a pike, I might find myself at the top of their persons-of-interest list. I'd rather stay off that list."

Penny made a horrified face. "That's nasty. You're not seriously . . . Never mind."

"No, my dear, I'm not seriously thinking about decapitating anyone. That would be far too gentle. I'll do something terrible to whoever I catch."

"Seriously, do you have a plan for finding whoever did this, or are you going to beat up everybody you see until someone confesses?"

"Oh, I have a plan, and it starts with Skipper."

In her typical style, Skipper answered my call quickly. "Hey, Chase. Any news on what started the fire?"

"It's a who, not a what," I said. "The FBI released their preliminary report, and it's definitely arson with multiple points of origin and likely multiple arsonists."

"I thought that's what they'd say. You're not surprised, are you?"

"No, I'm not surprised about it being arson, but the part about multiple arsonists wasn't what I expected."

"Yeah, that one isn't exactly what I would've predicted either."

"Have you had any luck on the hunt for Anya?" I asked.

She groaned. "No, and it's frustrating the crap out of me. It's like she just vanished into thin air. You're not thinking she had something to do with the fire, are you?"

"I'm not ruling anything out yet, but I can't come up with any reason why she would've started it."

"Yeah, and she's not exactly the type to do anything with a couple of pickup players."

"That's what I thought, too, but just because the feds *suspect* it was multiple arsonists, doesn't mean it was."

Skipper made a clicking sound with her tongue against her teeth. "Making it *look* like multiple arsonists when it was only one *does* sound like something Anya would do."

"But have you ever heard her talk about starting fires?"

She cleared her throat. "Have you ever heard her talk about her ability to disappear from Athens, Georgia, like a ghost? No, you haven't, but she did it."

I let Skipper's thought tumble around in my head. "Very true. Keep looking for her, but I need you on something else, too."

She laid down her phone and put me on speaker. "Okay, but make it quick. I've got a date."

"A date?" I asked. "With whom?"

"None of your business. Just tell me what you need."

"We're coming back to this date thing, but I'll let you off the hook for now."

She laughed. "I've never been *on* the hook. Just tell me what you need."

"I need you to find Jerald Davis's little brother. He was arrested with Davis and Carmichael. At the moment, he's at the top of my most-wanted list."

"That one's easy," she said. "I'll dig him up and send you his particulars. Anything else?"

"Yeah," I said, "back to this date of yours. . . ."

The line went dead.

Penny took my arm. "Let's go for a walk."

That's roughly the equivalent of "We need to talk," so I wasn't looking forward to our "walk."

"You're going after whoever did this, and there's nothing anyone can do to stop you, is there?"

I squeezed her hand. "They burned down our home."

She put on part of a smile and stepped in front of me. "No, only you and I could do that. They burned down our *house*."

She patted her palm against my chest. "Our *home* is in here. No matter how much of your family's history was trapped inside those walls, it was still just a house. You know what they say about digging two graves when you set out on a mission of revenge."

I held her hand against my chest. "Yes, but whoever did this was sending a message. I don't know what that message is yet, but there's more to all of this than simply being a fire."

"Whoever did it, and whatever the message was, it's not worth throwing away the rest of your life to get even. If you find them and kill them, you're not above the law, Chase. Losing you in a gunfight against terrorists halfway around the world is bad enough, but losing you to prison is something I can't bear."

I pulled her against me. "I have to find who did this, and I have to bring them to justice, but I promise you, I won't throw away our home. I won't throw away *us* to do it."

She smiled. "Thank you."

"Do you want to go back to L.A.?"

She blinked as if trying to focus. "Is that your way of saying you're welcome?"

"No, it's my way of saying, what's important to you is important to me. I understand how important your screenplay is to you, so if you want—or need—to be in California, I'm supportive of that. While you're chasing your dreams, I'll be catching the jackass who burned down our . . . house."

We shared a deep, understanding kiss, and then I pulled back and stroked her long hair. "I have a little gift for you that will make the trips back and forth to L.A. a little less stressful."

Her face glowed. "You bought a jet?"

"Not exactly," I said, "but if you agree, we'll buy part of a jet."

Her excitement turned to question. "Why would we want part of a jet?"

"It wouldn't be exactly like owning any one part of the jet. It would be a partnership with Singer, Hunter, and Skipper. I pitched the idea to them, and they love it. We can afford it. If we decide to do it, you and I would own two shares, and everyone else would own one."

"I love the idea, but why would we own two shares to everyone else's one?"

"There's a couple of reasons," I said. "First, with you flying back and forth to L.A., both you and I would be using it independently of each other. Second, we can afford a bigger investment than the other three. That's makes it possible to get a bigger, more capable airplane."

She wrinkled her brow. "Can you fly it?"

"I'll have to get the training, but yes, I'll be able to fly it. We'll also hire a crew for times when I won't be doing the flying. Sometimes, I like to sit in the back and have a cocktail. They frown on that sort of thing in the cockpit."

She rolled her eyes. "You're too funny. Yes, of course, I want us to have a jet, and the two-shares thing is good, but what about Mongo?"

"He's struggling a little with the whole disappearing-Anya thing. Now's not the time for him to make big decisions. We'll let him buy in when all of this washes out . . . if he wants to."

"I can understand that. So, sort-of buying me a jet is your way of saying you're welcome?"

I smirked. "Or maybe, thank you."

# Chapter 7
## *Remember the Maine*

It was Skipper's call that set us in motion.

"I found him, Chase."

"You found who?"

"Kindle Jefferson Davis."

I frowned into the phone. "Who is Kindle Jefferson Davis?"

She huffed. "Jerald Davis's brother. Try to keep up."

"Oh! Nice work. Where is he?"

She hit a few keystrokes. "You were right about the Saint Augustine PD not being able to hold him. He was out before his brother, believe it or not. Kindle runs a deep-sea fishing charter out of Cape Hatteras on the Outer Banks of North Carolina. I'll email the details of your reservation."

"My reservation?" I asked.

"Yes, you and three friends have reservations for an all-day offshore charter on Saturday with Captain Davis. You're booked under the name Knox Taylor. Take your foul weather gear. It's going to be chilly out there."

I chuckled. "Knox Taylor? Do you think he'll get the joke?"

She giggled. "I'm surprised you got it."

"Sarah Knox Taylor was Zachery Taylor's daughter and the first wife of Jefferson Davis. I'm a graduate of a fine Southern university, Miss Analyst. Did you really think I wouldn't make the connection?"

"Something tells me Kindle Jefferson Davis won't figure it out until he sees the familiar faces who step aboard his boat on Saturday."

"You said me and three friends, right?"

"Yeah, I figured you'd take Hunter, Singer, and Mongo."

I sighed. "Mongo probably won't be joining us for this little outing. He's a little messed up over Anya's disappearance, and if his head's not in the game, I don't want him downrange with us."

Skipper said, "I'm still working on finding her, too, but it's going nowhere."

"Keep at it. You found her in Siberia. If she can be found, I know you can do it."

She lowered her voice. "The difference is she *wanted* to be found in Siberia. I think she's hard underground now."

"We have to consider the possibility that she's run home."

She groaned. "Back to Russia?"

"Possibly. It'd be worth tossing some grenades into the water around Moscow to see what floats to the top."

She let out a whistle. "Okay, if that's what you want, I'll do it, but don't you think we should call in a favor from Langley before I poke my nose into Red Square?"

"Do whatever you think is best. You're the brains of this operation. I'm the pretty one."

"I'm the brains *and* the pretty one," she argued. "You're just the hired muscle."

I hung up before she could hurl anymore insults.

\* \* \*

Hunter and I found Singer at his church, hanging from a Swiss Seat some twenty feet below the belfry.

"What are you doing up there?" I yelled through the cavernous bell tower.

Singer shined his light down on us. "Oh, hey, guys. I'll be right down."

Our Southern Baptist Sniper rappelled down the shaft and landed at our feet.

Hunter dusted him off. "Santa Claus usually comes down the chimney, not the bell tower."

Singer swatted Hunter with the end of his rope. "Very funny, Air Force. I was replacing the old bell rope. It was quickly failing, and if it breaks, the boys who ring the bell won't have anything to do on Sunday morning."

Singer was impossible to explain. The Army had made him one of the deadliest snipers in history, but his faith made him one of the most devout Christians I'd ever known. He loved his God and his church above everything else. His brother, who lived at the monastery in Monks Corner, South Carolina, ran a close second. As children, Singer and his brother had witnessed the death of their mother at the abusive hands of their alcoholic father. Singer made use of the only weapon in sight, an old shotgun propped in the corner, to stop his father's rage, but he'd been too late to save his mother. The ordeal left Singer's brother mute and withdrawn inside himself for three decades. It taught Singer that sometimes, taking the life of another is the only way to bring peace. I don't believe pulling the trigger with a human in the crosshairs ever came easy to Singer, but I'll forever believe he bore the awesome burden of that responsibility so others wouldn't have to. He was likely haunted by the memories of the souls he'd sent into eternity, but his faith gave him the strength to soldier on in everyday life and on the battlefield.

As if remembering something he'd long forgotten, Singer turned to me. "Speaking of giving the bell ringers something to do, I've got a huge favor to ask."

"Sure. Anything. You know that."

"I'd like to show your Bible to my Sunday school class."

"My Bible?" I asked.

"Yeah, your family Bible. The one I pulled out of Bonaventure."

"Of course you can show it to your class. I don't mind at all. It's as much yours as mine. If you hadn't saved it from the fire, it would be forever gone."

"I really appreciate that. Is it on your boat?"

"No, I put it in the safe deposit box at the bank. It's too valuable to risk losing again."

"Oh, no, Chase. You can't lock it away. It's not a museum piece. It's a part of you, a part of your history, and a part of every day of your life."

I narrowed my eyes. "That Bible is nearly two hundred fifty years old, and I can't believe it's still in one piece. I really think it should be preserved somewhere safe."

Singer placed his hand on my shoulder. "Let's go get it from the bank. I want to show you something."

I glanced at my watch. "We've got a lot to do. We came by to—"

He squeezed my shoulder. "Let's go get your Bible, Chase. It won't take long. Then, we can go wherever you want and do whatever needs to be done."

Arguing with a man of Singer's enormous faith about the importance of something he wanted to show me in my family Bible would've been a colossal waste of time, so we headed for the bank, a block and a half south of the church.

The bank manager opened the heavy door and let us into the vault. My key opened the box, and the smell of smoke wafted from the drawer. Singer hefted the Bible from the bin and tucked it beneath his arm like a mighty sword. Perhaps to him, that's exactly what it was. He led us back to the church and unlocked the small library off the vestibule.

Singer slid the heavy, worn Bible onto the table and patted the cover. "What do you think makes this book so valuable?"

I glanced at Hunter, and he said, "He ain't talking to me. This is about you. I'm just here because I think something cool is about to happen."

I stared at the rugged binding of the Bible that had been handed down through generations of my mother's family for two centuries. It had fallen to me as a wedding gift from the hands of my great uncle, Judge Bernard Henry Huntsinger, the day he bound Penny and me together until death do us part.

Unsure what Singer wanted to hear, I said, "It's important because it's the Word of God."

He shook his head as if I'd forgotten the Pythagorean theorem in geometry class. "No, that's not it at all. The Word of God can't be contained in a book, no matter how old it is. The world is full of the Word of God. This thing burning to ash would've never changed that. There are millions of Bibles all over the world. It's the best-selling book of all time and always will be."

I was still a little confused. "Is it because it's old? It's probably the oldest book I've ever seen, and I know it's the oldest Bible I've ever seen."

Singer slid into a chair across the table from me and opened the Bible to the middle. He pressed against the pages where they came together at the binding. "It's partially because it's old, but it's not original."

"What do you mean, it's not original?"

He ran his finger down the seam. "Look at that discoloration."

I stared at the edges of the yellowing pages. "Okay, I see it. It just looks dirty to me."

He closed the Bible and stood it on its long side with the binding up. "Now, look down the edge. See how rough and ragged it looks?"

"Sure, I see it, but it's old. Isn't that how they made books in the seventeen hundreds?"

He shrugged. "I don't know how the printer of this Bible did it back then, but take a look at this."

He stood and stuck a key into an ornately carved cabinet in the corner of the library. Behind the heavy walnut cabinet door, he turned a pair of airtight locks on a glass enclosure and slid on a pair of white cotton gloves. Then, he lifted a leather-bound book from deep within the case.

"This is the oldest Bible *I've* ever seen. The first King James Version of the Christian Bible was printed in sixteen eleven. This one was printed in sixteen twenty-nine on the same press that produced that very first one. I bought it from a museum in Stockholm after you paid us for the oil rig job."

Hunter stopped being a silent observer. "How much was it?"

Singer smiled. "It doesn't matter, but this one is valuable because it's *really* old and in near perfect condition. If there's a better or older copy anywhere in the world, the Vatican probably has it."

I stared at the ancient book. Its leather was perfectly preserved, and the embossed print looked as if it could've been pressed into the hide yesterday. "It's astonishing, Singer."

He admired the book. "It is, isn't it? But I wouldn't run into a fire to save it."

"What?" I blurted out. "You risked your life to save my ragged, old family Bible, but you'd let that priceless piece of history burn? What are you talking about?"

He slid the nearly four-hundred-year-old treasure back into its airtight chamber and locked the cabinet. "Your Bible has done what it was meant to do, Chase. That priceless copy locked away behind me has never laid in the lap of a child and brought wonder to his eyes and salvation to his soul. It's never heard the cracks and pops of an oak fire in a Christmas fireplace as somebody's grandfather slid his calloused fingers across the pages of the Gospel of Luke and read the story of Jesus's birth in Bethlehem. It's never been shot at or rained on, and it's never had the name of a newborn child or a beloved grandmother who died of the Spanish Flu scribbled in it."

He slid my Bible toward me. "Take another look at that binding. It's not original. There's been at least half a dozen new covers put on that Bible, and it's been glued and pressed back together more times than any of us could count. Go ahead. Open it up to the eighth page and read me what you see."

I suddenly felt like I needed the white gloves he'd locked in the cabinet with the old King James Version. I dusted my clean hands against my pants and opened the book. The fading ink on the first few pages was hard to read, but when I found page eight, the cursive script was clear and strong.

*Feb 17, '98. Two nights and a full day of hell in Havana. The Maine is on the bottom, and I reckon two hundred and fifty or more of her complement lay with her. Prayed with as many as would hear me and over the ones who couldn't. I done my best. May Almighty now do His.*

*Lieutenant J.O. Huntsinger*

When I stopped reading, it felt as if the walls of the tiny library were slowly crushing in on me.

"Do you know what that passage is about, Chase?"

I nodded and whispered, "The sinking of the *Maine* in Havana Harbor in eighteen ninety-eight."

Singer slowly shook his head. "No, that passage is about the heart of the chaplain onboard the *Maine* the night she sank. That chaplain, Lieutenant Joshua Oliver Huntsinger, was your great-great-grandfather—or something like that. Have you ever heard of him?"

I sat in silence, shaking my head. Singer leaned in. "Have you ever heard of a lieutenant colonel named Theodore Roosevelt?"

"President Teddy Roosevelt?" I said.

Singer nodded. "That's the guy. Only, he was a lieutenant colonel when he grabbed one Lieutenant Huntsinger from an Army field hospital near Guantanamo Bay in June of eighteen ninety-eight and made him the regimental chaplain for an outfit known as the Rough Riders."

"Do you mean this Bible was on the *Maine* and at the Battle of San Juan Hill?"

He motioned toward the page. "Read the next entry."

*July 2, '98 Btl for SJ Hghts under Col Roosevelt. The Spanish Catholics gave up the hill, and a flight of souls, Spanish and American, met their God before yesterday's dark. And word of a son born and given my name in Virginia came by way of Captain Goddard.*

*Lt. Huntsinger*

Singer shot a thumb across his shoulder. "That book locked up behind that door holds the greatest story that this world will ever hear, but that beat-up, glued-together Bible in your hands tells stories the other one will never know. Don't lock it up, Chase. Protect it, but take it with you. You can't scare it. It's been through worse than you'll ever put it through. If we get it shot up or torn up, we'll find some more glue. God and Judge Huntsinger wouldn't have put it in your hands if they thought you couldn't bear its weight."

# Chapter 8
## *Baby Bird*

Singer's lessons about what's really important weren't always easy for me to swallow, but they were never forgettable. Having him as a cornerstone of the team gave me somewhere to run when everything in my world stopped making sense. Countless times would come when a round from his rifle would be the only thing between me and a pine box. But thanks to him, my soul knew that pine box was but a doorway beyond which I'd never have to deliver or receive another shot in anger, and the only place where true peace could ever be found.

"I don't know what I expected to find when Hunter and I came looking for you, but a history lesson taught from my own family Bible wasn't it."

Singer grinned. "That must be why you keep me around . . . to deliver the unexpected."

Hunter scoffed. "We keep you around because you can deliver a fifty-cal round through the eye of a needle at a thousand yards."

I tapped the table. "Hopefully, we won't be needing that particular skill in the next few days. Skipper has us booked on a fishing charter out of Cape Hatteras on Saturday."

Singer beamed. "Nice. A little R and R sounds like a great way to get our heads straight after the fire."

"Unfortunately," I said, "this isn't a pleasure trip. Our charter captain just happens to be one Kindle Jefferson Davis, the brother of Jerald Davis, aka Thumbprint from Saint Augustine."

"Oh, that's even better," Hunter said. "I thought we were going to have to hunt him down. Instead, Skipper scored us an invitation right through his front door."

Singer slapped the table. "Well done, Skipper!"

"Before we go, though, I've got a surprise for Hunter. I made you a promise, and I intend to keep it."

He cocked his head. "What promise did you make that you haven't kept?"

I said, "You'll see. File a flight plan for Miami in the Caravan for the three of us. We'll leave within the hour. While you're doing that, I have a couple of calls to make."

Skipper answered cheerfully. "Hey there, Chase. How's it going?"

"Your date must've gone well. You're in a good mood."

She giggled. "I'm sticking with my original position that it's none of your business. What's up?"

"Penny agreed to buying the jet. Get some brokers lined up, and let's see a few. At a bare minimum, we need a six-passenger with at least a fifteen hundred mile range, preferably single-pilot capable, under twelve million."

"Twelve million?" she almost yelled.

"Relax. Half will be carried by the company. That'll leave six million between five partners. Penny and I will be independent. That means a million two hundred thousand for each partner. I'll arrange the financing, so no one will have to write a big check. We'll need a good attorney to write up a partnership agreement and form a corporation to manage the ownership. Just find us a few options. I'll take care of everything else."

"I thought it was all just a *maybe* kind of thing. I didn't know we were going to jump right in, but I'm on board. I'll get to work."

"Don't worry. It'll all work out beautifully. In the meantime, I need you to charter something to get Penny back to the West Coast. It wouldn't be a bad idea to charter through a broker and let him know we'll be making a purchase soon."

"I like your thinking," she said. "I'm on it. Anything else?"

"One more thing. Book us a place on Hatteras for tomorrow night. It'll be Hunter, Singer, and me. It's possible Clark might come along, so get something big enough that I won't have to listen to him snore. Book it for two nights, in fact."

She huffed. "You could say *please*."

"I thought *please* was always implied," I said.

"No, *please*, *thank you*, and *you're welcome* are never implied."

"Got it. Please take care of the booking for us. Thank you for everything you do for me. And you're welcome for the privilege of being my secretary."

I hung up immediately to avoid her wrath, and Hunter hung up at the same time I did.

"Is the flight plan filed?" I asked.

"It is. Are you going to let me in on this surprise of yours?"

I shook my head. "Nope, but bring your pilot's license, logbook, medical certificate, passport, and foul weather gear for the fishing charter, and I'll meet you at the hangar in thirty minutes."

"You're the boss. Singer went home to pack a bag. You'll probably want to grab him on your way to the airport."

I pulled the library door closed behind us and followed Hunter onto the sidewalk.

An hour later, I was in the right seat of the Caravan with Hunter at the controls. As we climbed out to the east, I said, "Keep us below eight hundred feet until we cross the river. I want to take a look at the remains of the house."

He leveled off at six hundred feet and pointed the propeller toward Bonaventure.

I said, "Fly just south of the house and look out your window as we cross the property. Let me know if you see anything strange in the debris."

He followed my instructions and focused his attention past the massive pontoon beneath the left side wing. "I don't see anything that jumps out at—"

I pulled the power back. "Simulated engine failure. Where are we going?"

Hunter responded immediately by pushing the nose over to maintain best glide speed and scanned the area in front of us. "We're going in the water."

He continued through the emergency water-landing checklist and executed a flawless landing.

"Nicely done," I said. "Now, show me a confined area takeoff, and keep us south of the yellow Navy buoy."

Once again, his technique was perfect.

"Well done. Climb out over Cumberland Island, and I'll pick up our clearance."

Hunter set up the airplane for climb, and I keyed my mic. "Jacksonville departure, this is Cessna Caravan two-zero-eight-Charlie-Foxtrot, ten miles southeast of Saint Marys, VFR through one thousand niner hundred. Request IFR clearance to Opa-Locka Oscar Poppa Foxtrot."

"Caravan eight-Charlie-Fox, JAX departure, squawk seven-one-four-four."

"Seven-one-four-four, eight-Charlie-Fox."

"Caravan eight-Charlie-Fox, radar contact, position reported, JAX altimeter two-niner-seven-four, cleared to Opa-Locka Airport as filed, climb and maintain one two thousand and proceed on course."

Hunter activated the flight plan he'd preprogrammed into the GPS and set the autopilot. Fifteen minutes later, he ran the cruise checklist, and we settled in for the flight that would put us on the ground in Miami in less than ninety minutes . . . as far as Hunter knew.

Fifty miles out of Miami, the controller assigned seven thousand feet, and we started down. Hunter disconnected the autopilot and flew the standard terminal arrival route by hand.

As we crossed Fort Lauderdale International, I keyed the mic. "Miami Approach, Caravan eight-Charlie-Fox, we'll cancel instruments here and proceed VFR to the Miami Seaplane Base."

Hunter shot a look across his sunglasses. "Thanks. Getting to splash down at the Miami Seaplane Base beside the cruise ships is a big deal. I appreciate you letting me do it."

Pleased he hadn't caught on to my scheme, I leaned back in my seat and became a silent observer.

"Caravan eight-Charlie-Foxtrot, your cancelation is received. Maintain current squawk for VFR flight following, and maintain VFR at or above three thousand five hundred."

Hunter keyed up. "Keep the squawk, VFR at or above three point five, eight-Charlie-Fox."

The cruise ships came into sight, and Hunter did it by the numbers as if he'd been landing seaplanes in the fairway all his life. We powered out of the water and up the ramp, where Clark waited with his flight bag in hand.

Hunter shut down and began unstrapping from the pilot's seat.

I put a hand on his shoulder. "Not so fast. Take Clark for a ride. You've got an appointment this afternoon, and he'll prep you for it."

Singer and I disembarked, and Clark gave a knowing nod and a crooked grin as he climbed the ladder into the Caravan.

Singer stared back and forth between the plane and me. "What's happening right now?"

I motioned toward Clark's SUV. "You and I are having a nice meal at South Beach's premier restaurant while Hunter takes his seaplane check ride."

El Juez, Maebelle's Cuban-inspired Southern cuisine restaurant, fronted Ocean Drive, and the waiting list was full.

I leaned in and whispered to the hostess. "Tell Maebelle that Chase and Singer are here, and we'd love a seat in a closet somewhere if she has one."

The young lady smiled and motioned for us to follow. "Chef Maebelle told me you were coming, and your table is waiting."

South Beach's most celebrated new chef danced to our table, wiping her hands on her apron as she came. Hugs all around preceded rounds of cheerful greetings.

We finally took our seats, and Maebelle said, "Just relax, enjoy the show, and we'll take care of everything."

Daiquiris and tapas came first, and by the time the main course of steaming redfish over black beans and rice arrived, Singer and I had already begun thinking in Spanish. We ate until we could barely move, and then dessert arrived. A plate of pastelitos de guayaba, guava pastries, landed in front of me, and arroz con leche, a mouth-watering rice pudding, made its way to Singer.

He slipped a bite into his mouth while mumbling, "I don't think I can . . ."

The look on his face when the spoon hit his tongue said he most certainly could.

"So, how was it, boys?"

I took the chef's hand. "Maebelle, you are a genius. This was life changing."

Singer wiped his mouth and placed his napkin on the table. "It was almost a religious experience, and coming from me, that really means something."

She offered another round of hugs. "I'm so glad you guys enjoyed it. We've made up rooms for you at the house for tonight. I won't be home until midnight, but please keep Clark there with you. I *really* don't need him here."

"Thank you for everything, Maebelle. You're too good to us, and we'll definitely keep Clark out of your hair. In fact, we'll probably steal him for a couple of days if you don't mind."

She leaned down and kissed my forehead. "God bless you! You're a lifesaver. I have a food critic coming tomorrow night and . . . oh, it's a whole big thing. It would be fantastic if Clark was anywhere but here."

"We'll take good care of him. I promise. Now, get back in there and crack the whip before your staff thinks you've abandoned ship."

She waved as she backed toward the kitchen.

Even though no check would be coming, I slipped four one-hundred-dollar bills under the edge of my plate and forced myself to my feet.

When we arrived back at the seaplane base, Clark was sitting on the tailgate of a pickup truck near the wash rack.

"Where's our boy and my airplane?" I asked.

"He's up with Charles, the examiner. It's time for him to be back, though."

A few minutes later, the familiar sound of the Caravan whistled overhead, and Hunter splashed down like a pro. Before Hunter had everything shut down, the examiner climbed down from the plane and strolled toward the office. He shot Clark a wink and a thumbs-up as he ambled by.

Clark elbowed me. "I guess that means the world has a brand-new seaplane pilot."

"I guess it does."

Hunter made his way down the ladder. "I suppose the landing wasn't my surprise after all, huh?"

"Sooner or later, every baby bird has to get pushed out of the nest. Today was your day."

# Chapter 9
## *Ghosts in the Halls*

I've never known—or cared about—Clark's net worth, but his South Beach home left little room for doubt that he'd done well, and even less doubt that I'd seen the property before.

Hunter stood in the foyer and stared upward as if inspecting the ceiling of the Sistine Chapel. "This is some kind of place, Clark."

Clark slid his keys onto the marble-top table. "Miami's hottest young chef can't sleep in a cardboard box. Come on upstairs. I'll show you guys where you can crash."

He led us up the all-too-familiar curved stairway to the second floor, and my blood ran cold.

Clark twisted a knob and swung open a door. "This first bedroom is for Singer because if you crack the window, you can hear the bells at the Catholic Church around the corner."

Singer tossed his overnight bag inside. "Thanks, Clark. I'll make the bed in the morning."

"This next one is for Hunter because I know you like to sleep in, you lazy mutt. It's the darkest and quietest room on the second floor."

Hunter leaned into the room. "Some of us need our beauty sleep. We can't all be sexy right out of the box like you."

Clark brushed an imaginary fleck of dust from his shoulder and raised his chin. "Yep, that's what they call me, ol' Out-of-the-Box Sexy." He motioned across the expansive hallway. "These two rooms share a bath, but there's a full bath over there if you need it."

I stared at the heavy bathroom door that appeared obviously newer than the other doors in the hallway. My mouth felt like the inside of a vacuum cleaner bag as I took in the surroundings.

"And Chase, you're at the end of the hall on the right, through the double doors. That's the second-floor master." He snapped his fingers. "Chase? Are you all right?"

When I could finally speak, I grabbed Clark's elbow. "Who did you buy this house from?"

He frowned at the question. "What do you mean?"

"I mean, who owned this house before you?"

He shrugged. "I don't know, some property management company, I think. Why? What's wrong with you?"

"Do you remember the day we rescued Skipper from the porn shoot and Anya got shot?"

"Yeah, sure. I was babysitting that scumbag, Giovani Minelli."

I pointed toward the bathroom. "*That's* where I found Skipper wrapped in a bathrobe and trembling in fear."

His eyes went wide, and I pointed toward the staircase. "And *that's* where Anya took a bullet in the back after piling up two bodies, right where we're standing."

His eyes shot around the space as if he were trying to picture the chaos.

I motioned toward the doorway to Hunter's room. "And *that's* where I put every bullet I had into the bastard who shot her."

Clark, Hunter, and Singer stood in silent disbelief until I broke the trance. "Let's go back downstairs and have a drink. I think we could all use one."

Clark delivered whiskey on ice to Hunter and me, and a sweet tea for Singer. "Chase, I had no idea. I mean, I would've never bought the place if I had known."

I touched the rim of my glass to his. "Relax. It was just a shock. There's nothing evil about the house. It's a gorgeous property. Minelli and Paradise Productions were the evil, not the house."

Singer raised his glass. "Here's to living well. They say it's the best revenge, and Skipper and Anya definitely seem to be getting their revenge."

Glasses rose into the air, and grumbling agreements arose with them.

When we'd all had a swallow, Hunter said, "At least we hope Anya is living well, wherever she is."

Clark examined the group. "Anybody have any ideas where she might be?"

"Penny's got a theory," I said. "She suspects Anya is still working for the Russians and that she likely started the fire at Bonaventure and then ran home."

Clark leaned back in his chair. "I guess we can't rule it out, but it doesn't sound like her to me. Any other theories?"

I wasn't expecting it, but Hunter spoke up. "I'm not one for guessing, but something about it feels planned to me. It's like she knew she was never going back to Athens after Saint Augustine. I felt it when she claimed to be leaving after she scared the hell out of the guys who hit Earl's boat. Something about it just didn't smell right."

Clark frowned. "So, where do you think she is?"

Hunter took another sip of his whiskey. "Who knows? Maybe Defense Intelligence or the Agency has her. I don't have any answers. I'm just saying it smells funny."

Clark eyed our sniper. "Singer, what about you? Got any theories?"

"I tend to look at the world with less sinister intent than most. So, from my perspective, the most likely thing is that she's worried about being connected to the murders of the two escapees in Saint Augustine, so she's on the lam. I think maybe she'll turn up in a few days or weeks when things cool down."

Clark nodded in consideration and turned to me. "What do you think, Chase?"

"I want to believe Singer's right and she's just lying low for a while, but I'm leaning toward the sinister. I know this sounds terrible, but I hope Penny's wrong. I don't want to think about Anya going back to Moscow."

"None of us wants that," Clark said. "Is Skipper trying to find her?"

I glanced at my watch. "She's been working on it for a couple of days, but so far, she's turned up nothing other than a ping on her cell phone in Atlanta the day before she vanished."

Clark said, "I'll give Skipper a call and let her know she has our full support with anything she needs to find her."

"Who do you mean when you say *our* support?" I asked.

Clark almost grinned. "I didn't know what that word meant either before *they* promoted me. All of us work for a board of directors of a corporation. The board is made up of several members—I don't know how many—who must all unanimously agree on missions we accept. They are powerful men, and maybe women, too. I don't know. They're fully aware of Anya's disappearance and the fire at Bonaventure, and they've pledged their full support and almost limitless resources to find Anya and support you"—he pointed at me—"in finding the arsonists . . . plural."

I finished my whiskey. "Thank you for that. In the big scheme of things, it's likely that finding Anya is a lot more important than finding the jackasses who burned my house, but my focus is on finding the arsonists first, and then going after Anya. I just hope I don't accomplish both missions simultaneously."

Clark made a sound like a toy horn. "Toot toot. Let's talk about the fishing trip."

Hunter, Singer, and I stared at Clark as if he'd lost his mind. "Toot toot? Where did that come from?"

Clark held up his palms. "Everybody knows *toot toot* means we're changing the subject."

I shook my head. "No, Clark, nobody knows that. What's wrong with you?"

"What's wrong with me? I'm the one who knows things here. You guys are the ones who are lagging."

Hunter laughed. "Maybe it's a Mud Pie and Wanda Jean thing."

"Maybe," I said. "Anyway, with no toot toot involved, the fishing trip is going to be a lot of fun, and you're coming with us."

Clark pointed two thumbs at himself. "Me?"

"Yes, you. You're the only one of us who's been trained in waterboarding, and I think we may need some creative ways to get Kindle Jefferson Davis to talk."

Clark held up a finger. "I don't like the term *waterboarding*. I much prefer *tactical baptism*, but I see your point. Go on."

Singer jumped in. "Even God has a sense of humor, but tactical baptism? Really?"

Clark said, "I've never conducted one that didn't make the baptizee talk to God."

Singer rolled his eyes. "*Baptizee* isn't a word, but I'm starting to think you could use a few dips in the River Jordan."

"Anyway," I said, "Skipper has us set up for an all-day offshore trip on Saturday. I haven't decided how I want to play it yet. Part of me hopes Davis doesn't recognize us so we can spring the trap once we're fifty miles offshore."

Clark grinned. "I like where your head's at on this one."

I held up my empty glass. "The bar service around here stinks."

* * *

Dawn broke over the Atlantic, and Maebelle had made a breakfast spread fit for a king.

When I walked into the kitchen, I couldn't believe my eyes. "When did you have time to do all this?"

She wiggled her nose. "I'm a witch. Hasn't Clark told you?"

"You're anything but a witch. And as my way of saying thank you for all of this, I'm definitely taking your boyfriend fishing."

She threw her arms around me. "I love that man, I swear I do, but he needs a hobby."

A scratching sound came from outside, and Maebelle opened the door. Charlie, the black lab, came bounding through the door and squirmed in excitement at my feet.

"He's gotten so big," I said.

"He eats like a horse, and he clearly still remembers you."

I knelt and played with him until he ran off into the interior of the house.

"Oh, no," Maebelle said. "He's going to get his bumper. He'll never leave you alone now."

Seconds later, Charlie returned with a small boat fender in his mouth. He lunged toward me, encouraging me to take the once-inflatable fender. I did, and gave it a toss across the floor. His toenails clawed at the marble floor, and he skidded in pursuit of the toy. When he captured it firmly in his mouth, he sat erect by the back door, chewing violently on the fender.

"He wants you to throw it outside for him. I warned you."

I followed Charlie through the door and dived headfirst into a full-blown game of fetch with a world champion.

By the time Charlie had retrieved more tosses than I could count, Clark stuck his head through the door. "Get in here before breakfast gets cold."

I handed the fender back to Charlie, and he took it in his teeth. Instead of careening through the door back into the house, he lunged into the koi pond with his favorite toy.

After washing up, I joined the rest of the family at the breakfast table. I'd forgotten how incredible Maebelle's breakfasts were. No one took the time to speak. They just kept shoveling biscuits and gravy, strips of bacon, and eggs into their mouths.

When my plate was clean, I leaned back. "I don't know how you keep from weighing five hundred pounds, Clark."

He laughed. "Are you kidding me? She doesn't cook like this for me. She saves this for guests." He leaned in with conspiracy in his eyes and whispered, "Do you think you could come back more often? I really miss meals like this."

"I'll see what I can do."

Singer stood and lifted his plate. "Let me help you clean up."

Maebelle scoffed and waved her hands. "No, not a chance. You put that plate right back down and get out of here. You boys have a fishing trip, and I have all the help I need. Besides, you wouldn't wash dishes to suit me. I'm a little particular."

Fifteen minutes later, we crossed the causeway back toward the Miami Seaplane Base. We parked in the gravel near the fuel tanks and loaded our gear aboard the Caravan. As I headed for the cockpit, I discovered Hunter strapped into the captain's seat with the ink still wet on his newly-minted seaplane rating.

He looked over his shoulder. "You can chill out back there if you want. I've got this."

I slid into the co-pilot's seat. "It's a little hectic getting out of here, so I'll help you with the radios until we get north of Fort Lauderdale."

He slid his sunglasses down his nose and glared at me. "Okay, but try not to touch anything. A machine this complex requires expert handling."

I made a show of keeping my hands away from the controls. "In that case, get us out of here, expert. We've got some fishing to do."

## Chapter 10
# *Knight in Shining Armor*

The solid white obelisk that is the Ocracoke Lighthouse came into view on the northern horizon, and Hunter turned to make his announcement. "Ladies and gentlemen, this is your captain speaking. Please ensure your seatbacks and tray tables are in their upright and locked positions. We're now beginning our final descent into Cape Hatteras."

Every piece of scrap paper, candy wrapper, or debris the team could find became projectiles launched into the cockpit.

Hunter formed a pistol with his thumb and index finger. "I'm pretty sure it's a federal offense to interfere with the operation of an aircraft in flight. All of you are under arrest."

Clark draped his headset cord across Hunter's head. "You can add resisting arrest and assaulting a make-believe police officer to my charges."

Despite the jeers and verbal abuse from the peanut gallery, Hunter made another textbook landing at Billy Mitchell Airport with the barber pole black-and-white Hatteras Light in the distance.

I motioned toward the landmark. "Did you guys know the Hatteras is the tallest brick lighthouse ever built?"

Clark didn't miss a beat. "I'll take random facts nobody cares about for a thousand, Alex."

I stuck a backpack in his gut. "Oh, you're funny, broke back."

Hunter finally offered the respect I deserved by asking, "Did you say it's made of brick?"

"Yes, it's a hundred ninety-eight feet tall and made entirely of bricks. They actually moved it twenty-nine hundred feet in ninety-nine because of erosion at the old site."

Hunter widened his eyes. "Brick? Really?"

"Yes, really. It's brick," I said.

He turned to Singer and Clark. "Ready guys? One . . . two . . . three . . ."

In some sort of terribly off-key eruption, the three began singing The Commodores's "Brick House." And they held nothing back.

"You three are cultural barbarians, and only one of you can sing. Oh, and don't think I won't tell the preacher you were singing 'Brick House.' You're in big trouble when we get home."

Singer threw up both hands. "I was harmonizing, not singing. Get it right."

I shoved armloads of gear toward the barbershop trio—or whatever they were trying to be—and headed for the parking lot. "Would you look at that? Skipper's done it again."

Clark popped the rear hatch and tossed his load of gear inside. "How did she find a Range Rover out here on the Outer Banks?"

Hunter added his gear to the stack. "Leave it to Skipper. She's a miracle worker."

I checked my phone to find the address of our rented house and climbed behind the wheel. "Let's check into the house and then find something to eat."

We climbed to the widow's walk at the top of the three-story monster of a house. The view was breathtaking, even for the barbarians.

Clark shielded his eyes against the sun. "It really is pretty out here."

"It sure is," I said. "This wouldn't be a bad place to settle down."

He shot me a look. "Are you thinking about leaving Bonaventure?"

"No, not any time soon, but I'm glad you brought it up. I plan to rebuild, but not exactly the way it was. I'd love your thoughts on what I have in mind."

He hopped up onto the railing. "Let's hear it."

"I was thinking about making it look original from the outside, but I want to go ultra-modern on the inside, with an ops center, SCIF, bigger vault, comms center, and maybe even a bunker."

Singer turned to Hunter. "You see, Air Force, a SCIF is a Secure Compartmented Information Facility, where you can't take any cell phones or electronic devices so the grownups can talk about classified stuff."

Hunter grabbed Singer's belt. "I'm throwing you off this roof. You better hope you can fly."

Clark wasn't amused. "Chill out, guys. This is serious. How are you going to hide an ops center from random guests you might have in your house?"

I crossed my arms and leaned back against the railing. "I've already thought of that. If I rebuild the house as a three-story instead of the original two-story structure, I can put the ops center on the third floor, and nobody would ever go up there except the team."

Singer cocked his head. "How do you make a house that looks like a two-story plantation house have three floors?"

Bonaventure has . . . well, *had* ten-foot ceilings on the first floor and twelve-foot ceilings on the second floor, with attic space above that. There would be plenty of vertical space behind an identical exterior structure if we made the ceilings eight feet."

Clark seemed to consider my ideas. "What does Penny think of this plan of yours?"

I picked a pebble from the tread of my boot and tossed it over the rail. "We've not discussed the details yet, but she's definitely in favor of rebuilding."

Clark inspected his boots for debris. "Okay, then. I guess it's settled. You and your insurance company pay for the first two stories, and I'll talk the board into funding the ops center."

I held up a hand. "Not so fast. I'm not sure I want this mysterious board owning a third of my house. I think I'd rather foot the bill and not have any obligation to share my playroom with anyone outside our team."

"That's up to you," Clark said, "but I can get them to do it if you want. Just say the word."

"I'll give it some thought, but for right now, I'm leaning toward doing it myself."

Singer rubbed his stomach. "Didn't you say we were going to stow our gear and find some grub?"

"I did indeed. Come on. Let's do some scouting."

Hatteras is a sliver of sand about twenty-five miles off the east coast of mainland North Carolina. Strung together with barrier islands from Corolla to Portsmouth, the narrow dune-covered stretches of dry land make up the famed Outer Banks. Ocracoke, to the south, is accessible only by ferry, private plane, or boat. Hatteras is connected to the mainland by a series of bridges, but getting back to civilization from the island would be no easy task for most people.

Our Caravan simplified the process, but after dark, we were just as stranded as the rest of the island's inhabitants. No arrivals or departures are permitted after dark at the airport. I hoped we wouldn't bump our heads against that obstacle in the coming two days.

Hunter stuck his head between the two front seats. "What's the name of Davis's operation?"

"It's Lighthouse Charters, and according to Skipper's email, it's in this marina on the left."

"Let's buzz through there and get a look."

Hunter's idea was a good one, so I made the turn. The marina was minuscule by Florida standards, with perhaps twenty slips and no sailboats.

I spotted the sign. "There it is, all the way at the end."

Although there was no boat in the slip, the painted sign with a cut-out replica of the Hatteras Lighthouse marked the spot.

Clark rolled down his window and inspected the slip. "The dock's clean enough, and his lines are tidy. Maybe he runs a good boat."

"We'll find out tomorrow morning," I said, "but I suspect we'll be a charter he'll never forget."

Hunter grunted. "If he's our firebug, we'll be the last charter he ever sees."

Singer pointed around the corner of the marina. "There's a seafood joint right there. Why don't we get a table by the window, order up some oysters, and wait for the good captain to return to port?"

I tucked the Range Rover behind a palmetto bush, and we headed up the stairs. Just like every other building on the island, the restaurant was on stilts that put it above the likely storm surge from the next hurricane . . . and there was always a next hurricane.

As if drawn by some mysterious force even she couldn't identify, the waitress rested her hip against Clark's shoulder. "Hey, boys. I'm Heather. What'll it be?"

Clark looked up. "Don't be in too big a hurry to order, guys. The longer it takes, the longer Heather sticks around."

She draped a hand across his shoulder. "Don't worry. Even if I go away, I'll come back. I always do."

Singer cleared his throat. "I'm not sure your wife and the triplets would approve, Romeo."

Heather gave Clark a playful slap. "Triplets? You dirty dog. You're not wearing a ring."

He flashed her the crooked grin no woman can resist. "Relax. I'm pretty sure at least a couple of those triplets aren't mine."

Singer rolled his eyes. "Sweet tea for me, please, but I'm sure my heathen friends want a beer."

She giggled. "We've got Landshark and Nags Head Ale on tap. If you've not had the Nags Head, you should try it. It's really good."

Clark checked the table and received no disagreements. "Okay, then a pitcher of Nags Head and four dozen oysters to start."

"You got it, guys. I'll be right back." She gave Clark a hip bump. "And you behave, married father of triplets."

Clark tore the tip off a paper-wrapped straw and shot it at Singer. "You're telling lies on me, and you're supposed to be a man of God."

Singer grinned and pulled out his phone. "I'll give Maebelle a call. Let's see which one of us she's unhappy with when I tell her you're flirting with Heather and that I told a little white lie to get you back in line."

Clark waved both hands. "Okay, I surrender. Put the phone away."

The oysters weren't as good as Apalachicola's, but they certainly weren't bad, and the Nags Head turned out to be an excellent choice.

Hunter stole an oyster from Singer's tray. "Don't monks make beer, and didn't Jesus make a batch of wine out of water at a wedding a couple thousand years ago?"

Singer lifted the oyster back from Hunter's hand. "Yes, some monks make beer, and Jesus did, in fact, turn water into wine. I don't avoid alcohol because of my faith. I don't drink because I watched it turn my daddy into a monster."

Heather reappeared. "How are those oysters, boys?"

"Not bad," I said. "Do you have some kind of seafood platter and some hushpuppies?"

"We sure do. Grilled, fried, or blackened?"

"Blackened," came the overwhelming response from the table.

"Blackened, it is. How 'bout another pitcher?"

I glanced at the team. "No, I believe I'll have a glass of tea."

"Yeah, me, too," echoed Clark and Hunter.

Singer smiled. "Oh, and ma'am, I made that up about him being married with triplets."

Heather sidled up to Clark again. "So, you're not married after all?"

Clark held up his left ring finger. "Not yet, but I am committed, and we have a black lab."

"I'll be right back with those teas."

When our platter arrived, I asked, "Do you happen to know Captain Davis down there at Hatteras Light Charters?"

"Oh, yeah. I know everybody around here. Everybody knows everybody. Are you all going fishing with Kindle?"

Clark kicked my boot beneath the table.

"No," I said, "we were just thinking about doing some fishing and wondered who you'd recommend to take us out."

"Kindle would be a good one. He hauls in a lot of fish, but I'm sure you heard about his brother."

I raised my eyebrows. "No, we just got here today."

She placed her hands on the table and stage whispered, "Somebody killed his brother and a buddy of his down around Jacksonville not long ago. It's got Kindle pretty messed up."

"How does something like that happen?" I asked.

"You didn't hear it from me," Heather whispered, "but rumor has it his brother was into some money trouble and couldn't pay up, so somebody made an example. Kindle's been in some trouble too. Heck, all of us out here have been at one time or another."

"What kind of trouble?" I asked.

Heather blushed. "I got busted for having a dime bag of weed under the seat of my jeep, and I got caught shoplifting over in Chapel Hill when I was a kid."

"I didn't mean you. I meant Kindle."

She twisted her hair. "Oh, nothing, really. He likes to fight when he drinks, and I heard he got arrested 'cause somebody thought he stole a boat or something down in Florida right before his brother got killed. I heard somebody chopped him up with an axe or something like that."

"Drinking and fighting, huh? That's not so bad."

"No, it kind of comes with the territory, I guess. Can I get you guys anything else?"

"Just the check," I said. "And thanks for the info. We'll never tell a soul we heard it from you."

She winked at me. "You ain't got triplets at home, do you?"

"No, but I do have a wife, even *if* Clark doesn't."

"Oh, well, I guess I'll just keep slinging shrimp and oysters 'til my knight in shining armor comes riding up."

We paid the check and headed down the stairs just in time to see Captain Kindle Jefferson Davis backing into his slip.

## Chapter 11
# *Lady Two-Fifty-Seven*

My first instinct was to freeze on the steps in hopes our motion wouldn't catch Kindle Davis's eye, but the Green Berets and combat controller around me ducked into the shadows around the corner of the building. A hand caught the sleeve of my shirt and yanked me toward my team.

Clark put on his disappointed look. "Have you ever played hide-and-seek with a little kid?"

"Sure I have," I whispered.

"You know how they close their eyes and believe you can't see them because they can't see you? That's what you were doing on the steps, civilian."

"I've still got a lot to learn."

The team nodded in unison.

I ignored them. "That's our boy, all right. He looks a little healthier than he did lying on the floor with fish guts strewn about his belly."

When we brought Anya into our latest operation in Saint Augustine, she'd rendered Davis unconscious with a nasty vial of some drug I don't care to experience, and covered him with entrails of fish she'd commandeered from a pair of local fishermen. Her plan was to convince the three other "upstanding citizens" in the house that she meant business. It worked. They believed the fish guts were Davis's, and they spilled theirs in an eloquent confession for my audio recorder. Anya's ruse was outside her normal standard of violence of action. I'd never seen her pretend to kill anyone. She rarely hesitated to "gut someone like pig."

Hunter leaned close. "What do you think the chances are that he won't remember us?"

I shrugged. "I don't know. He was in pretty bad shape, and we kept it nice and dark in that house. I doubt he could pick us out of a lineup. If Mongo were here, I might have a different opinion. He's hard to forget."

Clark whispered, "I don't think there's any reason to spook him tonight. We know where he is and where he'll be tomorrow morning. If we show our faces tonight, that'll give him twelve hours to piece it together. I'd rather let him get us a dozen miles offshore before we spring the old 'Remember me?' trap."

"I think you're right. Let's hit the road before he comes off the boat."

With our bellies full and our target identified, we slept like the dead. I watched the sun break the eastern horizon from the widow's walk on top of the house and listened to the world come alive. The air was crisp and cool as it tends to be around Halloween on the Outer Banks of North Carolina.

We grabbed sausage biscuits and coffee from the gas station deli and pulled balaclavas over our faces, ostensibly to protect us from the morning chill in the air. The fact that the thin wraps helped conceal our identities was, of course, their true purpose.

Each of us carried a small, easily concealed pistol beneath our jackets and heavier firepower in our backpack. None of us had the intention of pulling a trigger, but making Davis believe we would shoot was critical to the success of our operation.

Before we dismounted the rented Range Rover, I called an audible. "Davis has heard my voice, so I don't want to let him hear it again until we spring our trap. Singer, I want you to make the introductions. Just use the name Knox Taylor."

Singer wrinkled his brow. "Whose idea was that goofy name? It makes me sound like a prep school yuppie. Hi, I'm Knox Taylor. Would you happen to have any Grey Poupon?"

"It's a little name game Skipper came up with. Sarah Knox Taylor was the first wife of Jefferson Davis, the first president of the confederacy."

Singer rolled his eyes. "Isn't that clever? Okay, I'll be Knox Taylor. Should I throw on my Oxford accent?"

It was my turn to roll my eyes. "The only thing being thrown will be you overboard if you screw this up."

With packs slung over our shoulders, we headed down the dock like four guys anxious for a cold, wet day on the Atlantic. Davis was cutting bait at the stern of his boat as we walked up.

Singer left the Oxford accent in the Range Rover. "Are you Captain Davis?"

The man wiped his hands and sheathed his filet knife behind his right hip. "You must be Mr. Taylor."

Singer stuck out his hand. "Yes, sir. I'm Knox, and these guys are Fulton, Johnson, and Stone."

*Brilliant*, I thought. Using our last names—and Hunter's first —was a stroke of improvisational genius.

"Welcome aboard *Lady Two-Fifty-Seven*, guys. Are you ready to catch a big one?"

Although I couldn't see his crooked grin behind his balaclava, Clark was no doubt wearing it. "Oh, you have no idea how ready we are to catch a big one."

Davis motioned for us to come aboard. "Then I've got a feeling today's your lucky day."

We stepped through the tuna door on the stern of his boat and stowed our gear well within easy access, should things escalate aboard *Lady Two-Fifty-Seven*.

Davis put away his cut bait and wiped his hands on a bloody towel hanging from the cleaning table.

Singer motioned toward the captain's hands. "It looks like you missed a spot."

Davis held up his hands and licked the back of his left one. "In this business, you can't be afraid to get a little blood on your hands."

Hunter chuckled. "I like that way of thinking. Do you mind if I steal that line?"

"It's all yours, my man. Stone, was it?"

Hunter held up his hands. "That's right. Stone. And it looks like my hands are clean . . . so far."

Davis started up the ladder to the topside controls. "We'll see what we can do about that. Now, what'll it be? You guys want to play it safe and stay inshore, where we can bag a boatload of kingfish? Or have you got the *stones* to head offshore for a big bluefin?"

The team turned to me, and I offered a slow nod.

Singer looked up at the captain. "We didn't come to play around. We're serious about catching what we came for."

Davis shot us a finger and thumb pistol. "I knew you guys were the real deal. Settle in. The ride's a little rough, and it'll take a couple of hours, but it'll all be worth it when we get out there."

He scampered up the ladder like a squirrel, and we made ourselves at home in the cabin.

I pulled down my balaclava. "He has no idea who we are."

The team unmasked, and Clark said, "I think you're right. This is going to be like shooting fish in a barrel."

Singer frowned. "I've never understood that saying. Who would shoot fish in a barrel?"

Hunter motioned for Singer to sit down. "Just because you could shoot a goldfish at half a mile with a pellet rifle doesn't mean we can all do it."

The interior of the boat wasn't luxurious, but it was more than comfortable. Pictures of Davis with a dozen grinning fishermen standing beside trophy gamefish lined the walls, and plaques boasting "Grand Prize Winner" in a dozen tournaments filled in the spaces not taken up by the pictures.

Singer, always the voice of reason, double-checked the chamber of his Colt Government .380. "So, do we have a plan, or are we going to improv this one?"

"Put away your BB Gun," I said. "Here's what I'm thinking. We'll play the first few hours nice and straight, just like regular fishing buddies. Maybe we'll hook one of those big bluefins he's talking about. If we do, the energy will be high, and his guard will be way down when we get it to the boat." I had everyone's attention. "Hunter, you've got the best hands, so you get that filet knife off his hip. I'd like to get him on his back on the deck. He's going to be sure-footed, but once we get him down, he'll be easy to keep down."

Nods told me the team agreed, so I continued. "Clark, that's when you go to work. A dose of salt water up the nose should get his attention, and I'll start a nice little game of twenty questions."

Singer held up a finger. "How far do we push it if he fights back?"

"Do you really think he's going to fight back against the four of us?"

Singer raised his eyebrows. "I don't think he's going to roll over and play dead. I just want to know the ROE."

I let the possible scenarios play out in my head. "Okay, the rules of engagement are simple. We're not going to kill him unless he gives us absolutely no other choice. We want him to confess and name his accomplices. If he does that, the three of you may have to restrain me, but we'll have what we came for."

Clark stood. "It's a solid plan. Now, let's go pretend like we're fascinated by a little boat ride."

We left the cabin and climbed the ladder to the topside, where Davis was sitting with his feet on the console and the boat on autopilot.

Singer almost yelled, "How much farther?"

Davis jerked as if he'd been shot. "Dammit, man! Don't sneak up on me like that. You scared me out of my skin."

Singer smirked. "Sorry. I'll ring a bell or something next time. How much farther?"

Davis pointed to the chart plotter. "We'll be on the trolling grounds in forty-five minutes. Is everybody's stomach feeling okay?"

Clark said, "Oh, yeah. We're all wearing the patch, so we'll be good. How about you, Captain?"

Davis laughed. "I've not been seasick in forty years in forty-foot rollers . . . and I ain't wearing any patch."

Clark feigned admiration. "Must be nice."

"It's just life at sea," he said. "A man can get used to most anything if he does it long enough. Say, do any of you guys know anything about boats?"

Clark motioned toward me. "He knows a little."

Davis looked at me and narrowed his eyes. "Say, would you mind pulling down that mask? I think I know you from somewhere."

My quick look at Hunter sent his hand toward his waistband.

I pinched my balaclava just below my chin and slowly slid it down, never taking my eyes off Davis's hands.

He stared at me with the intensity of a hawk eyeing a field mouse and then huffed. "I know who it is now. With your mask pulled up, you looked like Marshal Dillon from *Gunsmoke*. You guys ever watch that show? You ain't no lawman, are you, Marshal?"

I drew a make-believe pistol. "Stick 'em up, partner."

He laughed. "Here, take the wheel. Actually, just sit here and make sure the autopilot doesn't kick off. I'm going to set up the trolling rigs down below."

Davis hooked his heels and palms around the ladder rails and slid to the bottom like a submariner.

I shot a look at the team. "That was a little hairy."

Clark did his best John Wayne, which wasn't very good. "Well, I don't know, Pilgrim. Sounds to me like that hombre's got your number."

I threw an empty Mountain Dew can at him. "The Duke wasn't in *Gunsmoke*, you idiot."

He frowned. "That wasn't John Wayne. I was doing Festus."

"You've never actually seen an episode of *Gunsmoke*, have you?"

"Was that the one with Barney and Goober?"

Just as promised, forty-five minutes later, Captain Davis slowed to trolling speed, and we sent eight lines overboard.

"So, here's what's going to happen when we hook one," Davis began. "We're going to get all the empty lines out of the water as quickly as possible while we let the fish run with the hot line. Once we've only got one line in the water and the bluefin is convinced he's got a free meal, we're going to set the hook, and that's when the fun begins. Whoever's going to fight it will plant his butt in the fighting chair, and I'll back down on him."

"What does that mean?" Hunter asked.

"It means I'll put the boat in reverse and give you a chance to take up some of the line. Don't ever let the line go slack. If he starts running toward the boat, I'll power away. Keep that line taut all the time. Otherwise, he'll turn and snap it."

Singer said, "What do we do when we get him to the boat?"

"*If* you get him to the boat," Davis corrected. "If you get him up here, and if he's over forty-six and under seventy-three inches, I'll gaff him, tail-rope him, and we'll winch his bluefin ass right up on the deck."

Singer continued. "Then what?"

"Then we go home," Davis said.

Hunter protested. "Go home? Why would we go home if we're on the fish?"

"Because the law says we can keep one bluefin per day per boat."

Clark pointed at me. "And with Marshal Dillon aboard, we've got to follow the law."

Two hours later, after nothing even resembling a bite, Davis pointed astern. "Look at those birds. That's a good sign."

Before he could finish his prophecy, the rod on the starboard stern quarter bent as if Moby Dick himself had hit it.

"Fish on!" yelled Davis. "Get the lines out of the water!"

We cranked furiously on the unburdened lines until the rod with the fish on was the only one left in the water.

"Somebody, get on that rod and in the chair," Davis ordered.

All eyes turned to Singer, and he smiled. Soon, our sniper Sunday school teacher was fighting his first giant bluefin tuna.

Davis worked the controls of the boat like the seasoned seaman he was, and we cheered on our death-from-a-distance angler. As the fight continued and the excitement grew, I could have almost forgotten why we were on the boat. Seeing Singer completely lost in the thrill of landing the monster tuna was exhilarating.

Although Singer spent much of his time working with the church or the monastery, he put in just as many hours in the gym as the rest of us. He was in remarkable physical condition, but the look on his face said the tuna was winning.

Sweat poured from his face, and his arms trembled as if he were having a seizure. The way he gritted his teeth left me fearing Singer was wrestling with a demon rather than a giant tuna.

I pressed my shoulder into my friend's shuddering arm. "If you need a break, one of us can fight him for a while."

He shook me off and kept fighting. The battle raged for over two hours. We poured Gatorade down Singer's throat and even pulled off his jacket and two shirts while surreptitiously lifting his holster and Colt from his belt. Despite the cold October air, he looked like he was roasting in a sauna as he fought on.

Clark bent over the transom. "I see him!"

Davis abandoned the controls and ran to the stern with a long, razor-sharp gaff hoisted high above his head. With a mighty throw that would've made a Spartan proud, he hurled the gaff through the air and water until it pierced the flesh of the giant tuna just behind his gills.

He followed up the killing throw with a rapid flick of his wrist, landing a looped rope securely over the dying fish's protruding tail. He leaned back, drawing the slack from the rope, and whipped it around a cleat. "Fish landed!"

The captain turned and offered elated high fives all around until he came to Singer, who was leaning forward at the waist and gasping for breath.

The sniper reached out with his left, grabbed the captain by the collar, and yanked him to within inches of his face. His sweat dripped from his nose and brow, landing on Davis's cheek. "What on God's Earth does *Lady Two-Fifty-Seven* mean?"

# Chapter 12
## *Jurisdiction*

Captain Davis pulled the tail rope from the cleat and rigged it to the overhead winch. With the press of a button, and the whirring of an electric motor, the monster came, tail first, through the tuna door on the transom, and slid to a stop on the fiberglass deck.

Davis pulled the tail rope from the fish and looked up at Singer. "You fought a giant tuna for over two hours, landed him, nearly killed yourself doing it, and the first thing you say is, 'What on God's Earth does *Lady Two-Fifty-Seven* mean?'"

Singer's breath was coming easier. "Yeah. That's what I've been thinking about for two hours. What does it mean?"

Hunter took advantage of the distraction to lift Davis's knife from its sheath behind his right hip. Simultaneously, Clark snatched the tail rope from the captain's hand and looped it around his ankles. With one more touch of the button, the machine whined again, and Captain Kindle Jefferson Davis slammed facedown onto the deck as the winch yanked his feet skyward.

Hunter grabbed the man's shoulders and rolled him onto his back like he was trying to twist his spine from his body. Before Davis had stopped fighting against Hunter's pull, Clark sent a two-gallon bucket of seawater cascading over his torso and straight up his nose.

The hogtied captain spat and sputtered as if he were approaching death's door.

It was time for my solo, so I knelt beside the drenched captain turned prisoner. "You're going to answer some questions now."

He continued spitting salt water and blood from his nose and mouth as his eyes filled with terror. "It's the number of steps to the top of the Hatteras Light. That's all. I just thought it was a cool name for a boat. I swear. That's all it means."

I yelled. "Wrong answer. Wrong question. Hit him again!"

Before the words left my tongue, another deluge of water flooded the man's face. The sputtering and gagging came harder, and he shuddered in fear-induced tremors that consumed him from the waist up.

"I'm not your priest, and I'm not offering absolution, but it's time for confession, Davis."

He shook as if consumed by seizures, and his words came in soaked staccato. "Whatever you want, you can have it. The boat. Whatever. You can have it. Just don't kill me."

"Get his feet up higher," I ordered, and Hunter obeyed without hesitation.

Davis's feet rose eighteen more inches, leaving only his shoulders and the back of his head resting on the deck. His arms flailed wildly until Singer secured them with one hand in front and the other in back, with heavy fishing line running from wrist to wrist and directly across his crotch. Clark grabbed Davis's shirt and pulled it over his head until his face was hidden beneath the drenched material. More water followed, but not in a deluge. It came as if pouring from a garden hose with the spigot only half open. No matter where Davis sent his head, Clark followed with the solid, endless stream of water.

I stuck a knee on his forehead. "This is what my friend likes to call a *tactical baptism*, Captain Davis. It won't wash away your sins, but something tells me it *will* get you to confess them."

With every coughing gag, more water and blood spewed through the soaked shirt.

I held up one hand, and Clark stopped pouring. "The choice is yours. You can talk, or we can see how long it takes my buddy to pour the whole Atlantic Ocean up your nose."

"I don't know what you want," he gagged.

"Then here's a little drink to help you figure it out. Hit him again!"

Clark did.

I was impressed with Davis's resilience, but he would crack. Everyone does.

Begging is the first sign that enhanced interrogation is working.

"Please, just stop. Please. I don't know what you want. I can't give you what you want unless you tell me what it is. Please, just stop and tell me what you want."

"I told you what I want . . . a confession. Tell me all your sins, Kindle. It's the only thing that'll save your life."

Crying is always the immediate precursor to surrender. Davis's pleading turned to sobbing, and we'd won.

I tore the shirt from his face. "Innocent men don't cry under interrogation, so let's hear it."

He tugged against his restraints, and Clark moved toward him with the loaded bucket. "Okay! Okay! But I didn't do it. I swear. I needed the money really bad. I was just the driver. I swear to God."

"Names!" I ordered. "Who did it?"

"It don't matter, man. They're both dead."

"Who's dead?" I demanded.

"My brother and his government buddy. They did the whole thing, but they got cut up. They're dead, man. I've been through enough. You don't even know. I didn't do nothing except drive, I swear!"

I drew my pistol and pressed the muzzle beneath his bloody nose. "That cold steel you feel grinding into your face is a Makarov nine-millimeter. The last time you were this close to anything Russian, she could've added your guts to the fish entrails you were rolling in. She showed you some mercy. Nikolay

Fyodorovich Makarov and I will not. You just confessed to the wrong crime . . . again. The next thing out of your mouth better be exactly what I came to hear, otherwise, Nikolay and I will make it the last confession you ever make."

The tears turned to streams of submissive acceptance as recognition flashed in his face. Through sobbing inhalations, he moaned, "I swear to God, man. She said she was nineteen. I swear I didn't know."

His new confession sent a torrent of rage through me, leaving my right index finger aching to crush the trigger, but instead, I choked down my fury. "Who helped you start the fire, asshole?"

Behind the bloody, tearstained façade, his expression of guilt and terror gave way to utter confusion as the flesh of his philtrum parted beneath the pressure of my Makarov. "What fire?"

Innocence would never be a banner under which Kindle Jefferson Davis would reside. He was guilty of unforgivable sins, but burning my house to the ground wasn't one of them.

I glanced across my shoulder to see Hunter yanking Davis's pants from around his waist.

Hunter growled. "So, you're the kind of guy who likes messing with little girls, huh? You won't be doing that again."

None of us could get to Hunter's arm before the knife he'd lifted from Davis had done its gruesome work.

The muzzle of my Makarov was no longer a consideration in Davis's mind, so I holstered the weapon, and Clark yanked the tail rope from the winch. Davis's feet thudded to the deck, and he curled into the fetal position with blood trickling from his wound.

By the time the interrogation was over, Singer caught his breath, pulled his shirt back on, and knelt beside our captain. "Thanks for putting me on that fish. I had a lot more fun than you did today." He shot a glance toward Davis's wound. "I can stitch that up for you, but I didn't bring any Novocain, so it's gonna hurt."

Davis grunted like a dying animal.

Singer gave the captain's cheek a little slap. "I'll take that as a yes."

Clark marshaled me toward the cabin. "He's not our guy."

I stared at the scene on deck. "No, but he's somebody's guy. Did I push this one too far?"

He watched as Singer patched Davis back together. "I don't know, maybe. But there's nothing we can do about that now. We have to keep moving down the list. Who's next?"

"The more we eliminate, the brighter the light shines on Anya, and I don't like it."

"It doesn't matter what we like, College Boy. It matters that we find out who burned your house."

My satellite phone chimed from somewhere behind me. "You said you were going to put out some feelers for Russians on the loose. Have you had any bites?"

He shook his head. "Not yet, but we've been out of cellphone coverage for several hours. That sat-phone call you just missed might've been something."

I pulled the clunky, plastic phone from my backpack and unfolded the antenna. "It was Skipper," I said. "She wouldn't have called my sat-phone if it weren't important."

"Well, call her back. What are you waiting for?"

Hunter cleared his throat. "I'm sorry to interrupt, but I think one of us should get this boat headed west, don't you?"

Clark motioned up the ladder. "You're right. Get us underway. We'll clean up this mess down here."

Hunter scampered up the ladder and soon had the boat plowing through the rolling waves and headed back toward Hatteras.

The satellite connection took longer than it should have, but Skipper answered through terrible static. "Chase? Is that you?"

"Yeah, it's me. I missed your call. What's up?"

"Have you heard the news?" she yelled into the phone.

"What news? I can barely hear you."

The connection worsened. "Chase . . . somebody . . . shot . . ."

"Skipper, I can't hear you. We'll be back ashore in a couple of hours. I'll call you when we get back in cell coverage."

I stared down at the phone, but she never responded.

Clark leaned in. "What was that?"

"I don't know. The connection was bad. I think she was saying something about a shooting. What are we going to do with Davis?"

He rubbed his temple. "I've been thinking about that. Have you got your Secret Service cred pack with you?"

I pulled the black wallet from my backpack. "Never leave home without it."

He grinned. "Perfect. When we get in range, you'll call the sheriff. I think we'll play a little game of hot potato with the local law dogs, and Davis will be our spud."

The Hatteras Light came into view when we were eight miles offshore, and I dialed the non-emergency number for the sheriff.

"Dare County Sheriff's Office, how may I help you?"

"Good afternoon, ma'am. This is Supervisory Special Agent Chase Fulton with the U.S. Secret Service. Is the sheriff available?"

"Yes, sir, Agent Fulton. One moment, please."

The phone clicked. "Sheriff Randolph."

"Sheriff, I'm Special Agent Fult—"

"Yes, I know. Glenda told me. What is it?"

"Sheriff, I'm on a detail aboard Captain Kindle Davis's boat out of Hatteras, and there's been a development that falls under your jurisdiction."

"Go on."

"During a series of routine questions aboard *Lady Two-Fifty-Seven*. . . . Do you know the boat?"

"Yes, I know it."

"Well, as I said, during a series of routine questions, Mr. Davis became agitated and visibly nervous. Ultimately, he confessed to having some involvement with a minor female recently. That sort of matter is outside the purview of my assignment, but as you know, I'm required to report any such discovery to you."

Sheriff Randolph huffed. "Agent Fulton, I can't say I have any love for you federal boys, but I do have a special kind of hatred for child molesters. I assume you've got that bastard in cuffs."

I glanced at Davis. "Cuffs aren't particularly necessary in this situation, Sheriff. The captain suffered an unfortunate accident in which he slipped and fell onto his filet knife. One of my agents has the bleeding under control, but the subject of your special kind of hatred isn't going to be doing any running off any time soon."

"I'll meet you at the marina with a set of handcuffs, just in case. How soon will you be ashore?"

I gauged our speed and distance. "We'll be backing into the marina in twenty minutes. Oh, and Sheriff . . . I'd appreciate it if we could keep the commotion to a minimum. My protectee doesn't need his picture on the front page of your local paper, if you understand what I'm saying."

Randolph grunted. "After what's happened in South Carolina, I imagine you Secret Service boys are a little jumpy and anxious to get back to D.C., huh?"

I tried to make sense of his question but couldn't. "Sheriff, my job is to provide security to the protectee under my charge, regardless of what's going on elsewhere."

"Yeah, whatever. You feds sure are something else. I'll see you in eighteen minutes. No lights, no cameras."

I turned to Clark. "Find a jacket with a hood. Pull your balaclava over your face, and pretend like you're important. Sheriff Randolph is meeting us at the dock, and I need a dignitary to protect."

Hunter backed Davis's boat into the slip somewhat clumsily, but he didn't break anything. Two plain-clothed detectives stepped aboard, and I flashed my credentials. "I'm taking my protectee off now. Davis is all yours."

Clark ducked his head between Singer and me, and we hustled up the dock and deposited him into the right rear seat of the

Range Rover. Hunter slid behind the wheel, and we left the marina—and Singer's tuna—in the rearview mirror.

I shucked Clark's hood off his head. "Okay, you can stop pretending to be important now."

"Who's pretending?" he argued.

I pulled my cellphone from my pack and ignored the voicemail icon. "Skipper, it's Chase. We're back ashore. Davis didn't—"

She cut me off. "Chase! The president's been shot."

# Chapter 13
## *Aftermath*

I swallowed hard. "Is he alive?"

Skipper's voice cracked. "Chase, we had a drink and shot skeet with him."

"Yeah, I know. I'm having trouble wrapping my head around it, too. I remember the first time I met him. He was larger than life. Is he alive, Skipper?"

She pulled herself together. "He was alive a few minutes ago, but he's in a coma. The chief justice swore in the vice president about an hour ago."

"Hang on a second. I'm putting you on speaker."

I laid the phone down on the console between the front seats of the Range Rover. "The president's been shot. Skipper's going to brief us."

Every face in the car went pale, and questions roared.

"I don't know any more than you. Just hang on and let Skipper brief us."

I pressed the speaker button. "Okay, Skipper. I'm here with Clark, Singer, and Hunter. Let's hear it."

"Here's all we know so far. The president was doing a campaign speech for Senator Haller in Columbia. A sniper got off one shot from about twelve hundred yards." Singer let out a slight grunt, and Skipper kept talking. "The round hit the rim of the podium and struck the president in his left hip."

Singer interrupted. "That's a terrible shot. What do we know about the bullet and the shooter?"

"The shooter's dead. A countersniper put a fifty BMG round through the top of his head the instant after he pulled the trigger on the president. There wasn't much left of the shooter."

"Wait a minute," Singer huffed. "The Secret Service counter-snipers don't use fifty BMG."

Skipper raised her voice. "I didn't say anything about a Secret Service countersniper. Shut up and listen."

In a lighter moment, that would've been hilarious, but we did as we were told, and we shut up.

"As I was saying, the sniper who shot the president used a three hundred Winchester magnum round. His name was Landon Edgar Barrier, a Canadian who spent time in the French Foreign Legion. I'll have more on him in a few hours, but he's not the important player in this thing."

She paused, apparently expecting one of us to interrupt again, but we held our tongues in spite of the thousands of questions screaming inside us.

"The countersniper who put the fifty-cal round down Barrier's spine took the shot from an antenna over twenty-eight hundred yards away."

Singer couldn't sit still any longer. "You could fit every sniper on Earth who could make that shot inside this car. They have him in custody, right? What's his name?"

Skipper sighed. "There you go, interrupting again. They do not have him—or her—in custody. In fact, the existence of the countersniper hasn't been released to the media yet."

It was my turn to interrupt. "Let me get this straight. This Barrier guy shot the president, and then an unknown sniper shot Barrier from over a mile and a half away the same instant he shot the president. Is that what you're saying?"

"That's exactly what happened," Skipper said. "The Secret Service is publicly taking credit for the counter-snipe, but they're doing it in political doublespeak."

"Who made that call?" Clark asked.

Skipper said, "I guess it was the White House, but I don't know."

Singer whispered, "They'll never catch him."

Clark nodded. "You're right. There should be a huge manhunt underway right now, but if they're keeping it quiet, that means they're not even telling the local and state police."

Skipper spoke up. "There's no way to contain a lie this big for long."

Singer said, "He—and the sniper *is* a he—is dust in the wind. If they didn't catch him before he made it to the base of the antenna, he's gone for good."

I turned to the best sniper I've ever met. "Could you make that shot, Singer?"

He chewed on the inside of his cheek. "Maybe. A couple of Canadians made shots close to that last year in Afghanistan, but they were shooting standing targets, not the bowling-ball-sized heads of concealed snipers in the prone position."

I lowered my gaze. "Other than you, how many snipers could make that shot?"

He pursed his lips. "Maybe fifty or so would confidently take a twenty-eight-hundred-yard shot knowing they could hit a man, but fewer than a dozen would even attempt it on an eight-inch target like the top of a dude's head."

"Whoever took the second shot knew he'd make it," I said.

I opened the glove compartment and found an envelope with rental paperwork. I threw the envelope to Singer. "Make a list."

Skipper said, "We have to stay out of this. It's the Treasury Department's game. We're not even supposed to know about it."

"I'm not going to start searching the woods around Columbia for a sniper, but I want to find out where the twelve guys who could do this are on Earth, and you're the only person I know who can make that happen."

She protested. "If I get caught messing around in this. . . ."

"Relax," I said. "If anyone asks, I'm looking for another sniper for our team. That's all."

Singer slid the envelope to me with eight names on the back. I read them to Skipper.

"Okay, I'll get on it, but guys like this aren't easy to find. It'll take some time."

"Speaking of hard to find," I said, "any luck finding Anya?"

She let out a long breath. "Until the assassination attempt on the president this morning, I've done nothing but look for her. She's gone, Chase. I mean, gone gone."

I gathered my thoughts. "What about the Kremlin?"

"I'm monitoring everything in and out of Moscow, and there's not a whisper about her."

"How does someone just disappear?" I asked.

"To be honest," she said, "disappearing from my perspective isn't terribly hard if someone is well trained, which Anya definitely is, but for someone like her to *physically* disappear is another story."

"What do you mean, someone like her?"

I could almost hear Skipper rolling her eyes. "Come on, Chase. She's a beautiful Russian woman with a definite accent. Unless she goes back to Eastern Europe, she's going to stand out wherever she goes."

I scratched my chin. "We can't exactly put out a nationwide A-P-B on her, but we can throw out a local net and see what we catch."

"What are you talking about?" she said.

"I'll explain it later. We're heading back to Saint Marys. Get to work on that list."

"Hey!" she scolded. "I don't really work for you anymore. I'm kinda rich now, so I don't need this crummy job."

I grinned. "Get to work on the list . . . please."

"Since you asked nicely, I'll have something for you by the time you get back to Bonaventure."

I groaned. "Bonaventure doesn't exist anymore."

She sighed. "I know. I'm sorry. It's just habit."

"It's fine. I'll call you when we land."

I hung up, and the four of us sat in stunned silence for a long moment.

I finally asked, "Did anyone leave anything at the house?"

Everyone said no, so we drove straight to the airport.

The rest of us loaded our gear and climbed aboard while Hunter conducted the preflight inspection. "We're going to need fuel," he said.

I threw my feet into the empty seat across from me. "Okay. You're the pilot in command. I'm just a passenger."

"A passenger who'll be paying for fuel when we land at Beaufort."

The wind off the Atlantic made the Caravan a handful on take-off, but Hunter managed it as well as I would have, and we landed at Michael J. Smith Field in Beaufort, NC, twenty minutes later. The lineman wouldn't refuel the airplane with passengers aboard, so we wandered into the pilot's lounge while we waited.

The television in the lounge showed a pair of talking heads yelling at each other. "If the Secret Service sniper could kill the assassin after he shot the president, why couldn't he have stopped him before he took the shot?" one of them said.

I pressed the mute button on the remote. "He called him an *assassin*. Does that mean the president is dead?"

A man with epaulets on his shoulders stuck his head into the lounge. "The president died just before you guys landed. Good riddance, is what I say. This country will be a lot better off with-out—"

I was on my feet before the man could finish his insult. I'd sprung from behind home plate dozens of times to protect my pitcher from an angry batter, so the motion was purely muscle memory. On the baseball field, no one was fast enough to stop me before I pummeled the furious batter to the ground, but I wasn't on a baseball field. I was in a pilot's lounge only feet away from three elite covert operatives. Hunter planted his shoulder beneath my right arm an instant before a right cross would've landed on the man's jaw.

Clark was moving, too, but when he saw Hunter knock me off track, he stepped in front of the man at the door and grabbed him by the shirt. "You listen to me, you S-O-B. You were a half second away from a lesson in respect for our country and our president. The president was our friend and the best thing that's happened to this country in a long time."

The man struggled to free himself from Clark's vise-like grip but failed miserably. "Get your hands off me. I'll press charges."

Clark laughed. "Press charges? That's your threat?"

He hung a heel behind the man's left knee and gave him a Green Beret shove. The man tumbled to the floor, the contents of his pockets emptying around him. He looked up, and his voice trembled. "I'm warning you. . . ."

Clark held up one finger. "Hold that thought." He then turned back to face the three of us. "This genius here is in the process of warning me. You guys may want to hear this."

Singer, Hunter, and I flanked Clark and stood over the frightened man. "Warn somebody who you can intimidate, you piece of crap, but keep your mouth shut about our president."

I landed a heel against the edge of his knee as we stepped over him. It wasn't enough to do any real damage, but it would leave a nice strawberry for a few days.

The man behind the counter was laughing and leaning in to watch the show. "Why did you stop? That guy's had it coming for a while, and I didn't see nothin'."

I paid the fuel bill, and we blasted off. The news of the president's death made me feel like I'd been kicked in the gut. None of us had a word to say on the two-and-a-half-hour flight back to St. Marys.

We towed the Caravan into the hangar, and I pulled my phone out to call Skipper. The screen told me I'd missed a call from the 202 area code, Washington, D.C.

I pressed the voicemail icon and stuck the phone to my ear.

"Mr. Fulton, this is Special Agent Briscoe with the FBI. There's been a development in your arson investigation. Please call me when you get this message."

I dialed his number. "Agent Briscoe, Chase Fulton here. I'm sorry I missed your call."

"Ah, Mr. Fulton. Thanks for calling me back. The lab results on the accelerant likely used to start the fire at your residence are in."

I waited for him to continue, but the line was quiet. "Okay, are you going to tell me the lab results?"

"Oh, yes, of course. I don't know how detailed you want me to get. I'll email you a copy of the lab report, but the accelerant was made from the resin of a Pinus sibirica tree and a complex petroleum compound. The resin provided a base compound that slowed the burn rate of the petroleum but allowed the temperature of the accelerant fire to reach over a thousand degrees."

I squeezed my eyes closed, trying to picture such a compound. "So, somebody started the fire with pine tar and gasoline?"

"Well, no, not exactly. The petroleum compound was more closely related to dicyanoacetylene or more commonly called carbon subnitride. Think of it like the welding gas acetylene, except replace the two hydrogen atoms with cyanide groups."

Squeezing my eyelids became as painful as the headache Agent Briscoe was causing. "I wasn't great in chemistry, so you may have to break it down even further for me. Are you saying somebody mixed welding gas with pine tree resin? Is that a typical technique for arsonists?"

Briscoe cleared his throat. "Again, Mr. Fulton, it's not that simple, and it wasn't just any pine tree resin. Carbon subnitride is the hottest-burning petroleum compound known to man. The process to create the compound is incredibly complex. As fascinating as that aspect of this case is, the resin from the Pinus sibirica is even more intriguing."

"Come on, Briscoe. I'm not a chemist or botanist. I get that the carbon nitrate stuff burns hot—"

"Carbon subnitride," he corrected.

"Okay, whatever, but what's so special about the tree sap?"

"Mr. Fulton, it's not sap. It's resin. When combined with the carbon subnitride, the resulting compound would burn incredibly hot, but also slowly, making it possible for one person to place and ignite multiple samples inside your house without an accomplice, and then escape before the fire consumes the residence."

I could feel my heart pounding inside my chest. "Are you suggesting the arsonist likely worked alone?"

"I'm saying it's *possible* the arsonist worked alone, but more importantly, you need to know that the Pinus sibirica is the Siberian cedar, and it only grows in Russia."

# Chapter 14
## *Wrong Ponies*

The couch inside our hangar at the Saint Marys Airport instantly became the safety net into which I fell. I glared into the phone in disbelief as the knot in my stomach turned to nausea. "She did it."

Hunter stared down at me. "Who did it?"

"Anya started the fire."

He set his jaw and slowly shook his head. "Tell me about it."

I held up my phone as if I were back in third-grade show-and-tell. "That was Briscoe. He said the lab report on the accelerant came back. It was some sort of crazy hot carbon hydro-something mixed with sap from a tree that only grows in Russia."

He groaned. "But that still doesn't nail Anya as the arsonist. What about the accomplices?"

I shook my head. "That's the worst part. The concoction used to start the fires made it possible for one person to light them, position them, and still get out before the fire began roaring. Everything about it points to Anya."

"But why would she burn your house down? It doesn't make any sense."

I twirled my phone in my palm. "I don't know. Why does she do anything? She's mysteriously disappeared. That's a problem in itself. The Russian tree sap is another. Who else would use something like that to start a fire? It screams SVR."

He pushed my feet off the couch and slid onto the seat beside me. "I want to argue with you, man, but it looks like Anya."

My heart sank in my chest as I tried to digest the unthinkable realization that the woman I'd once loved, and who claimed to have loved me, would do something so utterly horrific.

I drove my fist into the cushion. "Damn it. We took her in and made her part of the team. We trusted her."

"Maybe a pony ride would make you feel better and help clear your head."

I scoffed. "The last thing on Earth I want to deal with right now are those horses."

"Wrong ponies." He pointed toward my P-51D Mustang nestled in the corner of the hangar. "I meant that one."

I gave his thigh a punch. "I think you're onto something. Come on. Let's go for a ride."

As I stood from the couch, Hunter didn't move. "I think you could use a little time *alone* with *Penny's Secret.*"

The Mustang had been Dr. Richter's pride and joy. When he owned her, she wore the nose art of a stunning woman with the sharp, unmistakable features of an Eastern European beauty. She'd been *Katerina's Heart* before I got her shot up and nearly destroyed by Russian gunfire just twenty miles off the Georgia coast in a ridiculous battle with a Russian intelligence-gathering ship. I'd managed to limp her home and get the sixty-year-old warbird back on deck without killing myself, but she was near death. Earl's brother, Cotton, the best airframe and power plant mechanic I knew, rebuilt the World War Two queen of the skies piece by piece, and I christened her *Penny's Secret* after the sparkle in my wife's gorgeous eyes that made everyone around her believe she knew a secret she'd never tell.

The twelve-cylinder, supercharged Merlin engine not only left its mark in the skies high over Europe in 1944, but it also left an indelible mark on the memory of anyone who ever heard it roar past. I'd loved that sound—and feeling—since the first time I'd ever experienced it. It was the spring of 1997, my senior year at the University of Georgia in Athens, when Dr. Robert "Rocket" Richter put me in the cockpit and transported me to another life and another world—a world in which I would stand between the enemies of freedom and my beloved country, and draw my sword until my dying breath, in defense of the very foundations on which our nation was built.

Dr. Richter was gone, but his sacrifices and lasting impressions lived on in me, and in men *like* me who'd been inspired by his devotion, wisdom, and bravery. He survived the Cold War, loved only one woman, and died believing the child of that love, the daughter of Katerina, the beautiful woman on the nose of his airplane, had turned her back on the Kremlin and become an American through and through. I was thankful he couldn't see what his daughter had become. I was thankful that he'd never know his daughter, Anastasia Robertovna Burinkova, burned my house into a pile of rubble and debris.

I eased the throttle forward and felt the tail wheel leave the ground. A thousand feet later, the main gear left the concrete of the runway, and my pony and I were soaring into the sky. The gear came up, and I set the manifold pressure and RPM for my climb over Cumberland Island. Kings Bay Nuclear Submarine Base lay just to the north, so any turn in that direction was a no-no. Straight out to the southeast not only kept me from having to deal with the repercussions of overflying a top-secret naval facility, but also provided some of my favorite views of the coastal Georgia low country.

Flying purely for the joy of flying is one of the world's most rewarding endeavors, and there's no better airplane in which to do it than the Mustang. Fewer than one hundred airworthy Mustangs remain of the thousands produced during WWII. I made a promise to *Penny's Secret* that I'd never intentionally put her in peril again. The day might come when some unforeseen mechanical condition or mistake on my part left her choking and desperately seeking something hard on which to land, but I'd never again roll her on her back above a Russian warship, no matter how close the comrade captain chose to lay his vessel to the American coastline. She'd seen her last combat, even though I had not.

I pushed the nose over just north of Fernandina Beach and let the warbird stretch her wings and accelerate to two hundred fifty knots five hundred feet above the Atlantic. No one on the beach could ignore the sight or sound as I roared southward. The Mustang seemed to enjoy the attention as much as I had as every head on the beach turned and peered skyward, hands forming sunshades on foreheads and fingers pointing into the heavens. With just enough back pressure on the stick to keep her from sinking beneath me, I performed a pair of barrel rolls to the left and one back to the right. I did this for two reasons: First, as much as people love watching fascinating airplanes, they love watching fascinating airplanes do something cool even more. Second, I loved the feeling of the world twirling around me instead of the other way around.

Fifteen minutes later, the Usina Bridge and the Saint Augustine Inlet came into view. With a pull of the throttle and a little elevator trim, I slowed the Mustang to 140 knots and flew down the Matanzas River and over the Bridge of Lions. Earl's new boat appeared exactly where her old one had been, at the end of the floating dock at the Municipal Marina.

My old friend replayed the actions of the hundreds of gawkers on Fernandina Beach. She appeared on deck, hand on forehead, and stared skyward. I rocked the wings and added enough throttle to complete another barrel roll just for her. Although I couldn't see the smile on her round face, it was there.

With the power and propeller set for climb, I turned eastward over Saint Augustine Beach and headed out over the blue North Atlantic, where I'd done battle with Commander Krusevich, the master and commander of the *Viktor Leonov*. I relived the battle, putting the Mustang through the same dance we'd performed that day, with one important difference. Our dance partner, the Russian spy ship, was nowhere in sight, and for that, I was thankful. *Penny's Secret*, on the other hand, seemed to yearn for a target to engage. For all of her elegance, she was a machine of war. No matter how gracefully she presented herself, beneath the paint and flawless skin lay the heart of a warrior, a gladiator yearning for battle. Perhaps she and I had that in common. No matter how badly I wanted to pretend I was just like everyone else, beneath my flesh lay a spirit forged for combat, a weapon honed to a razor's edge, and left humming with lust for a target, for one more dance partner like Commander Krusevich.

The last time I'd flown *Penny's Secret* from the battlefield, she'd been pouring black smoke and limping like a wounded animal westward toward the coastline. I'd prayed with every revolution of the propeller that we'd make the beach. Losing her in the Atlantic would've been an unbearable fate for both me and the airplane.

Unlike that day, the Mustang roared her guttural expression of power and determination. No black smoke trailed behind, and no prayers in desperation left the cockpit. A three-point landing that would've made Dr. Richter—and Chuck Yeager—proud, ended our afternoon in the air, and my head was clear. My thoughts were rational. And my refusal to be defeated by fire, or the one who started the fire, was resolute.

With the Mustang back in her stall, I checked my phone to find a message from Skipper.

"Hey, Chase. I know it's weird timing with the president's assassination, but I found a couple of jets for us to look at. One is near Knoxville, Tennessee, and the other is in Orlando. The same broker has both listed, and he says he'll bring either or both to Saint Marys and apply the cost to the purchase of either one. Call me back, and I'll set it up."

I pressed the button to call the only woman in my life more important than Skipper, and Penny answered on the first ring.

"Hey, you," she said. "I've been wondering if you were going to call anytime soon."

"You can stop wondering. Here I am. Listen, I have some

news. Davis is not our guy. He didn't start the fire, but it turns out he did a few other things the local sheriff found interesting, so we left him in handcuffs."

She sighed. "Does that mean you're going after the guys from the Saint Marys shooting next?"

I swallowed the knot in my throat. "No, the lab results came back on the accelerant used to start the fire, and it doesn't point to the shooters. Someone used a compound of petroleum and resin from a tree that only grows in Russia."

The sound she made wasn't the sound of triumph. It was sincere sorrow. "Oh, Chase. I know how badly you didn't want it to be Anya. I'm sorry."

"Never be sorry for the truth," I breathed. "We can't change what happened."

"Yeah, I know," she said, "but this is tough for you to swallow, I'm sure. Are you going after her?"

I considered her question. "What would I do if I found her? Skipper says she's in the wind and leaving no tracks."

Penny groaned. "You found her before in Siberia."

"We only found her because she wanted to be found. She left a trail of breadcrumbs we couldn't miss. This time, she's deep underground."

I don't know what I expected Penny to say next, but what came out of her mouth was an absolute surprise.

"Have you told Mongo?"

I slapped my forehead. "I haven't even thought of Mongo. It's bad enough for him that she's gone. This is going to kill the poor guy."

She lowered her voice. "You have to tell him before someone else does. He needs to know."

"I'll call him when we hang up. How's it going in Hollywood?"

She let out a long sigh. "Exhausting. I had no idea it was so much work to pick a cast. I've sat through about a million auditions, and nobody is even close to how I picture my characters. I don't think they care about my opinion, though. The casting director, film director, and producers will make the selections. I still give them my opinions, but in the end, it probably won't matter. Oh, but I did meet some other writers, and they're amazing. I'm learning so much from them already."

That was the high-speed Penny I loved. "It sounds like you're having quite a time. Do you know when you'll be home?"

"Hopefully, we'll wrap up casting this week and start preproduction next week. I don't know if I need to be here for that, but I think it's important for me to learn as much about the process as I can. The more I learn, the easier it'll be next time, and the time after that."

"Oh, so there's already a next time, huh?"

She giggled. "Well, yeah, of course. Especially if this one is a hit."

"There are a couple more things we have to talk about. I'm sure you heard about the president."

She sounded deflated. "Yes, and it's so sad, but the Secret Service guys being able to shoot the guy like that . . . that was amazing. At least there won't be a long, expensive trial, and the guy will never get his fifteen minutes of fame."

I wanted so badly to tell her the truth about the snipers, but I couldn't, especially not on an unsecure cell phone. "Yeah, it's terrible. I just wanted to make sure you'd heard."

"It's all over the news. The whole world knows everything there is to know as soon as it happens these days. You can't keep anything a secret anymore."

"Oh, I don't know. You might be surprised."

She hissed. "What do you know that you're not telling me?"

I ignored her question. "We need to talk about the house. I want to build it back so the outside looks just like it did before the fire, but I want to shorten the ceilings inside and build a secure operations center on the third floor."

"The third floor?"

"Yes. If we shorten the ceilings to eight or nine feet, we can build a third floor that's invisible from the outside. We'll have an

Agency contractor do the design and construction, but you'll have to pick the colors and finishes. I'm a complete dummy when it comes to decorating."

"Does that mean you're not going after Anya?" she asked.

I grimaced. "Like I said earlier, I don't know what I'd do if and when I caught her."

"What's to keep her from doing it again after we rebuild?"

As badly as I wanted to be able to give an answer, nothing came. "I don't know, but if the Agency designs it for us, it'll have a state-of-the-art security system."

"I don't get the feeling Anya is afraid of security systems."

"You may be right," I admitted, "but at least the cameras will catch her if she does it again."

I could hear someone talking in the background.

"I've got to go," Penny said, "but I can call you later if there's more to discuss. I love the rebuilding idea if we can put machine guns on the roof to cut down anybody who tries to burn it again."

I laughed. "Machine guns, noted. I'll tell the architect. The only other thing is the airplane. Skipper found a couple of jets for us to look at. Do you want to be involved in that process?"

She slid her hand over her phone, and her muffled voice said, "Yeah, yeah. I'm coming. Just a second." She returned to our call. "Sorry. They're doing a dinner thing for the potential cast. I really have to go, but I trust you to pick an airplane for us. You seem to like Cessnas. Do they make a jet?"

"As a matter of fact, they do. You've been aboard a couple of Cessna Citations already."

"Okay, great. I'll have one of those, please."

I laughed. "You crack me up. We'll talk soon. Enjoy your dinner thing. Just don't fall for any of those chiseled-jaw, Hollywood types."

She almost choked. "Ha! Those pansies can't hold a candle to my man. I love you, silly boy."

"I love you, too."

*My Hollywood wife*, I thought.

# Chapter 15
## *I'll Take That One*

Sleeping alone aboard *Aegis* gave me more time to think, but thinking may not have been what my brain needed. I lay awake the first half of the night consumed by rage.

*If she burned my house down, I'll kill her. I'll hunt her down and put a bullet through her gorgeous Russian skull.*

The second half of my sleepless night was spent plummeting into a bottomless pit of disbelief and despair.

*I saved her life more times than I can count. I broke every international law imaginable to break her out of the Black Dolphin Prison. I went to the ends of the Earth to bring her back to America, where she could live the life of freedom everyone should experience. I loved her, and part of me always would. How could she . . . why would she destroy my house?*

At some point, merciful sleep took me, and I awoke to the sound of Skipper banging on my cabin door.

"Chase! Wake up!"

I dragged my weary mind from the depths of sleep. "What is it? What do you want?"

"Chase, it's nine thirty. What are you doing still in bed?"

I shook off the sleep I so desperately wanted and stumbled my way to the door. "Okay, I'm up. What are you doing here?"

She stood in the passageway with her hands on her hips. "You look terrible. The first jet will be here in thirty minutes, and the next one, an hour after that. You need—"

I pressed my finger to her lips. "You know how well I respond to the words *you need*, so let's use some other phrase."

"Okay, fine. If you want to look at the jet, you have to get cleaned up and pretend to be awake. How's that?"

"Much better," I said. "Please tell me you made coffee."

"Clark made coffee three hours ago, but I'll start a fresh pot. Do something with yourself. You're a mess."

So, I did something with myself—namely, a shower and shave. I almost felt human afterward, but lingering thoughts of Anya and Russian tree sap nagged from somewhere behind my ears.

"Here's your coffee, Rip Van Winkle."

I took the cup from Skipper and blew across the black surface of the liquid. "Thanks. I didn't get much sleep. I've got a lot on my mind."

Skipper looked up. "Apparently. I've never seen you sleep this late."

"It's Anya."

She frowned. "What's Anya?"

A tentative sip. "She burned down my house."

An eye roll. "You don't know that for sure. All you know is that someone started the fire with sap from a tree that's native to Russia. That's your only foundation for thinking Anya did it. She has absolutely no motive."

A less tentative sip. "Trying to figure out what motivates her is an exercise in masochism. To her, it could make perfect sense to burn down my house and vanish."

"That doesn't make perfect sense to anyone, not even her," Skipper argued.

"So, this jet . . . tell me about it."

She pulled a file from her case. "The first one is a Bombardier Learjet Forty-Five. It's just over ten million."

I slid the file toward myself and thumbed through the paper-work. "What else?"

She pulled out another file. "I still can't believe we're talking about spending ten million dollars, but this one is cheaper."

I pulled the file from her before she could open it. "Cheaper isn't always better. Sometimes, you get what you pay for." I read through the specifications. "This one looks interesting. I like it, and it's a Cessna. Penny likes Cessnas."

Skipper checked her watch. "If we're going to be there when the Learjet lands, we should go now."

I poured the last of the coffee down my throat and pulled on my shoes. We picked up Hunter and Singer in the VW Microbus and pulled up to the hangar just as the Learjet was taxiing to the ramp. I waved my arms, motioning for the pilots to park the jet in front of my hangar instead of the ramp in front of the FBO.

The door opened, and down the stairs came the epitome of a used car salesman. His hair was perfect, and his suit probably cost more than all the clothes I owned. He stuck out his hand before the engines stopped whining. "Vinnie Castellano. Which one of you is Mr. Fulton?"

I took his offered hand and looked him up and down. "I'm Chase Fulton, and this is Elizabeth."

He yanked his hand from mine and stuck it toward Skipper. "Oh, yeah, I talked with you on the phone. How you doing?"

"I'm good. Thank you, Vinnie. This is Singer and Hunter."

The handshakes and how-you-doings continued until Vinnie said, "Well, we ain't here to look at the outside. Come on aboard your new jet."

We followed him up the stairs and into the cabin. It was cramped, but well-appointed. The leather was nice, and every-thing worked.

"It's a beautiful cabin," I said, "but I'm more interested in the front office."

Vinnie slid between a pair of seats and motioned toward the cockpit. "Make yourself at home. Don is in the left seat. He'll answer any questions you have about the avionics and performance."

I carefully folded myself into the right cockpit seat and scanned the panel. "Good morning, Don. I'm Chase. Tell me about the airplane."

He was an excellent tour guide after we established that I wasn't aeronautically illiterate. "It's a sexy ride," he said. "Think of it as a flying Ferrari. It'll do everything you ask almost before you ask it."

"I'm more of a Porsche guy, myself. Great performance at half the price."

He shot a glance across his shoulder and into the cabin. "What's the asking number on this one?"

"Just over ten," I said with a hint of conspiracy in my voice.

He pursed his lips. "It's probably worth that if you plan to fly it fifty hours a month or more, but if not, the Citation that's on its way may be just the ticket. What sort of business are you in?"

I grinned. "My wife is a Hollywood screenwriter. I'm a bit of a kept man, you might say."

He winked. "Gotcha. Sounds like good work if you can get it."

"You know how it is," I said. "Chicks dig pilots."

He chuckled. "Yeah, some of us are fun for the weekend, but a bad long-term investment."

Back on the tarmac, I did the walk-around with the copilot, and he told me everything I ever wanted to know about the preflight inspection of the Learjet.

As we stood from beneath the nose of the jet, I heard the whine of the Pratt and Whitney turbofans of the Citation turning onto final approach. The landing gear chirped, and two puffs of white smoke twisted from the main landing gear.

Vinnie yelled, "Hey, you got a tug?"

I nodded, and he pulled a cellphone from his jacket pocket. Soon, the Citation Excel was sitting nose-to-nose with the Learjet. The Citation loomed over the Lear with just over three feet of additional height. The domination didn't end there. The Citation's wingspan outstretched the Lear by six feet.

*Who says size doesn't matter?*

It quickly became clear the size of the check is what mattered most to Vinnie.

He motioned up to the Citation. "As you can see, you're going to spend a lot more on hangar space for the Citation, so the Lear is the obvious long-term choice."

"That's your sales pitch?" I said. "Hangar space?"

"It adds up," he insisted, and brought up the calculator function on his phone. "Here, let me show you."

I pushed the phone away and pointed to my hangar that would easily contain both jets and still leave room for my other toys. "Hangar space isn't an issue, Vinnie. I'm going to have a look at the Citation."

Undaunted, he twisted the handle of the Citation's hatch and deployed the stairs. "This one is owned by Consolidated Foundry, a steel company out of Ohio. They're moving up to a Gulfstream as soon as we find this one a new home."

The team followed me into the cabin and made themselves at home. The leather wasn't flawless, and a few of the overhead lights didn't always come to life every time we pushed a button, but something about the airplane felt like it already belonged to us.

The yoga required to wedge myself into the cockpit was less demanding than it had been in the Lear, and I felt like I'd be spending a lot of time in the seat.

The pilot pointed out the window toward the Learjet. "Are you comparing this to *that?*"

I smiled. "No, I'm just sitting here structuring my offer on this one."

He leaned back and pulled a Clive Cussler novel from beneath his seat.

"Sorry to interrupt your book," I said, "but do you work for Consolidated Foundry or the broker?"

He dog-eared a page corner. "Neither, as soon as you write the check."

I threw him a look of confusion.

"Consolidated Foundry is going toes up," he said. "They're liquidating their assets. This airplane and me, well, I guess we're two of those assets. The airplane will keep working, but I'll go back to teaching kids to fly until I can pick up another corporate gig."

"So, you're a CFI?"

"That's right, a CF double I. I taught the turbine transition course at Flight Safety for three years after I retired from the Air Force. Now I'm just a lowly high-speed bus driver."

He was getting better by the minute.

"What did you fly for the Air Force?"

"The A-Ten Warthog for eighteen years, and the LGMD for two years after that. I guess you could say that's why I retired. If they'd left me in the cockpit, I'd probably be wearing colonel's wings by now."

I frowned. "LGMD?"

He winked. "Large gray metal desk."

I called into the cabin. "Hey, Hunter. Get up here and see if you can remember how to salute an officer."

Hunter took a knee at the cockpit door.

"Stone Hunter, meet . . ." I glanced up. "I'm sorry. I didn't get your name."

The pilot stuck out his hand. "The name's Disco, 'cause I like to dance with the ugly girls at the party."

I couldn't stifle my grin. "Disco, meet Stone Hunter, former Air Force combat controller."

Disco lowered his gaze. "I should be the one saluting you. CCT is the toughest gig there is. I was just telling your buddy here that I drove A-Tens for eighteen years. I've thrown many a round downrange with a combat controller whispering in my ear."

The two shared a moment of mutual respect, and I said, "Disco is looking for work. It seems the company he's been flying for just sold their jet. He just happens to be an instructor."

Hunter smirked. "You don't say."

"How about your copilot?" I asked.

Disco said, "Oh, him? He's got a right-seat job with a charter company. He's an aeronautical whore. He'll fly anything they pay him to."

I crawled from the seat. "Excuse us, if you don't mind. We've got to talk about buying an airplane and hiring a pilot. You're welcome to hang out in our hangar if you'd like. There's a relatively comfortable couch, a refrigerator that works, sometimes, and a couple of airplanes you might like to take a look at."

Hunter shuffled back into the cabin, and I followed. Disco took me up on my offer of relaxing in the hangar.

I spun one of the seats to face the rest of the team. "I think this is the one, guys, but I've got a proposal for you. This one is six million dollars. That's the check I was planning to write for the company's half of the airplane. What do you think of me writing that check, and you guys keeping your checkbooks in your pockets? We'll work out an hourly rate for personal use, and you pay that into the pot when you use the airplane. It'll be an asset of the team, but we can all use it whenever we want."

Singer was the first to speak. "I'm not sure that's fair to you, Chase, but if you're okay with it, there's a lot of good things I can do with the money I would've spent on my share of the purchase."

"Is Disco going to teach us to fly it?" Hunter asked.

Skipper's eyes widened into saucers. "Do I get to learn to fly it?"

I laughed. "Can I take that as a unanimous yes vote?"

There was no hesitation, and we had a deal.

I found Vinnie inside the Learjet, talking on his phone. He held up one finger. "I'm going to have to call you back."

"So, it's the Learjet, am I right?"

"Sorry to break your heart, Vinnie, but we like the Citation. I'll make an offer pending inspection of the records and the airplane by my mechanic. If it is what it's advertised to be, and my mechanic gives it the thumbs-up, I'll give you five point five, plus your expenses of getting it and the Learjet here."

Vinnie grimaced. "I don't think Consolidated Foundry will accept five point five. They're pretty rock solid on six."

I shrugged and turned for the stairs. "Consolidated Foundry is belly-up, Vinnie. I'll either give them five point five, or I'll buy it from the bankruptcy court for three, and I don't think the court pays a broker's commission, but I could be wrong."

Haggling complete, we agreed Vinnie would present my offer to Consolidated Foundry, and Skipper arranged for Cotton Jackson, the only airplane mechanic allowed to touch the Mustang, to bring his truckload of tools and head for Saint Marys.

November-five-six-zero-Charlie-Foxtrot fit nicely beside the Caravan, and I called Penny to let her know we were on the verge of adding another Cessna to the family.

"That's great news," she said with the excitement of a kid on Christmas Eve.

"It's a beautiful airplane and less than half of what we'd budgeted, plus, if it all works out, it comes with a pilot."

My phone chirped, and I glanced down to see a 202 area code on the caller ID. "I'm going to have to call you back, Penny. Somebody from D.C. is calling."

I pushed the button to accept the call. "Hello, this is Chase."

"Mr. Fulton?"

The voice sounded vaguely familiar, but I couldn't place it.

"Yes, this is Chase Fulton."

"Mr. Fulton, this is the vice president. We haven't been formally introduced, but I've heard a great deal about you."

I stammered. "Uh, Mr. Vice President? Aren't you the president now?"

He let out a long sigh. "Yes, I suppose I am, but that's going to take some time to get used to. Do you have access to a secure telephone line, Mr. Fulton?"

"Yes, sir. I have one in my hou—" Suddenly, I could smell the ashes of what remained of my house. "Actually, sir, I don't have a house anymore, but I think I can gain access to a secure line at Kings Bay Naval Submarine Base."

The president cleared his throat. "Very well. You get on over there to the base, and when you get to a secure line, you call this number, two-zero-two, five-five-five, two-six-two-three. Have you got that?"

"Yes, sir, I've got it."

"Good. A young officer will answer, and you are to tell him *code twenty-one*. He'll then place you on hold and find me. We have something critically important to discuss. Please, Mr. Fulton. Don't waste any time getting to the base."

# Chapter 16
## *The President's Man*

I immediately yelled for my partner. "Hunter! We need to get to the base, pronto. I need a secure line."

There are two kinds of men on Earth: those who would ask questions at a time like that, and those like Stone W. Hunter.

He was behind the wheel of the VW Microbus before the words left my tongue. Minutes later, a well-armed Marine waved us through the main gate to the Naval base. Hunter pulled to a stop in front of a nondescript, squatty building that could've been an abandoned bank branch from the 1970s.

I slid from the seat. "What is this place?"

My partner grinned. "You'll see."

He pulled a keycard from his pocket, slid it through a reader, and typed in a ten-digit code. A series of clicks followed, and we pushed through the heavy door.

A Marine only slightly less well-armed than the man at the gate stood just inside the door. "Good morning, Mr. Hunter. What can we do for you?"

"I need the commo officer and a secure line for Special Agent Fulton."

The young Marine pressed a combination of buttons on a panel and lifted a handset to his ear. "Captain, this is Sergeant Mills. Mr. Hunter is escorting a special agent and is requesting to use a secure line."

Another series of clicks resounded from a set of locks, and the Marine held the armored door open for us.

Hunter gave him a slap to the shoulder. "Thanks, Mills."

A Marine captain stepped from a doorway. "Good morning, Mr. Hunter. Right this way."

We followed him through a passageway and finally into a small room with no windows and a bank of communications equipment dominating one wall.

The captain motioned toward the gear. "There you are, sir. I'll post a guard on the door."

Hunter stepped aside, but I put a hand in the middle of his back. "Oh, no. You're coming in with me."

Again, no questions came, and he led the way into the room. We settled into chairs no one would ever classify as comfortable, and I lifted the handset to the only piece of equipment in the room I knew how to use.

I dialed the number the president gave, and I waited. A progression of tones rolled through the handset until a sharp voice came on the line. "Duty officer."

Pretending as if I knew exactly what I was doing, I barked, "Code twenty-one."

"Standby, sir."

The line went silent, and I slid a hand over the mouthpiece. "I don't know what's about to happen, but I don't want it to happen exclusively to me. I intend to share the love, so pick up a handset."

Hunter pulled black headphones from a hook and slid them over his ears. Obviously, he had no intention of doing anything other than listening.

"Is this line secure, sir?" came a monotone voice.

Hunter pointed to a pair of green lights illuminated near the bottom of the panel and gave the thumbs-up.

I said, "Line is secure."

"Standby for the president."

Hunter palm-slapped his forehead.

"Mr. Fulton, thank you for the efficiency. I won't waste your time with pleasantries. We have a crisis, and based on what I've been told about you and your team, you are exactly the man I need."

He paused, so I said, "Go on, sir."

The president made a clicking sound with his tongue. "There's a conspiracy afoot, Chase. May I call you Chase?"

"Of course, Mr. President."

"Good. As I'm sure you know, the president was assassinated yesterday, and the killer was shot immediately thereafter by a member of the Secret Service anti-sniper team."

He paused again, but I didn't take the bait. "If you say so, sir."

I'd never met the man, but I swear I could almost hear him smiling. "I *don't* say so. That's part of the reason I'm calling."

"I'm listening, Mr. President."

"As I said, there's a conspiracy of proportions this country has never seen, being perpetrated against the American people, and I may be powerless to stop it."

The sounds coming through the line made it clear the president was having a drink, so I sat, silently waiting for him to continue. Finally, he did.

"The Secret Service didn't shoot the sniper, Chase. I've been under their protection long enough to know and understand their tactics and capabilities. One of the things I've learned is that the CS teams—that's countersniper teams—use the Remington seven hundred or the KAC SR-Twenty-Five in seven-six-two, but the fifty-cal is not in their arsenal."

I cut my eyes toward Hunter. "You seem to know your weaponry, Mr. President."

"Damn right I do. I was a SEAL for over a decade before running for the Senate. I wasn't at the event when the president was killed, but I've watched the footage a thousand times, and the round that took out the president's killer was no thirty-cal."

"Why are you telling me this, Mr. President?"

"Cut the crap, Chase. The president and I were brothers-in-arms long before we wore red neckties and rode in armored limousines. We talked about things that mattered. You're one of those things. You were the president's man, and now, I'm the president."

A chill ran down my spine, but I didn't say a word.

He continued. "Finding people you can trust inside the Washington Beltway is like finding ice cream in Hell. The president trusted you. He told me all about the Pan America Oil Rig. The work you did could've never been done by anyone else without it showing up on the six-o'clock news. I've just got one simple question for you, Mr. Fulton."

I shifted in my chair. "What is it, sir?"

"Are you still the president's man, Chase?"

"I'm not sure I understand what you're asking, sir. If you want me to find the countersniper, I'm not sure I'm capable of doing that. The Secret Service has resources and assets I'll never dream of having. I can't even scratch the surface of the investigation they're going to conduct."

He cleared his throat. "That's just it, Chase. There is no investigation. The case is closed as far as the Secret Service is concerned. The whole world, except for you and me, believes a sniper killed the president and a Secret Service countersniper killed the shooter. Case closed."

I shook my head. "That can't be the case, sir. The Secret Service knows your background. Surely, they know you're not going to swallow that explanation, don't they?"

"The conspiracy that I believe is underway is far bigger than the Secret Service. I believe whoever killed the president isn't finished killing, and I'm next on the list."

"Mr. President, the person who killed the president had his head blown into microscopic pieces before he felt the recoil of his own rifle. That man isn't going to do any more killing."

"Stop playing small ball, Chase. I'm talking about the people behind the headless sniper."

"I'm sorry, sir, but I still don't understand what you're asking me to do."

"I'm almost out of time," the president said, "but are you familiar with the Twenty-Fifth Amendment to the Constitution?"

I racked my brain but couldn't piece it together. "I'm afraid I'm not, sir."

"Do a little Constitutional study, and we'll talk again soon. I may need your help, Chase. Can I call on you if I do?"

Without hesitation, I said, "Of course, Mr. President. I'm at your service."

The line went dead, and Hunter shucked off his headset. "What the hell was that?"

I stared into the handset. "I wish I knew. Do you remember what the Twenty-Fifth Amendment says?"

Hunter scoffed. "I don't think I can tell you what the first ten amendments say, let alone the Twenty-Fifth. It's too bad the Judge isn't still around. I'm sure he could tell you all about it."

I snapped my fingers. "He's not around, but I just happen to know a couple of bright young law clerks who studied in the Judge's shadow."

Hunter stood and pushed the rigid chair beneath the console. "It sounds like you've got a phone call to make."

We thanked the Marine captain on the way out and headed back for my boat. We found Skipper back aboard *Aegis*, pecking away at her computer.

"Hey, Chase. What's up?"

I filled her in on the talk with the president, and she bit her bottom lip. "So, what does he want us to do?"

"That's where I'm a little unclear. He told me to study up on the Twenty-Fifth Amendment. Do you know what that is?"

She nodded. "Duh, it's the one right after the Twenty-Fourth."

Useless as it was, I launched a pillow at her head, but she easily blocked it. "You'll have to do better than that. I'm not afraid of throw pillows, no matter who throws them."

"Since you clearly aren't up on your Constitutional amendments, we need to find someone who is. How about the two clerks who worked for the Judge? Do you remember them?"

She said, "Sure, I remember them. How could I forget? Ben Hedgcock and Jeff Montgomery are their names. They both work for the same law firm in Savannah now. Ben calls me at least twice a month trying to get me to go out with him, and Jeff always calls right behind him to remind me what a dog Ben is."

I chuckled. "I don't want to get in the middle of that triangle, but I do need to talk with the one who knows more about the Constitution."

"That's definitely Ben," she said. "Jeff is chasing ambulances or something sleazy like that, but Ben is doing some civil rights stuff. Do you want his number?"

"I do."

She scribbled down a list of numbers on a yellow pad. "Here you go. That's their office and cell numbers."

I took the paper from her hand. "You're the best. How's the sniper hunt coming along?"

"Don't ask," she said, rubbing her forehead. "Guys like that aren't easy to find when they want to be found, and almost impossible when they don't want anyone to know where they are."

I feigned throwing the pillow back at her. "For a lesser analyst, they may be impossible to find, but it should be child's play for you."

She rolled her eyes. "It's one thing for you to be cocky about what you can do, but don't put that on me. Even I have my limits."

"Limits are for losers. How many of them have you found?"

She clicked her mouse, and pages shuffled on her computer screen. "Here's what I have so far. I've found three of the eight names Singer gave us. They're confirmed and alibied. It couldn't have been any of them."

"Three down, five to go," I said. "Keep at it." I stuck the phone to my ear and listened as it rang.

Finally, the young lawyer picked up. "Hello, this is Ben."

"Ben, it's Chase Fulton. Do you remember me?"

"Of course I do, Chase. How are things down at Bonaventure?"

I stared up the yard at the blackened remains of the majestic house. "Things have been better, Ben. I'm sad to say, the house burned to the ground."

"Oh no! Was anyone hurt?"

"Thankfully, no. We weren't home. The investigators say it was definitely arson, though."

He sighed. "I'm sorry to hear that. I'm sure they'll catch the guy."

A wave of anger poured over me as I pictured Anya slinking away from Bonaventure with flames lapping into the sky behind her.

"Listen, Ben. I need a little help with some research I'm working on. Could you give me a little primer on the Twenty-Fifth Amendment?"

He stammered. "Well, yeah, sure I can, but what . . ." When it finally hit him, he said, "Oh! Yes, of course. Wow, I hadn't thought about that, but I guess we should all be talking about who'll be the vice president now."

I scratched my head. "What?"

Ben said, "You called about the Twenty-Fifth Amendment. That's the one that outlines what to do when the president is no longer able to fulfill the duties of the office. It also covers what to do when there's a vacancy in the vice president's position. The president will nominate a VP, and then it requires a majority vote in both the House and Senate to confirm a new vice president. That's essentially all the Twenty-Fifth Amendment says."

I let his words roll around in my head before asking, "So, does that mean we have no vice president until one is nominated and confirmed by congress?"

"Yes, that's exactly what it means."

"So, if something happened to the president while we have no vice president, the Speaker of the House would become president, right?"

"Yes, exactly, but that's tenth-grade civics stuff."

"Has that ever happened?" I asked.

"Has *what* ever happened?"

I groaned. "Try to keep up, Ben. Has the Speaker ever become president?"

"Only once, but not because of the Twenty-Fifth Amendment. James K. Polk was *elected* to the presidency after serving as Speaker of the House."

"Thanks, Ben. You've been a lot of help. Send me a bill."

I turned to my partner. "They're going to kill the president again."

# Chapter 17
## *Should I Stay, or Should I Go?*

I dialed the number the president had given me, and I waited for the duty officer to pick up. Instead of the crisp voice of a young military officer, a nasally, high-pitched female voice came on the line. "White House switchboard."

I cleared my throat. "Code twenty-one."

"Excuse me, sir?"

"Code twenty-one," I repeated.

"I'm sorry, sir. You've reached the White House switchboard. This line is for official business only."

"This *is* official business," I demanded. "I need to speak with the president. Get the duty officer on the line, and tell him it's code twenty-one."

"This call will be logged and reported to the United States Secret Service. Goodbye."

I closed my eyes and tried to imagine what was happening at the White House.

Hunter leaned in, wide-eyed. "What happened?"

I shook my head. "The number went to the switchboard and not the duty officer. They said they were going to report me to the Secret Service."

"What does that mean?"

I sighed. "It means the president of the United States is in grave danger."

"What are we supposed to do about it?"

"I don't know," I admitted, "but I know where we're going to start."

Skipper was buried in her computer and typing furiously when I interrupted her. "I'm sorry, but I really need to know where those snipers are."

She glared up at me. "I'm working on it, but I'm only one person. There's only so much I can do."

I laid a hand on her shoulder. "What can we do to help?"

"Clone me," she said.

I stuck my phone to my ear. "I can't do that, but I know how to do the next best thing."

"What is it? I'm busy," came the curt answer to my call.

"Ginger, it's Chase Fulton. I need your help."

Her tone lightened. "You don't need anybody's help. You've got Skipper. She can do anything I can do."

Ginger was one of the world's greatest intelligence analysts. She didn't examine aerial photographs or listen in to intercepted, encoded transmissions, but she could run an operation better than any analyst alive. She had run one of the most high-risk operations I'd ever worked. It involved the insertion and extraction of an eccentric operative named Diablo de Agua, aboard a Chinese intelligence ship masquerading as a cargo vessel in the Panama Canal. Following the operation, the firecracker with supermodel looks and a brain the size of Texas took Skipper under her wing and created the next generation of super analyst. If anyone could help Skipper find the remaining snipers, it was Ginger.

"I agree," I said. "She can, and she's proven it time after time, but the clock is ticking on this one, and we need your help."

"You've got the worst timing on Earth, Chase Fulton. I have a stack of work over my head."

I laughed. "You're four foot seven, Ginger."

She huffed. "I'll have you know, I'm four eight, and when I wear heels, I'm five feet."

"Forgive me," I begged. "I missed it by an inch, but I think you'll change your priorities when you hear what the mission entails."

She relented. "Okay, fine. What is it?"

"I can't tell you on the phone."

"You mean, you called me up to tell me you've got a mission that you can't tell me about?"

"No, I can tell you, but not on the phone. This one needs to be face-to-face."

"Fine, but you're coming to me. And bring Skipper. She'll get more work done from here than anywhere else, so if this mission is as critical as you seem to think it is, you'll be glad you did."

"Done," I said. "We'll be there this afternoon."

I hung up before she could protest, and I turned to Skipper. "Pack up everything you'll need to continue. I'm taking you to your clone."

Ten minutes later, her computers, files, notes, and whatever else she keeps in her boxes and bags were packed and ready to head north.

I was on the phone with Vinnie Castellano, the airplane broker. "I'm taking the Citation to Silver Spring, Maryland, as a maintenance test flight. I'll cover the expenses, and I've already added the plane to my insurance policy."

"I'm afraid that's highly unorthodox, and we'll need a significantly more significant deposit."

"Significantly more significant? Really? Is that airplane salesman speak for 'Write me a bigger check'?"

"It's just that . . ."

"Relax, Vinnie. The full purchase price is in escrow." I gave him my Cayman Islands banker's number. "Just call him. He'll set your mind at ease. I'm buying the airplane as long as it checks out. If it doesn't, I'm buying it minus the cost to bring it to the condition you claim it's already in. Either way, you've made a nearly six-million-dollar sale. That's not a bad day."

"But you'll need a crew," he said.

"I have a crew. Disco now works for me, and I'll fly right seat. We're not a low-rent operation, Vinnie. Just take it easy, and you'll get your commission check in a few days. I gotta run."

He was still talking when I hung up the phone, but I wasn't interested in whatever he was saying.

I found Disco asleep on the worn-out couch in the hangar, exactly where I liked my chief pilot to be. "Wake up, Air Force. We've got a mission."

He rubbed at his eyes and swung his legs off the couch. A long stretch and yawn preceded his answer. "Where're we going, boss?"

"Silver Spring, Maryland."

"There's no airport in Silver Spring. The closest general aviation airport with enough concrete for us to get in and out is Montgomery County Airpark. I think the identifier is GAI. When do you want to leave?"

I glanced at my watch. "Ten minutes ago. You do the preflight, and I'll file the flight plan."

He tied his shoes and stood from the couch. "You're the boss, but we need gas."

I pointed through the hangar doors at the fuel truck pulling up outside.

He grinned. "I guess this ain't your first rodeo."

Hunter towed the Citation from the hangar and signed for the fuel while Disco did the walk-around.

Twenty minutes later, we were climbing out of Saint Marys, bound for Montgomery County, Maryland. The total flight time would be eighty-eight minutes if we didn't get routed all over the sky over Washington D.C.

I did the flying while Disco manned the radios and kept me from killing us. The jet was a delight to fly. It seemed to know what I wanted before I moved the controls. We leveled off in cruise at flight level three-five-zero, and I watched our speed settle on four hundred forty knots, the fastest I'd ever flown anything. Theoretically, my Mustang could make three hundred seventy-five knots, but I'd never push her that hard. The Citation seemed to settle into cruise speed as if it were nothing more than a leisurely stroll.

Potomac Approach took us over Washington Dulles at eleven thousand feet, and I flew the RNAV approach to runway one-four by hand. It wasn't the best instrument flying I'd ever done, but Disco said, "That wasn't bad for your first time. I'm impressed."

"Don't be impressed," I said. "Even a blind hog finds an acorn every now and then."

He taxied us to the FBO. "You're anything but a blind hog. You'll have this thing mastered in no time."

We shut down and made our way into the terminal. I slid my credit card across the counter. "Top off the fuel, if you will. We'll be a two-hour turnaround at most."

The young lady took my card, and Disco found his way into the pilot's lounge.

Hunter, Skipper, and I caught a cab into Silver Spring and pulled up in front of a nondescript house on a narrow, tree-lined street.

"This is it," Skipper said.

We bailed out, and Ginger met us at the door with a pencil stuck into her red ponytail.

She and Skipper shared a long hug, then Ginger eyed Hunter. "Who's this?"

"Ginger," Skipper said, "meet Stone Hunter. Hunter, this is Ginger, my mentor and favorite teacher."

Hunter looked at the woman who would've graced the cover of Vogue had she been a foot taller. He stuck out his hand. "Nice to meet you, Ginger."

She slapped it away. "I'm a hugger, especially when it comes to good-looking men like you."

Hunter returned the hug, somewhat awkwardly, before Ginger threw her arms around me.

"Thanks for this," I said.

She glared. "You're welcome, but it's going to cost you. Now, what's this top-secret mission of yours, and how'd you get here so fast?"

"I'll tell you about the mission inside, and we bought a Cessna Citation jet."

"It's about time," she said. "I wondered how long you'd be content with that slow, lumbering Caravan of yours."

"Hey! Don't disrespect the Caravan. The Citation may get there faster, but she can't land on the water."

"She can once," Ginger argued. "Now, let's hear this mission of yours."

Skipper pushed past me and began setting up her computers. "It's not our mission, yet. We're just doing the preliminaries. We have a list of eight of the best snipers on Earth. Our job is to find them, alibi them, and see who's missing."

Ginger shot a look between Skipper and me. "Alibi them for what, exactly?"

Skipper looked over her shoulder. "Chase, I'll leave that one for you."

"We're trying to find the countersniper who took out Landon Edgar Barrier, the president's killer."

Ginger narrowed her eyes. "How many of your eight names are Secret Service agents?"

"None," I said.

Ginger pursed her lips. "Oh."

"Now you know why I need help," Skipper said.

Ginger held out her hand. "Let's see the list."

In a matter of minutes, the two women were side by side and pounding away at their keyboards.

I leaned across Skipper's shoulder. "How long do you think . . ."

Ginger shoved me away. "It'll take a lot less time if you two weren't here. We'll need forty-eight hours if you go. Ninety-six if you stay."

Without another word, Hunter and I ordered up another cab and headed back to the airport. When we found Disco asleep in the pilot's lounge, the thought occurred to me that he and Clark shared the same skill. Both of them could fall asleep almost any-where.

I nudged his bare foot. "Get up, Flyboy. We're heading home."

Just like he'd done back in the hangar, he rose, stretched, reshod his feet, and was ready to go. "Moving, boss."

We blasted off and climbed to the southwest, remaining clear of the complex D.C. airspace on our way out. The tailwind that had added thirty knots to our groundspeed on our northbound leg was on our nose and made the flight time back to Saint Marys less impressive.

On approach to Saint Marys, we overflew Cumberland Island and what remained of Bonaventure. I was on the controls, while Disco looked for other traffic in the vicinity.

Suddenly, he leaned forward and pointed toward the charred remains of the house. "I'll bet that was a pretty place before the fire."

"It was," I said. "It used to be my house."

He turned with awe in his eyes. "Seriously? That's your place?"

"It is. We're going to rebuild as soon as we get the debris cleared."

He leaned toward the side window. "I guess that's what that guy is doing, huh?"

"What guy?" I asked, suddenly curious.

"There's some guy kicking around in the debris."

I almost shouted. "You have the controls."

Disco took the yoke and throttles in his hands. "I have the controls. What's wrong?"

"There shouldn't be anyone kicking around the ashes."

I contorted to pull my phone from my pocket. "Singer, are you at home?"

"No, I'm at the church. Why?"

"There's some guy messing around at Bonaventure. If it's not you, I don't know who it would be. Can you get over there?"

"I'm on my way," he said. "I'll be there in five minutes."

"We're on final into the airport. Hunter and I will be on our way as soon as we land."

I was speaking into dead air. Singer had, no doubt, already pocketed his phone in his haste to get to Bonaventure.

Disco rolled the Citation onto the ramp in front of our hangar, and Hunter and I were on the tarmac before the jet's wheels stopped rolling. The VW Microbus had its limitations, but I pushed the old ride as fast as it would go.

I roared up the driveway between the lines of aged pecan trees and saw a figure disappear around the northern end of the only remaining structure—my vault.

Hunter had obviously spotted the man before I did because he was out the door and sprinting around the burnt foundation before I could shut off the engine.

Instead of stopping, I accelerated through the grass and gave chase around the end of the foundation. When I rounded the vault, I saw a dark figure dive from the end of the dock and into the North River.

Hunter paused only long enough to tear off his shirt and yank his feet from his boots. Outswimming Stone Hunter, former Air Force combat controller, would be like outeating Mongo.

My partner sprinted the length of the dock and dived into the black water like a falcon diving on defenseless prey.

# Chapter 18
## *Manhunt*

I brought the Microbus to a stop beside the gazebo and leapt from the seat. I threw open the side door and pulled a Heckler & Koch MP5 9mm submachine gun from beneath the seat. Unlike Hunter, I wasn't going in the water. Whoever the trespasser was had an enormous head start, and I had a much better chance of catching him with a barrage of 9mm rounds than with my breaststroke.

I made it to the end of the dock in fifteen sprinting strides. The white foaming splashes of the pursuit shone on the surface of the black water like moonlight on lingering snow. I pulled the MP5 to my shoulder and sighted down the short barrel. Hunter was directly in line between my muzzle and the perp. If I pulled the trigger, I had a greater chance of clipping my partner than hitting the fleeing man.

I pulled the muzzle a few degrees left and buried the trigger. A barrage of water-splitting lead peppered the surface of the river three feet to the swimmer's left. Any sane human would surrender and face the perils of capture rather than continue swimming in the assurance of the next volley of fire falling on his back, but the swimmer only intensified his strokes.

He was headed for the marsh grass, a tall, dense, broadleaf grass that thrives in the brackish water of the river. The density of the grass made it nearly impassible for anything short of an airboat at full speed. There was no question that as soon as the swimmer hit the grass, Hunter would be on him in seconds. Not only was Hunter the best swimmer on the team, but his endurance was second to none. When he did catch the man, he wouldn't be winded, and he'd be more than ready for a fight.

To my surprise, when the man hit the marsh grass, he stayed low – too low for me to get off an effective shot—but he didn't stop. He powered onward, parting the grass in long powerful sweeps of his arms.

Thundering footsteps sounded from the floating dock behind me, and Singer thudded to a stop at my side. "Where is he?"

I motioned toward the disturbance in the marsh grass. "That's him. Hunter's on him."

Singer shot a look toward my catamaran. "I need a rifle."

I handed him the MP5 and started for *Aegis*.

"This isn't a rifle," he protested.

"It'll have to do for now. I'll be right back!"

I shoved my key into the lock on the companionway and slammed open the sliding hatch. The clamps holding the 308 sniper rifle into the locker clicked and surrendered the weapon into my hands. As I rushed back to the cockpit, Singer was climbing the ladder to the upper deck. I tossed the rifle toward him, and he caught it without missing a stride. I followed him up the ladder as he took up a prone position on the deck, sighting out across the river.

The sound of an engine twisting to life wafted across the river as Singer squirmed left and right in a desperate effort to get a clean angle of fire. "I can see motion in the grass, but I can't tell if it's Hunter or the runner."

I yanked a pair of binoculars from their case and scanned the area. My vantage was no better than Singer's. The motion in the grass was definitely human, but it was impossible to tell who.

The starting engine I'd heard seconds before roared into high RPM force, and a glimpse of white shot through the grass.

"He's on a Jet Ski!" I yelled.

Singer peered over the rifle's scope. "Which way is he running?"

"He's moving left to right."

"Man or machine?" came Singer's barely audible question.

"Shoot the Jet Ski if you can. I want to have a talk with whoever that is."

Without another word, Singer squeezed the trigger and sent a 30-caliber, 180-grain chunk of lead whistling through the air toward the fleeing perp. We listened for the engine to falter, but it continued to roar, growing fainter as the man escaped down the river.

"Did you miss?" I yelled in disbelief.

Singer never missed, but the look on his face said there was a first time for everything.

"Get the RHIB in the water," I ordered as I pulled my phone from my pocket.

Disco answered on the first ring.

I said, "Get the One-Eighty-Two airborne, now! We're chasing a guy on a white Jet Ski, heading south away from Bonaventure. We'll be in a white RHIB and monitoring one-twenty-three-forty-five."

Singer had the rigid hull inflatable boat descending from the davits by the time I made it to the cockpit, and Hunter was swimming back toward the dock. We leapt into the RHIB and freed the davit lines. The fuel-injected engine spun to life at the touch of the key, and we powered toward Hunter, who was stroking his way across the surface.

I accelerated, bringing Hunter down the starboard side, and Singer hooked him in a perfect frogman pick up. The maneuver hefted Hunter from the water and deposited him on the deck of the RHIB as we picked up speed and headed downriver.

Hunter spat out a mouthful of water. "Whoever this guy is, he's good and must be a pro. He never flinched when you peppered the water beside him."

The river northeast of the town of Saint Marys winds like a snake, making 180-degree switchbacks every two hundred feet. The RHIB made short work of the winding course, but even a RHIB with the power of mine is no match for the agility of a Jet Ski. The man was getting away, but if I could get even a glimpse of him, I was confident Singer could cut him down.

"Get on the bow," I ordered. "I'm going to try to get you another shot."

Singer took up a firing position on the bow with the 308 pulled snuggly into his shoulder. As the RHIB rolled through every turn, Singer scanned the next straightaway for any sign of the runner. His wake was evident in front of us, but he was outmaneuvering us at every turn.

The radio crackled. "Chase, it's Disco. I'm airborne and over the river."

I shot a glance into the sky to see the Cessna 182, with her landing gear tucked neatly away, racing through the air, barely a hundred feet over the water.

I keyed the mic. "We're the white RHIB under your nose at a thousand feet."

"In sight," came Disco's confident response.

Hunter pulled the mic from my hand. "This is our playground. You just drive the boat."

Hunter keyed the mic. "Disco, Hunter . . . fly heading one-one-zero and track outbound to the Cumberland Sound. The gun run is two-seven-zero. Push him to the west when he clears the mouth of the river."

Disco replied, "One-one-zero . . . gun run two-seven-zero."

Hunter ordered, "Wet the tips on the gun run."

Although I had no clue what he was talking about, Disco clearly understood. "Roger. Tips wet."

Hunter's plan was solid. We weren't going to catch the Jet Ski, but he couldn't outrun the Cessna. Calling on his training and experience as a combat controller and Disco's days as an A-10

Warthog pilot, Hunter set a trap into which our prey was destined to fall.

Disco lowered the nose of my Skylane and dived for the tops
of the marsh grass. At well over a hundred knots, he parted the
grass and left a foaming wake on the dark water as he raced to
the southeast. When the grass gave way to the open water of the
sound, he pulled up and sent the airplane into a teardrop maneuver that would've made a crop duster cringe.

The radio crackled again. "Disco's on the gun run. Target ac-
quired. Tips wet."

Hunter gripped the stainless-steel handrail above the console
of the RHIB and stood on the starboard tube, straining to see
the action unfolding just south of us. I held the throttle full forward and leaned into every turn. Singer lay like a stone on the
bow, absorbing every wake, and never moving even when the
RHIB's bow wave sent walls of water cascading over him.

My airplane disappeared beneath our line of sight as Disco
drove the Skylane westward at full speed, toward the town of
Saint Marys. Anyone on the waterfront was only seconds away
from getting an airshow they'd never forget.

If our plan worked, the runner would emerge from the mouth
of the North River and discover the propeller of a Cessna Skylane
in his face. Unless the man was thoroughly insane, he'd turn to the
west, giving us the advantage of driving him into water we knew
well, and hopefully, away from his intended route of escape.

If insanity prevailed, he'd turn east and face certain death at
the spinning blades of the propeller. The third possibility was
that he'd bring the Jet Ski to a stop in the mouth of the river, or
even turn back to the north. Though unlikely, that's what I was
hoping for. If he made the northward turn, Singer would demol-
ish the Jet Ski with at least a pair of 308 rounds, and the man
would be left to our mercy—something I was quickly running
out of.

As we rounded the second turn above the mouth of the river,
I watched my Skylane flare into the sky at an impossible angle

and heard the engine fall to idle. Seconds later, the nose fell, and Disco dived the airplane back toward the water as the radio came alive.

"He's headed west, and he's shooting at me." Disco's tone could have been that of a man discussing a grocery list. There was no hint of anxiety, fear, or excitement in his voice.

Hunter's tone was nearly identical when he keyed up. "Don't get shot down."

I exploded through the mouth of the river and turned west toward Saint Marys with the throttle fully open and the RHIB skidding across the surface of the water. He had the advantage of speed and agility, but I had air support and firepower. I also had the runner essentially cornered in water I knew like the back of my hand.

There were three 180-degree turns and one 90-degree bend in the river before the first fork. I wouldn't gain on the runner in the straightaways, but I'd have a slight advantage in the turns, and as long as he didn't shoot Disco out of the sky, I wouldn't lose sight of him.

I made the first 180-degree bend and caught a glimpse of the Jet Ski entering the next turn. Singer sent a questioning glance across his shoulder, and I shook him off. A missed shot from that angle would send a thirty-caliber round racing through the river-front of downtown Saint Marys. The next turn would be an entirely different story. After another bend, Singer could send a cannon shot downrange and hit nothing except marshland and thousands of acres of emptiness.

Disco made another evasive maneuver, sending the Skylane into a climbing right circle tighter than I believed possible. When he rolled out of the maneuver and headed back for the deck, he put the airplane into a sideslip and sent a series of six pistol shots toward the Jet Ski.

I had definitely hired the right pilot, but I wished I'd told him to bring the Mustang with her fifty-caliber machine gun in the left wing.

Despite Disco's onslaught, the runner kept running.

I yelled, "Get ready, Singer. Next time you see him, put him down."

My sniper's response was a single nod of acknowledgment, followed by the opening verse of "The Old Gospel Ship." I wondered just how many Southern Baptist hymns he knew by heart.

I hugged the southern bank to gain as much advantage in the turn as possible, and silently begged my engine for more speed. The depth sounder screamed its shallow water warning, but I ignored it. At our speed, there were less than six inches of hull and propeller in the water. The bottom was not my concern. My only thought was stopping the runner, but I should've had at least one additional concern.

As we rolled out of the turn, I looked up into the rigging of an enormous shrimp boat anchored in the shallows. To my left was mud, muck, and marsh grass. Right was my only option. I spun the wheel hard over, sending the RHIB into a skidding turn to the right that was going to be insufficient to avoid the shrimp boat. The collision was imminent, and it was going to be nasty.

Recognizing the catastrophe I'd created, Singer made the split-second decision to roll overboard to avoid being the battering ram at the bow of the RHIB. Surviving the collision in his position wouldn't have been possible. Hunter made the same decision, but it was an instant too late. The portside of the RHIB struck the hull of the shrimp boat in a skidding turn, sending both Hunter and me flying through the air toward the wooden hull. I felt myself collide with the unforgiving hull the second before Hunter's body crashed into mine.

# Chapter 19
## *Word-Salad and Show Ponies*

When the lights finally came back on, they were pulsating and blinding. Every inch of my body hurt, and my head felt like it was in a vise. I was wet, cold, and confused.

The world around me was moving mostly in circles, but also fading in and out of focus. I thought I could make out the outline of my partner kneeling beside me, but I wasn't sure.

An echoing voice that sounded as if it were being thrown down a well said, "Try not to move. We'll have you ashore in a couple of minutes."

*Ashore?*

A hand landed on my chest, and Hunter's face materialized in front of me. "Hell of a place to anchor a shrimp boat, huh?"

Nothing made sense. Why was I wet, and what did a shrimp boat have to do with anything?

"Kiss trampoline forward toboggan, no?"

Hunter came into momentary focus and faded again. His voice sounded like the flexing blade of a handsaw. "Try not to talk. You're going to be all right. Just hang on."

"Tomatoes spring a catapult to nightmares."

He patted my chest. "Just relax, and try not to move."

I couldn't get my mouth to form the words my brain was trying to get out. I wanted to ask where I was, but it came out, "Escape temple and side path."

Every breath felt like swallowing razor blades, and everything was the wrong color. Deep purples and oranges filled the air in front of me just as the lights went out again.

The next time I saw a light, it was bright white and probing into my eye like the light of a freight train through a tunnel.

"Mr. Fulton, can you hear me?"

"Ketchup," I muttered.

"Do you know what day it is, Mr. Fulton?"

"Poison sinking trees binders line artist."

"You've had an accident, Mr. Fulton, but we're going to take care of you. My name is Mike. I'm a paramedic. You hit your head, and you're a little confused, but we'll get you to the hospital, and the doctors will get you fixed up. If you can understand me, I want you to blink your eyes once for me. Can you do that?"

I understood him, but he sounded like he was yelling down a long hallway. I blinked and said, "Cleave?"

"Is your name Cleave?" I heard him ask.

"No, I'm Hunter. Stone Hunter."

I called out for Hunter. "Cleave."

My partner squeezed my hand. "Just hang on. The paramedics are going to put a C-collar on you and get you on a backboard. You're going to be all right."

The word-salad that kept coming out of my mouth made it impossible to communicate more than simple yes-and-no answers and left me with no way to ask questions. Although I couldn't focus well enough to pick out details of Hunter's expressions, his tone made it clear that I was in trouble. A C-collar and backboard were not a pair of accessories I ever wanted.

"Are you in pain, Mr. Fulton?"

*Pain* was the wrong word for what I was feeling, but I blinked rapidly enough to leave little doubt in the paramedic's mind.

"I'll take that as a yes," he said. "As soon as we get you on the backboard, I'll make a call to the E-R, and we'll get you some relief. Just hang on, buddy. We're going to take good care of you."

What was supposed to be *thank-you* came out as "Nectar purpose."

A second medic slid half of the plastic collar beneath my neck and Velcro-strapped the front in place. The device was designed to immobilize my cervical spine in case of a fracture. Moving a broken neck tends to make a bad day a lot worse. Although I was in agonizing pain, the collar didn't add to the anguish. But what came next was a different story altogether.

"On three. One . . . two . . . and roll him."

The two paramedics rolled me onto my left side, and a billion shards of glass exploded into my back. I made a sound that resembled something a grizzly bear in a spring steel trap might make if he were being beaten with a thousand clubs.

When they rolled me onto the backboard, the spikes of glass ceased their onslaught, but every muscle above my waist felt like it was being torn from my skeleton.

"All right. The worst is over. We'll get you off this shrimp boat and into the bus."

*Shrimp boat? Why did they keep talking about a shrimp boat?*

The slats of the pier jolted the wheels of the gurney and sent lightning bolts down my spine and spikes into my skull. There was nothing gentle about the ride, nor the way the medics shoved me into the ambulance. I assumed it was an ambulance based on what little my brain was capable of putting together about the scene unfolding around me.

*Why had I been on a shrimp boat, and how could I have gotten hurt this badly on any boat, let alone a slow, lumbering shrimp boat?*

The paramedic started an IV that I couldn't feel and spoke to someone on a radio I couldn't see.

"Med base. Med one-four. We're in route with one thirty-year-old Caucasian male boating-accident victim. Confusion, aphasia, lower extremities unreactive, probably spinal injury, probable concussion, cooperative, but in extreme pain. I-V fluids hanging, and I'd like to give him a little morphine for the ride."

*Concussion, spinal injury, boating accident? Why couldn't I re-member what happened, and where on Earth was I?*

Everything the medic said was unnerving, but the aphasia concerned me more than everything else combined. Following a stroke or traumatic head injury, the brain sometimes forgets how to communicate. I'd learned at UGA the clinical concept of the disorder, but I never thought I'd experience it firsthand.

The three types of aphasia are global, Wernicke's, and Broca's. If I were experiencing global or Wernicke's aphasia, I wouldn't understand what the paramedics were saying, but I seemed to understand language. My problem was I couldn't create language that made sense to anyone around me. That left Broca's, or com-prehensive aphasia, as my likely diagnosis. No diagnosis would be good, but Broca's was likely the least bad of the possible three.

The morphine helped with the pain, but it robbed me of what little comprehension I had of the world around me. I tried to re-member every important detail of my life, but they ran together like letters in a bowl of alphabet soup.

I was a baseball player and an assassin. That didn't make any sense, but the smell of a house fire kept pouring into my nose, and that made even less sense. I knew Hunter was my partner, but his name was supposed to be Clark. Was he a pitcher, an in-fielder, or another assassin? A pair of faces flashed in my mind—beautiful and mysterious.

\* \* \*

All hospitals smell the same, and they all make the same noises. Beds rolled on tiled floors, curtains slid on metal rails, footsteps trod—some fast and others slowly, as if the walkers were unrelated and unaware of the situation around them.

The beams of punishing light poured into my eyes again, one at a time.

"Mr. Fulton, I'm Doctor Eggert. Can you tell me what hap-pened to you?"

"Philadelphia," I said, but couldn't understand why.

"Philadelphia, huh? All right. We'll see what we can do about that. Tell me . . . can you feel this?"

I said, "*Nevesta.*"

*Nevesta? What the hell did that mean?*

"What was that?" the doctor said.

"*Prekrasnaya nevesta.*"

Dr. Eggert laid his hand on my shoulder. "Mr. Fulton, what language are you speaking?"

I could understand him, but I couldn't understand my own voice, my own words. "High bottom tomorrow."

"Let's try something else," the doctor said. "Blink once for yes and twice for no. Can you do that?"

I blinked once.

"Good. Can you feel this?" He squeezed the fingers of my left hand, and I blinked once. "How about this? Can you feel this?"

He wasn't doing anything, so I blinked twice.

"Hmm. How about this?"

Again, he wasn't touching me, so I blinked twice.

Even though I couldn't focus on his features, I could see him leaning in closely. "Do you speak any languages other than English, Mr. Fulton?"

I didn't know if I spoke any other languages, but something had come out of my mouth that certainly sounded foreign, so I blinked three times.

"Remember," he said, "one blink for yes, and two for no."

I blinked once, reminding him I knew the rules.

He leaned back and spoke to someone else. "How's the other guy who came in with him?"

"He's in exam three. He's ambulatory and coherent."

The doctor said, "Bring him in here."

Sometime later, it could've been a minute or an hour, Hunter said, "I don't need a wheelchair. I'm perfectly capable of walking."

"I'm Dr. Eggert. I understand you were in the accident with Mr. Fulton. Is that right?"

"Yes, I was, and so was Singer."

*Singer?* I thought. *He's my priest.*

"Can you tell me what happened?" the doctor asked.

"We hit a shrimp boat that was anchored someplace it never should've been."

"You hit a shrimp boat? With what?"

"We were in the RHIB, and we came around a bend in the river and hit the shrimp boat broadside."

"How fast were you going?"

"I don't know. Fifty, or maybe a little faster."

"And you were in the accident, as well? Are you injured?"

Hunter patted himself down. "I'm okay, thanks to Chase. He hit the boat first, and I flew into him. Our other man, Singer, he went over the side before the collision. He's all right. He's dealing with the RHIB."

The doctor nodded. "Well, Mr. Hunter, your friend here has sustained a serious concussion, at least. We're going to run some tests to determine the severity of his injuries and then formulate a treatment plan. I'm an emergency medicine physician, so it's my job to stabilize him and refer him to the specialists. In my opinion, his injuries present no immediate life-threatening conditions. Whoever pulled him out of the water likely saved his life."

Hunter turned to me. "I'll just add one more to your tab. Did you copy what the doc said? You're not gonna die in the next few minutes, and they're gonna poke and prod you. Are you okay with that?"

One blink.

I spent the next few minutes—or perhaps the next several days, I couldn't be sure—enduring MRIs, CT scans, X-rays, and limitless confusion. Hunter said we'd hit a shrimp boat in the RHIB, but what was left of my brain couldn't piece that information together with anything it had stored away. I had my wits about me. I knew what was happening, but what I didn't have was my memory or the ability to communicate. I was trapped inside a prison of my own sanity.

The radiology tech rolled my bed into a waiting room and patted my chest. "If you can understand me, hang in there, buddy. We've got one of the best neurosurgeons around."

I gripped the technician's wrist and tried to ask what he saw on the images that told him I needed a neurosurgeon, but it came out, "Giraffe turn-about compound."

He frowned. "Hang in there, man. We've got you."

Dr. Eggert came in with a clipboard and a scowl. "Okay, Mr. Fulton. As I told your friend, I'm an ER doctor, but it looks like you have what's known as an intracerebral hemorrhage. Essentially, that means your brain is bleeding, and you're going to require surgery to stop the bleeding and relieve the pressure inside your skull. I imagine you have a pretty good headache, huh?"

I blinked a long, slow blink.

The doctor tapped the edge of my bed with his clipboard. "I've paged the on-call neurosurgeon, and he'll be here any minute. He'll explain what's going on and what you can expect from this surgery. The good news is, your neck appears to be intact, so he'll probably get you out of the collar. There's some inflammation in your lower spine. I think that's what's causing your paralysis."

*Am I paralyzed?*

I concentrated with every ounce of strength inside me and tried to ask for Hunter, but instead, I said, "*Okhotnik?*"

Dr. Eggert narrowed his eyes. "Are you speaking Russian, Mr. Fulton?"

*Why would I know Russian?*

I blinked twice, and the doctor said, "Well, it certainly sounds like Russian."

He lifted the clipboard from the bed. "Don't go anywhere. The surgeon will be in shortly."

Again, my inability to process the passage of time left me dangling between reality and an unimaginable realm of existence that felt like a Salvador Dali painting.

A man in his mid-fifties with salt-and-pepper hair ambled into the room. His white lab coat hung open over a Nike golf shirt. If I could've moved my head, I suspect I would've seen khaki golf shorts and maybe even a pair of spikes on his feet.

Without looking up from the clipboard, he said, "I'm Gary King, the neurosurgeon. You have yourself one hell of an intracerebral hemorrhage. That's why you're spouting a word-salad every time you open your mouth. It's called aphasia. There's damage to a region of your left frontal lobe called Broca's Area. That's the part of the brain that allows us to speak rationally. Dr. Eggert tells me you understand what's happening around you and you can communicate with blinks."

That wasn't technically a question, but I answered with a single blink.

He pulled the Velcro from the C-collar. "We can get this thing off. That'll make you a little more comfortable. Dr. Eggert also told me it sounded like you were speaking Russian. Do you know Russian, Mr. Fulton?"

Something led me to believe I did know Russian, but I couldn't be sure if I could trust my own belief. Before I could blink, I said, "*Da.*"

Dr. King pulled his glasses from his nose and stared down at me. "*Da* is Russian for *yes*, isn't it?"

I blinked once. "*Da.*"

For the first time, Dr. King smiled and whispered, "Fascinating."

I wanted to ask him if I was paralyzed, and my mouth spat out, "*Ya paralizovan?*"

He held up one finger. "Hold that thought."

He pulled his phone from the pocket of his khaki shorts, just as I'd predicted, and dialed a number. "Alex, Gary King here. Listen, I have a patient who is a native English speaker, but he's got an intracranial hematoma in Broca's Area, causing aphasia. When he tries to speak English, it's word-salad, but I think he can speak Russian. Here, listen to this."

He pressed the speaker button on his phone and held it toward me. "Say that last thing again."

I asked, "*Ya paralizovan?*"

The voice from the phone said, "Is he paralyzed, Gary?"

"Yes, from the waist down for now, but I think it's temporary. Why do you ask?"

The voice said, "I didn't. He did. He's definitely speaking Russian. Have him say something in English and then in Russian."

Dr. King looked down and nodded. "Go ahead."

I frowned. "Upstage laughter time cushions slipping."

"Now say that again in Russian," came the voice through the phone.

I said, "*Ya ne vystavochnaya poni. Vosstanovite moy mozg.*"

Dr. King pulled the phone toward his face. "What did he say, Alex?"

"He said, 'I'm not a show pony. Fix my brain.'"

# Chapter 20
## *Warrior Angels*

I tried to sign the informed consent forms so Dr. King could drill a hole into my skull and plug the leak, but my ability to sign my name had gone off to play with my ability to speak English. I considered signing in Cyrillic, but what little logic I had left told me that would never do.

Somehow, Hunter managed to convince the hospital's legal department he had sufficient authority to consent to my surgery. After accomplishing that Herculean task, he and a man my eyes didn't recognize flanked my bed.

My eyes may not have known the stranger, but my soul recognized him immediately. It was my priest, Jimmy "Singer" Grossmann. He laid his hand on my shoulder and stared down at me with a look of sadness from the depths of his heart. "It's going to be all right, Chase. Disco's gone to get Penny, and you're in good hands . . . God's and Dr. King's."

I knew God and Dr. King, but Penny and Disco didn't ring any bells.

The surgeon came through the door, rubbing his hands together. "Okay! It's time to open you up and teach you to speak English again. Are you ready?"

I nodded and blinked once. "*Da.*"

The operating room was bone-chillingly cold and filled with masked, gloved participants who all appeared interchangeable.

They milled about as if working at some mysterious task perhaps even they didn't understand. A pair of minions identical to the others started IVs and connected a bevy of equipment to every corner of my body.

A woman I imagined I recognized leaned toward me and placed a rubber mask over my mouth and nose. "Breathe normally for me, Mr. Fulton. I'm going to help you go to sleep. When you wake up, you'll feel like a whole new man."

I didn't want to go to sleep. I didn't want to endure the surgery. I wanted to escape from the chasm into which I'd fallen. I wanted to talk to Alex on Dr. King's phone. I wanted everything to be . . .

Whatever the woman fed me through the plastic mask did far more than help me go to sleep—it gave me no choice. Darkness enveloped me, but the world into which I'd floated, or perhaps fallen, wasn't a realm of silence. As the light vanished, sound replaced its presence, but there was no way to know if what I was hearing was real or imaginary. I felt no pain; in fact, I felt nothing at all. There was no anxiety, no knowledge of anything other than the perception of sound: mechanized tones, the shuffling of feet in paper booties, metallic instruments slapped into gloved palms, and the whirring of a machine grinding perhaps into bone. Calm, confident voices spoke barely above a whisper, and the grinding ceased.

The sounds and darkness faded in unison as if conjoined and inseparable, and gave way to soft, pale light. I was at perfect rest, afraid of nothing, longing for nothing, and feeling as if I were somehow home in a place I'd never been.

*Could this be Heaven? Will I spend eternity suspended in perfect slumber? Have I arrived where I've been destined to be since the dawn of time?*

As the soft, gentle light absorbed my body and soul, angels appeared as if born of the farthest reaches of the light. They came ever closer, moving as one, though they were countless in number. Their flowing robes and ivory wings moved like the wind as they grew ever closer with each passing moment. The angels continued their seemingly endless progression, morphing and joining as they came, many becoming few, and their features growing clearer. Their flowing hair trailed and danced across the velvet tops of their wings, and their flawless complexions came into perfect focus. Each wore an identical face, perfect and confident. I knew the face as if it were my own, its eyes calling to me, and every curve, every expression, was more beautiful than the last.

As their approach continued, I believed the angels would soon consume me, but when they came so close I could feel their spotless robes and taste their strength, they turned as one and spread their downy wings, shielding me from everything beyond. I'd never felt safer, more loved, or more protected from every harm, from every evil the world or beyond could threaten.

Suddenly, I relived the moment of my mother wrapping me inside her coat and running down a long corridor with my legs and bare feet bouncing against her hips and thighs. I could hear and feel her heaving breath as she ran, carrying me from some unseen danger that lay behind.

"You're safe, baby boy. You're safe."

I felt, more than heard the words, and I believed that assurance as if it were spoken from God's own lips. The rushing wind from the wings of angels seemed to echo my mother's promise. "You're safe, baby boy. You're safe." And perhaps this time, the words were falling directly from the lips of God.

The legion of angels turned as if driven by a force mightier than all of Heaven, and each drew a gleaming sword as their wings froze like a wall of stone. Though unable to see beyond their mighty wings, I heard the unmistakable sounds of battle, sounds I somehow knew and understood.

The realm in which I lay seemed devoid of time, and perhaps even of space. Nothing appeared to be up or down. Everything was merely in its place. The battle raged on, and fire exploded from beneath the angels' robes. Slowly, the phalanx of warring spirits pressed ahead, driving ever forward, deeper into the battle and away from where I lay in solace and wakened slumber. Just as they'd morphed from many into a mighty few, as they distanced themselves from me and fought on, farther into the battlefield before them, they became, once again, a number impossible to count.

The echoing sounds of the terrible battle softened as the light seemed to absorb the angels back into the space from which they'd come. The face of the greatest of these angels, these otherworldly warriors who surrounded and protected me, began to form at the limits of my vision, perhaps at the edge of all that exists. Her face was laced in clouds, and her hair flowed like wispy smoke across placid waters. She drew ever nearer, and the same perfect face I'd seen on each of the angels became more than a vision, more than an apparition. It became a face I could touch and feel and know.

"Chase? Are you awake?"

Her lips moved in time with the voice, and I knew every tone as if the sounds from her lips were the very breath in my chest. I knew every strand of her hair and every curve of her face.

"You're an angel," I whispered.

She beamed, and tears fell from her enchanting eyes. "I'm no angel. I'm just your wife, and I'm so glad you're back. You had us worried sick. They told us you might not make it, but I told them they didn't know Chase Fulton like I did. I told them you were a fighter and that you'd—"

I raised my hand and cupped the face that had waged a relentless battle for me when I could not. "Shh. I have so much to tell you."

The realm from which I'd come held no concept of time, but the world into which I'd returned seemed dominated by it. Nurses and doctors and God only knows who else shone lights into my eyes, squeezed my fingertips, prodded every inch of me, and asked the most ridiculous questions.

"Can you tell us your name?"

"I'm Chase, and I'd like for you to stop shining that light in my eyes. I have a nasty headache."

"Can you feel this?"

"Yes, and it hurts. Stop doing that."

"How many fingers do you see?"

"Five, but three of them, including your thumb, are tucked away. Can I please have something to drink?"

My angel, the perfect, flawless Penny Fulton, waded through the throngs of tormenting practitioners and held a plastic cup to my lips. The water tasted like life itself and felt better than anything I ever remember flowing down my throat.

Behind my angel stood Dr. Gary King with a smile the size of Penny's home state of Texas across his face.

I locked eyes with him. "Did you stop the bleeding, doc?"

If possible, his smile broadened. "It would appear we did. Welcome back, young man. You had us a little concerned for a few days."

"A few days?" I said. "How long have I been out?"

The doctor looked down at his watch. "It's Pearl Harbor Day. You've been in a coma for almost sixteen days."

"That's impossible," I insisted. "I remember you taking me into surgery this afternoon."

He pressed a series of buttons on the monitor above my bed and stuck his stethoscope into his ears. After listening to my lungs and heart, he said, "I'm afraid it's been over two weeks since we rolled you into my OR, but I'm sure you have no memory of the past sixteen days."

"Actually," I said, "you'll never believe what I heard and saw."

He shoved the stethoscope back into his jacket pocket and smiled. "I can't wait to hear all about it, but there will be plenty of time for that. Something tells me your wife would like to scold you for oversleeping. I'll be back in to talk with you in a bit, and I'll see that you get something to eat. It's been a while since your last meal. I do, however, have one question before I go."

I squirmed in the bed in a wasted effort to find a comfortable position. "Sure, what is it?"

"Do you speak Russian?"

I nodded. "Yes, and German, and enough Spanish to find a bathroom and a cerveza."

He smiled again and offered a quick nod. "We'll have a talk about that when things settle down. I'll see you a bit later."

Penny slid onto the bed beside me and squeezed my hand. "I'm not going to scold you, but if you ever do anything like this again, I'm going to kill you. Okay, I probably won't kill you, but I'll do something to make you wish you were dead."

"We were chasing some guy—at least I think it was a guy—who was messing around in the debris at Bonaventure."

"I know," she said. "Hunter and Singer told me all about it."

"I guess he got away, huh?"

She brushed my hair off my forehead. "Yeah, he did, but not before putting a half dozen bullet holes in our Skylane. Disco got it back to the airport, though, and Cotton will probably finish the repairs today or tomorrow."

"Is Disco okay?"

She shook her head. "I can't believe you. Here you are, just five minutes out of a coma, and you're worried about everybody else. Yes, Disco is fine, and so is the new Citation. Cotton says it's in great shape. He even fixed the lights that weren't working in the cabin."

The flood of regained memories left me reeling and drowning in unanswered questions. It was like trying to drink from a firehose. As I struggled to prioritize the flood of information my brain was devouring, the terrifying reality of the time I'd lost struck me like a bullet to the chest. I scanned the room for my partner. Although my vision was still less than perfect, Hunter—*Okhotnik*—stood near the window beyond the crowd, his arms crossed and the slightest hint of a smile on his face.

I met his stare and mouthed, "Is the president alive?"

# Chapter 21
## *The Pink Panther*

Hunter stepped to my bedside and scanned the remaining faces in the room. "Is Chase going to die if all of you leave the room?" he asked.

A nurse in Pink Panther scrubs took charge and herded up her flock of nurses and technicians. "I'll be back to check on him in ten minutes. Is that long enough?"

Hunter lowered his chin. "Can he survive twenty minutes?"

Pink Panther checked her watch. "I'll see you in twenty minutes."

Unlike the nurses, Penny didn't budge. I doubted if a crane could've lifted her from my bed and the death grip she had on my hand.

When the last nurse made her way into the hallway and closed the door, Hunter cleared his throat. "The short answer is yes, the president is still alive."

I repositioned a pillow behind my head. "What's the long answer?"

"The long answer is the president would like for you to call him back. For entirely different reasons than all of us, he's quite concerned about you."

"You spoke with him?"

"Yes, three times, and I'll never get used to it. It's like talking to the Pope if the Vatican had a nuclear arsenal."

I eyed my partner. "What makes you think they don't?"

He shrugged. "Good point. Anyway, I have a number, a private number, and he wants to hear your voice."

I turned to face my wife. "It's good to be back, but you'll never believe where I've been."

She wrapped her arms around me as if we'd spent a lifetime apart. Perhaps we had. As she ran her fingers through my hair, she couldn't take her eyes from mine. "You need a haircut."

I tried to imitate one of Clark's crooked grins. "Ah, I've been busy."

"Chase, you had us so worried. They told me you couldn't talk before the surgery, but now it's like you never left."

"I remember," I said. "After the accident, I couldn't make a coherent sentence in English, but I could speak Russian. And on top of that, I couldn't remember anything."

She ran her palm across my face. "They let me give you a shave yesterday. You looked like a woolly mammoth."

I laid my hand on top of hers as she traced the line of my jaw. "You'll never believe it, but it was you."

She squinted. "What was me?"

"It was you who fought off death when he came for me."

She frowned. "What are you talking about? Should we get the nurse back in here?"

I squeezed her hand. "No, we don't need the nurse. There were a billion angels surrounding me and fighting off whatever was trying to take me. Each of the angels had your face and some serious sword skills."

"I'd fight a million demons for you, Chase. I just don't ever want to lose you again."

"You're not going to lose me," I said. "How's the movie coming along?"

She waved me off. "That's not important right now."

"Sure it is. It's important to you, so it's important to me. Tell me."

She left my bed only long enough to retrieve a binder from her shoulder bag propped in the corner of the room. She unfolded the binder and took out a stack of glossy photos. For the next ten minutes, I listened as she described every character and actor who'd been chosen for each role. She was alive and beautiful and in her element. Penny Thomas Fulton was born to make movies. I knew it as surely as I knew I was born to draw my sword, just like those angels when the demons came calling. Seeing my wife so deeply in love with her work left me feeling as if all was right with the world. At my core, though, I knew that was a condition in which the world would never find itself, and people like Hunter and me were the thin, barely visible line between Penny's world and chaos of the highest order.

Hunter checked his watch. "We've got two minutes before the Pink Panther and her little cult invade again. Is there anything you need, want, or need to tell me?"

He had a way of cutting through the crap of the world around him and getting right to the point. We all need a Hunter in our lives.

"I need a shower, and apparently a haircut, but nothing else."

He nodded. "All right, then. I'll go make some calls and let the world know the great Chase Fulton has returned from the dead."

The nurses returned, but not in a drove. Only the Pink Panther and one other showed up. She checked my temperature, took my blood pressure, and counted my breaths. "Dr. King has ordered that we remove your catheter and get you ready to stand up. How does that sound?"

I looked down to see the rubber hose running from beneath my gown to somewhere beyond my line of sight. "I didn't realize I had a catheter, but now that you mention it, I'd love for you to take it out. As for the idea of standing up, I like it in concept, but when I went into surgery, I was paralyzed from the waist down."

She pulled the cover from my feet. "Look away and tell me which foot I'm touching."

"Left, and it tickles."

"You're not paralyzed anymore," she said as she pulled a syringe from her pouch and lifted the bottom of my gown.

I flinched, not liking the idea of a syringe being anywhere near where the catheter, undoubtedly, entered my body.

She held up the plastic tube and plunger. "Relax. It's just a syringe, no needle. I have to deflate the balloon in your bladder. Trust me, you don't want me pulling on the tube while the balloon is still inflated."

She made me count to three, but before I'd gotten fully through two, she gave the tube a yank as if she were starting a Weed Eater. It wasn't pleasant, but I suppose it wouldn't have been pleasant for someone to change my diaper for sixteen days, so I endured the pull-start like a champ.

Pink Panther said, "Let's get you sitting up on the edge of the bed." She lowered the bedrail, and I turned ninety degrees, allowing my legs to hang from the hospital bed. "Don't try to get up yet," she scolded. "Dr. King will be in here in just a minute."

I followed her orders and tried to imagine what it would feel like to stand after sixteen days in a coma. The doctor came in and tossed his trusty clipboard onto the bed. "There are two schools of thought on getting patients on their feet after an extended period in a coma. A lot of doctors like to let their patients take baby steps back into the real world. I'm not one of those doctors. Baby steps are for babies, so let's get you up."

He and the nurse flanked me, but Penny didn't go far. She was never out of reach throughout the whole ordeal. I slid forward and let my feet touch the cold tile floor, then I leaned forward and pushed off the bed. I hoped I didn't look as much like a baby giraffe as I felt. A few steps across the room and back was all I could manage, but that seemed to thrill Dr. King.

He stuck two fingers into his mouth and let out a shrill whistle as if calling a dog. Through the door came an orderly pushing an empty wheelchair, which he rolled behind me. I took the offered seat, thankful to be off my trembling legs.

Incapable of masking my concern, I looked up at the doctor. "Will I have to learn to walk again?"

His laughter did little to comfort me. "You've been asleep for sixteen days. You've not forgotten how to walk. You're just drowsy. This fine young man is going to take you to get a few pictures of that brain of yours. I want to take another look at it without opening you back up. I'm sure you'd prefer that method."

I chuckled. "Yes, that'd certainly be my preference."

Penny shoved her way between the orderly and my new set of wheels. "You lead the way. I'll drive."

The orderly shot a shocked look between the doctor and the wheelchair.

Gary King, my new favorite brain surgeon, said, "If you think you can wrestle that chair away from her, be my guest, but I'd recommend doing what the lady says. It's likely you wouldn't win the fight."

The orderly made a wise decision, and my wife propelled the chair and me through the corridors of the hospital until we finally found the radiology department. The technician in the MRI lab insisted that Penny couldn't be in the room during the imaging. He was wrong. There was little question that Penny and I were joined at the hip for the foreseeable future.

The results of the MRI, CT, and the rest of the alphabet soup of tests I endured arrived on the clipboard every doctor in the hospital seemed to carry no matter where they were. Dr. King strolled into my room as if he were enjoying a leisurely walk through the park.

He stared through the glasses perched precariously on the tip of his nose and studied the contents of the almighty clipboard that seemed to be the sole source of information inside the walls of the hospital. "I'm afraid I have some disturbing news."

Penny's face fell into instant despair, and my heart sank into my stomach.

He pulled the glasses from his nose and slid them into the pocket of his lab coat. "I'm afraid you're going to have to find someplace else to sleep. You've worn out your welcome here."

Relief replaced terror on Penny's face, and my heart began beating again.

Penny yanked a newspaper from a corner table, rolled it into a tight wand, and brutally attacked the doctor as if he were a puppy who'd just peed on her new carpet.

Dr. King took the deserved beating well. When my wife had sufficiently taken out her hostility, he said, "Are we finished abusing the guy who put your husband's brain back together?"

"I don't know yet," Penny huffed.

He chuckled and handed her his clipboard. "In that case, use this if I do anything else to deserve a lashing. Perhaps I'll have a worker's comp claim afterward, and I can finally get a few days off."

She shook the clipboard at him as if warning of things to come.

He pulled a tuning fork from his pocket, and I wondered how many obscure items he could have in that apparently bottomless cavity. He pounded the tuning fork against his palm and placed it against my skull, just behind my ear. "Can you hear that?"

"Yes. I can answer in Russian if you prefer."

He pointed toward my chest with the tuning fork. "I'm glad you brought that up. I've been doing a little reading on the phenomenon you exhibited. What do you know about the brain?"

I glanced between Penny and Dr. King, wondering where the conversation was headed. "I have a psych degree from UGA, so I know a little about how the mind works, but I'm no neurosurgeon."

"It's interesting that you said *mind* instead of *brain*. Do you believe they're the same thing?"

I cast my eyes to the institutional ceiling overhead and pondered his question. "No, I don't believe they're the same thing. I believe the mind is the collective human consciousness while the brain is a biological organ of the body."

It was Dr. King's turn to stare at the ceiling. "Okay, I'll buy that, and it's a pretty good answer, especially for a psychologist, but specifically what I want to talk about is the part of the brain that gives us the ability to convert thought into coherent words and sentences. The region of the brain with that responsibility is called—"

"Broca's Area," I said.

"Very good. That skill is primarily developed in the first decade of our life. Of course, our vocabulary grows throughout our lifetime, but we generally learn verbal communication in those first ten formative years. How old were you when you learned German and Spanish?"

"My mother spoke fluent German, so I picked it up from her. And we spent a lot of time in Spanish-speaking parts of the world during the first fourteen years of my life, before my parents were killed."

That revelation caught his attention, and the briefest look on his face said he'd made a mental note to revisit my parents' death.

"And how about Russian? When did you learn to speak that messed-up little language?"

"In my early twenties," I said.

He snapped his fingers and pointed toward me. "Any ideas why you didn't start speaking German or Spanish instead of Russian after your accident?"

I was a student of the human mind, but Dr. King was a student of the brain. That's why he found my case particularly fascinating.

"It's not nice to point," I said, "but I do have a theory."

He added his left index finger to the offense and pointed at me with both hands. "Let's hear that theory of yours."

"I think I learned English, Spanish, and German in those formative years you mentioned, and that would put all of those language skills into Broca's Area, but Russian came to me as a purely academic practice and not an early-life development. I don't speak Russian from Broca's Area. I speak it from long-term memory, which is stored all over the brain, but generally managed by the hippocampus. That's why I could speak Russian using the hippocampus, and probably the amygdala to some degree, but I couldn't speak the other languages that were stored in Broca's Area."

He exaggerated his double-fingered pointing at me and then flashed his thumbs toward himself. "It sounds like *you* don't need *me* at all. You probably could've done your own surgery."

I shrugged. "Maybe I wouldn't have been in a coma for two and a half weeks if I'd done it myself."

He raised his eyebrows. "Two weeks, two days."

"So, when are you kicking me out?"

"We'll hang onto you for one more night." He leaned in and spoke in a conspiratorial whisper. "That way, we can bill you for another night at the Empty Arms Hotel and Medical Center. I'll take another look at you in the morning, and we'll finish my tuning-fork game. If everything checks out, you'll be home in time for lunch."

"Thanks for everything, Dr. King."

"What kind of work do you do, Chase? We'll need to make arrangements for some occupational therapy to make sure you can still earn a living."

I put on Clark's crooked grin again and pointed at Penny. "She's the breadwinner. I just bum around and slam my boat into bigger boats for kicks."

# Chapter 22
## *Back at the Mill*

Twenty-four hours later, my legs had regained their confidence, and I was at home aboard *Aegis* with my favorite screenwriter, who just happened to be my wife.

In addition to potentially being the next great screenwriter in Hollywood, Penny Fulton made the best old-fashioned in existence. She placed the tumbler in my hand and snuggled beside me on the settee as I stared out over the North River from the upper deck of our catamaran.

"I want to hear your version," she said.

I poured the first sip of the cocktail across my tongue and savored the smoky essence. "My version of what?"

"Oh, I don't know. Maybe your version of the boat accident that landed you in the hospital for seventeen days."

The placid water flowing slowly to the Cumberland Sound, and finally into the blue Atlantic, made it difficult to imagine the recent scene that had resulted in my experience behind the protection of the legion of angels.

I laid out the story for her in explicit detail, right up to the moment the sky in front of me turned into the hull of an anchored shrimp boat.

"That's the same story Hunter and Singer told me," she said. "By the way, Disco is apparently the real deal."

I enjoyed another sip of the old-fashioned. "Yeah, I think he is. I need to have Clark vet him, but if he checks out, I plan to put him on the payroll."

She stuck her finger in my cocktail, gave it a stir, and seductively licked the bourbon from her skin. "Do you think the world stopped turning just because you took a two-week nap?"

I kissed her softly and tasted the drink on her lips. "I hope you don't expect me to talk about work while you're doing things like that with your fingers."

She put on her sweet and innocent Southern-belle face. "Why, I wouldn't know *what* you're talking about, sir."

I found myself lost in everything about her. "I've missed you."

She closed her eyes and let her forehead touch mine. "I've missed you, too . . . for a long time. I don't like that you got hurt, but I love that we seemed to have found *us* again."

"Me, too. I'm sorry I let the rest of the world come between us."

"It wasn't your fault," she whispered. "We're not exactly the typical family next door, so I don't think our lives will ever be normal. I'm just glad we realize what's really important when it all starts falling apart around us."

"I am, too. Thank you for not giving up on me, but what did you mean about the world stopping while I was napping?"

She leaned back, took the tumbler from my hand, and enjoyed a sensual sip. "I meant you have some pretty amazing people around you who don't exactly stop being amazing just because you're playing Rip Van Winkle."

"What do you mean?"

"Clark and Skipper already ran Disco's background. He left out a few things."

That old, familiar sickening feeling returned to my stomach. "What did he omit?"

Penny smiled. "The fact that he has two Purple Hearts and a Distinguished Flying Cross, for starters."

176 · CAP DANIELS

Suddenly, my stomach felt better. "Yeah, he did fail to mention that. Anything else?"

"According to Skipper and Clark, he's squeaky clean. Air Force, twenty years, retired as a lieutenant colonel, married once, wife died of complications from lupus ten years ago. Owns a house outside Knoxville, Tennessee, no debt, and should be an easy go at reestablishing his Top Secret clearance."

I nodded my approval. "I guess the world *didn't* stop turning while I was away. It sounds like we'd better get this guy under contract before somebody else snatches him up."

"We've just been waiting for you to wake up and get back to work. Skipper had Ben Hedgcock write up a contract and nondisclosure agreement. They're in the safe downstairs."

I finished my drink. "In that case, I guess it's time to get back to the mill."

The rest of my day was spent catching up on everything I'd missed during what Penny continued calling my "Rip Van Winkle phase." My headache was gone, the surgical wound was healing nicely, and she gave me a much-needed haircut. The shaved area around the incision made me look like Frankenstein, but my hair would soon grow out, and no one would ever know.

The call I'd been dreading and anticipating finally happened. I swallowed my anxiety and dialed the president's private line.

He answered after thirty seconds and six rings. "Yes."

"Good afternoon, sir. Chase Fulton here."

"Oh, Chase, of course. It's good to hear your voice. I trust you're out of the hospital and back on your feet?"

"Yes, sir. They released me this morning."

"Good . . . good. Last time we spoke, I left you with the charge of researching the Twenty-Fifth Amendment. May I assume you've done so?"

"I have, sir, and I think I understand your concern. I do have to ask, Mr. President, do you have a VP selection in mind?"

"If I had a dollar for every time I've been asked that question over the past three weeks, I'd never need to raise another dime for my campaign. Because I feel I can trust you, Chase, I can say I do have a couple of names, but I'm not sure I'll make any public statements about either of them anytime soon."

"My partner said he'd spoken with you on three occasions while I was incapacitated and that you wanted to hear from me as soon as possible. That's the reason for the call, sir."

As if I'd made no mention of why I was calling, he said, "I hear you're building a new house."

I shook off the dramatic change of subject. "Well, not yet, but we plan to rebuild Bonaventure as soon as the smoke clears, so to speak."

"The way I hear it, you're planning to build a covert ops center. I understand you turned down an offer from my predecessor for full financial support in return for constant availability of your team to the White House. Why would you do that?"

I wasn't prepared for an inquisition, but I took it in stride. "I would've been proud to be at the beck and call of the former president, and for you, sir, but I was hesitant to make such a commitment, potentially leaving my team hanging out to dry if the election didn't keep him and you in power."

"I can respect that position," he said. "In fact, putting the team first is one of the marks of a great leader. Even though you turned down our financial support, I'd like to extend an offer in helping you rebuild your home."

"Thank you, sir. I sincerely appreciate your kindness, but we're well insured, and we have the financial—"

"I'm not offering to buy you a house, Chase. I want to send down a couple of intelligence-service guys to help design the ops center, and when you're ready, we'll put a builder in your hands who understands the sensitive nature of your project."

"CIA guys?"

"No, not exactly," he said. "Are you on your boat?"

"Yes, sir. We are."

"Good. Stay there, and expect a design team tomorrow. Goodbye, Chase. I'll be in touch."

With that, the line went dead, and I was left with my mouth hanging agape.

"What did he say?" Penny demanded.

"He said he's sending down an architect to design our new house, and then he's sending a builder who understands projects like ours."

She frowned. "I wasn't expecting that. Were you?"

"No, not remotely, but I can't say I don't welcome it."

Her tone became almost accusatory. "Is this a quid pro quo?"

"It always is," I said. "I don't know how much Skipper and Hunter told you about what's going on inside the Secret Service, but it's safe to say the new president is going to ask for a favor sooner rather than later."

* * *

Politicians keeping promises is like the sun rising in the west, but to my surprise, a pair of visitors arrived on the Bonaventure dock at ten the next morning.

"Can I help you?" I called down from *Aegis's* upper deck.

The two looked up, shielding their eyes from the morning sun. "Good morning. Are you Mr. Fulton?"

"That depends on who's asking."

"We're from the design firm about your reconstruction project."

That was purposefully vague enough to be a federal government answer, so I said, "Come on up."

Hands were shaken, and coffee was distributed.

"I'm Clint Nielson, and this is my associate Carrie Phillips. I'm an architect, and Carrie is a structural engineer."

"It's nice to meet you both. I'm Chase Fulton, and this is my wife, Penny."

We took our seats around the table.

Carrie said, "Before we talk about your new house, I have something for you." She pulled a metallic container from her briefcase and slid it across the table.

I opened the box and discovered a cell phone inside. "I already have a cell phone."

Carrie shook her head. "Not like that one, you don't. That phone dials only one number and receives calls only from an extremely select set of numbers. That is the only method of communication you are to use with our boss from this point forward. Do you understand?"

I stared across the table. "Your boss?"

"Yes," she said. "Our boss, and your friend."

I pulled the phone from the case and examined it closely. "Is it encrypted?"

"Of course. It uses the latest Advanced Encryption Standard two-fifty-six-bit encryption. There's no more secure encryption system in the world."

I pressed the phone back into its case. "I see. Am I expected to keep this phone with me at all times?"

"No, of course not. You're expected to regularly check the phone for messages and only use it for the purpose I described."

"Regularly check it. Does that mean once a day or once a week?"

She placed her briefcase back on the deck. "That depends on what's going on in the world and in your world. Use your best judgment. If our boss didn't believe you had excellent judgment, you wouldn't be holding that phone. Now, shall we talk about your new house?"

Whoever these people were, they were far more than architects and engineers.

"Sure, let's talk about the house," I said.

Clint pulled a roll of drawings from a case he'd carried aboard and rolled them out in front of Penny and me. On the first page of the roll was an architectural rendering in near-photo quality of Bonaventure as it existed before the fire.

I stared down at the page. "How did you . . ."

Clint flipped the page. "Never judge a book by its cover. When your house is finished, the exterior will be practically in-distinguishable from the original. The inside, however, is quite another story."

As he flipped through the drawings, I couldn't believe my eyes. There must have been ten different sets of floorplans for each level of the house.

Clint said, "You may like some of the ideas I've come up with for the interior, but, of course, you're welcome to design any interior you'd like as long as it fits inside the shell of the original house and the doors and windows align with the origi-nals."

Penny slid her hand across the pages. "Do you mean we can make the interior look any way we want?"

Clint smiled. "Yes, ma'am. I'm an architect, and she's an en-gineer. If you can dream it up, we can design it, but that's not all. Anything we design can and will be built. That's the point of all of this."

I saw the light in Penny's eyes as the ideas poured like water through her mind, and I turned to Clint. "So, who's paying you two?"

Clint and Carrie shared a look. "Let's just say we're part of the interior department."

"Department of Interior?" I asked.

Carrie smiled. "If you say so."

I leaned back in my chair. "I want a secure, fireproof arsenal on the ground floor with access from both inside the house and from the exterior. I'd like an absolute minimum of three hun-dred square feet—preferably more—and a five-ton ceiling-mounted, rolling crane. I want the ops center to be designed by our analysts, Elizabeth and Ginger. Outside of that, the remain-der of the interior is up to my wife. What she says, goes."

Clint placed his empty coffee mug on the table. "Too easy, but I think anything smaller than a twenty-by-twenty arsenal would quickly become cramped."

I rose from the table. "I like your style, Clint. I've got work to do, so I'm leaving you in Penny's capable hands. I have a pilot to hire and an arsonist to catch."

# Chapter 23
## *Chicken Fried*

I met Hunter and Disco for lunch at a hole-in-the-wall diner I loved. When the sweet tea and paper-lined basket of homemade biscuits arrived, I slid a short stack of paperwork toward the man who would, hopefully, become the chief pilot for our operation.

"Disco, we've done our homework. First, I want to express my condolences for the loss of your wife. I can't imagine enduring such a tragedy."

He ignored the paperwork. "Thank you, Chase. She was the love of my life, and I miss her every day. There will never be another, and I appreciate your kindness."

I said, "Before we get into the details, I have a question that you will both find amusing, but I've never worn the uniform, so I'm at a disadvantage in your world."

Disco shot a glance at Hunter and then back to me. "Sure, let's hear it."

I took a sip of the tea that almost qualified as syrup based on its sugar content. "You're a remarkable pilot. You proved that in the One-Eighty-Two during our little escapade over the river. The thing I have to know is, what on Earth does the phrase *tips wet* mean?"

He and Hunter burst into simultaneous laughter. When they caught their breath, Disco said, "It's an old term left over from Vietnam. The L-Nineteen Bird Dog pilots would fly so low down the Mekong River they were afraid the tips of their propellers would hit the water. Thus, tips wet."

I raised my glass. "Makes perfect sense now. Thank you for indulging a civilian who still has a lot to learn."

Disco bit his bottom lip. "I guess it's my turn for confession. I've been curious, to say the least, about what kind of operation you're running down here on the Georgia coast. You've got a hangar full of airplanes that run the gamut from basic to exotic and everything in between. You can write a check for a six-million-dollar Citation, but something tells me you don't own a necktie."

I patted the collar of my T-shirt. "I knew I'd forgotten something when I got dressed this morning."

Disco chuckled. "I've been hanging out with Cotton for a couple of weeks, but he wasn't forthcoming with any details about what's going on down here. You mentioned there might be a job for me flying the Citation, but I'll need to know who—and what—I'm going to work for."

I pulled the nondisclosure agreement from the bottom of the stack and gave it a tap. "Read through this, and sign the bottom. Hunter will witness it, and then I can answer *most* of your questions."

He pulled his glasses from his shirt pocket and scanned the document. "An NDA? Really?"

Hunter and I nodded. "Yep. Really."

Disco looked over the rim of his glasses. "Is it illegal?"

"No, quite the opposite, in fact. We're the good guys."

He pulled out a pen, signed the bottom of the agreement, and slid it toward Hunter.

My partner witnessed Disco's signature, turned the paper over, and slid it back to me.

"Here's my thirty-second elevator spiel," I began. "We're a team of highly-specialized operators—all with combat experience —who solve problems most people never know are problems. We do this on behalf of the federal government . . . mostly."

"Mostly?"

"We occasionally take on private work, but never on the wrong side of the law."

"Private work? Like mercenaries?"

I waggled a finger. "Absolutely not. We're not soldiers for hire. We're problem solvers with the philosophy of 'Walk softly, but carry a big stick.' Except we don't walk softly, and our stick is heavy firepower."

Disco looked up. "Like the Mustang with the Ma Deuce fifty-cal in the wing?"

I grinned. "Yeah, exactly like that."

He removed his glasses and dropped them onto the table. "So, you're the ones who wrangled that Russian spy ship a while back."

I feigned innocence and used one of Penny's lines. "Why, I wouldn't have any idea what you're talking about, sir."

Hunter and I smiled like the cat who ate the canary while Disco sat in silence, shaking his head. He replaced his glasses on his face and picked up the contract I'd placed in front of him. Two minutes later, he leaned back in the booth and let out a long sigh. "Is this one of those hidden camera shows? Is some announcer going to pop out with a microphone and a fake grin?"

I said, "No cameras, no microphones. Just an offer to put you to work flying the airplane you know better than most pilots on Earth, and a chance to maybe have a little fun on the side."

It was Hunter's turn to pitch. "You've already proven you're not afraid to jump into somebody else's fight. You took and returned fire a couple of weeks ago from the cockpit of an unarmed Cessna One-Eighty-Two. You're already one of us. We're just offering you a chance to get paid for that kind of stuff."

Disco pointed to a blank space on the contract. "There's no salary on the offer."

"Sure there is," I said. "You just have to write it on that line."

He jacked his thumb toward himself. "Me? I'm supposed to name my price?"

"You're the one with the pen," I said.

He eyed me hesitantly, apparently waiting for me to crack a smile, but I ignored him and enjoyed another sip of my sweet sweet tea.

"You're serious, aren't you?"

I replaced my plastic cup onto the ring of condensation on the table. "Yes, Disco. We're serious."

He flipped to the third page of the document and pointed at a paragraph. "It says here I have to obtain and maintain a Top Secret clearance. I don't know how to do that. The Air Force always took care of that for me."

"Don't worry," I said. "All you have to do is avoid doing anything that would put your clearance in jeopardy. We'll take care of the rest."

He shrugged, wrote six figures into the blank space on the contract, and signed the bottom of each page.

Pulling the paperwork from beneath his hands, I snatched his pen and immediately lined through his number. I doubled his figure and wrote my initials by the new figure. With the pen back in his hand, I said, "Initial here, and we've got ourselves a new chief pilot and flight instructor. Welcome aboard the crazy train."

We shook hands as gentlemen should do upon agreements such as ours.

Disco planted a palm on the table. "Now, will you please tell me why we were chasing the guy on the Jet Ski and who he was?"

I turned to Hunter. "Why didn't you tell him already?"

Hunter threw up his palms. "It wasn't my place. You're the boss. I told him we were chasing the guy because you told us to."

Disco suppressed a grin. "I guess you could say that's why I never made full-bird colonel. I was never good at blindly following orders unless they sounded like fun. Chasing a runner on a Jet Ski with a Skylane definitely *sounded* like fun, and it was, right up until the getting-shot-at part. That part . . . not so much fun."

"I'm not much at giving orders," I said, "so blind following isn't something we do around here. Generally, we make decisions together. We were chasing Jet Ski boy because he was messing around in the remains of our house, and no one should've been there. There was obviously some sinister intent; otherwise, he wouldn't have run and shot at us."

"What happened to the house?"

I laid out the arson, the investigation, and our efforts to find the fire-starter ourselves.

He listened to every word. "So, is this one of those private missions you mentioned?"

I shrugged. "I guess it is. I never *expect* anyone to jump into the pit with me when I go off on these quests, but I appreciate when they do. Everything we do is absolutely volunteer. You're never required to climb aboard. If you're opposed to what we're doing, you're welcome to stay home, and there will be no hard feelings . . . unless you stayed home because you're scared. If that happens, you can expect no mercy from our merry band of idiots."

"I think I'm going to like this merry bunch, idiots or otherwise. By the way, I was a little busy when you decided to mate with that shrimp boat, so I didn't see the crash. I kept chasing Jet Ski boy, as you called him."

"Where did he lead you?" I asked.

Disco sat up straight in the booth and took a look around the nearly vacant diner. "I chased him across the interstate and up a creek to the north. I've been studying the local maps, and apparently, every body of water within fifty miles of here is called the Saint Marys River. It's a little frustrating, but I finally found the name of the creek. It was May Branch. Whoever the guy was, he's a good shot, and he had no shortage of ammo. I chased him up the branch of the river until I started losing oil pressure. At that point, I had no choice. The engine wasn't going to survive long, so I pulled the power, flattened the prop, and headed for the airport."

I was leaning in as if hanging on his every word. "Do you have a guess where he was going?"

The waitress appeared with our chicken fried steak, mashed potatoes, and green beans.

Disco watched her place the plates on the table in front of us. "We didn't order this. It must be someone else's."

The waitress giggled and nudged my shoulder. "Who's the new guy?"

"This is Disco," I said. "He's going to do some flying for us. Disco, meet Edith. She doesn't take food orders. She just brings out what she thinks we want, and so far, she's never been wrong."

"It's nice to meet you, Edith. I was just thinking how much I wish I had a plate of chicken fried steak."

She nudged me again. "I think I like this one. Try not to get him killed like them last three or four."

"I'll do my best," I said. "Besides, what are the chances of four pilots all getting hit by lightning?"

"Eat up, boys. It's nice to meet you, Disco. I'm sure I'll be seein' you around . . . if these two don't get you killed."

We dug in, and once again, Edith had guessed correctly. The meal was fit for a king, if that king was hoping for clogged arteries.

Disco finally continued. "Anyway, I chased him as far as I could before I had to cut and run. I did some snooping around on foot a couple days afterwards and ended up on Lindy Lane off Scrubby Bluff Road. Do you know where that is?"

"Yeah, I know where it is. Go on."

"Well," he continued, "unless he was lost, there was only one place he could've been going. I think he had a truck staged in the woods back there, but I doubt if it was his primary egress route."

"If it was his plan all along," I said, "it was a terrible plan, and he did too many things right to have a crappy egress plan." I turned to Hunter. "Was he wet before he went off the end of the dock?"

Hunter cast his eyes to the ceiling. "I don't think so, and that would mean he had help."

Disco frowned. "I'm not following."

"It's simple," I said. "The guy had a Jet Ski stashed in the marsh grass, and he likely had a vehicle stashed off Lindy Lane. That takes preparation. If he wasn't wet before he dived into the river from the dock, he arrived dry. If he came up the river by Jet Ski, he would've had to swim ashore. If you put it all together, he pre-positioned some assets, showed up dry, and knew exactly where to run when confronted. Either somebody dropped him off, or he hiked into Bonaventure."

Understanding flashed on Disco's face. "Ah, I get it. But what if he drove himself to or near Bonaventure and planned to drive away after finding what he was looking for? Come to think of it, what *was* he looking for?"

"It's an interesting theory," I said, "but there's no way for us to know if he drove in, was dropped off, or if he hiked in. In the big scheme of things, it doesn't really matter."

Hunter held up one finger. "Unless the vehicle he drove in is still somewhere around Bonaventure."

"No way," I said. "We all agree this guy is a pro. He'd never leave a vehicle behind."

"You're probably right. But it wouldn't hurt to do a little aerial surveillance just to be sure."

"If we only had an airplane and a pilot," I said.

Glancing across the table, I expected at least some response from Disco, but instead of a reaction to my jab, he took in a long breath, puffed out his jaws, and exhaled audibly.

"What is it?" I said.

"It's probably nothing, but I noticed something about the guy on the Jet Ski."

Hunter and I leaned in.

"There was something about the way they moved. Whoever it was had on a watch cap, so I couldn't see their hair, but when they turned around to shoot at me. . . ." He waved a dismissive hand. "Never mind."

Hunter spoke up before I could. "No, we don't play 'never mind.' One of the tactics we use better than any team I've ever worked with is piecing together a scene by combining what a dozen eyes saw at any particular time. Whatever it is, say it."

He took a drink. "I don't know, but when the runner looked up at me, I could've sworn it was a woman."

# Chapter 24
## *I Know a Guy*

In unison, Hunter and I said, "Anya."

Disco scowled. "What's an Anya?"

"Anya is a long story," I said. "We're going to need a better nondisclosure agreement before I tell you about her."

I placed two twenties under the edge of my half-empty plate and slid from the booth. "It's time for that aerial surveillance."

We found Cotton Jackson on his back beneath the starboard float of the Caravan.

I peered beneath the float. "Is everything okay down there?"

Cotton jumped, dropped his flashlight, and hit his head on the keel of the aluminum float. He dug his heels into the floor and pulled himself out from beneath the airplane. "You scared the hell out of me. I didn't know anyone else was here."

"Sorry about that. Are you all right?"

He rubbed the knot on his forehead. "Yeah, I'm okay. Salt water plays hell on those floats. I'm just checking for corrosion. It's almost time for the annual inspection, so I thought I'd get a head start while I was up here."

"What about the One-Eighty-Two?" I asked.

He pulled a dirty rag from his back pocket and wiped his even dirtier hands. "Why do you keep bringing airplanes home with bullet holes in them?"

"It wouldn't be any fun if nobody shot at us. Besides, I wasn't the culprit this time." I pointed toward Disco. "It was his fault."

Cotton raised a hand. "Hey, Disco. How's it going? Chase is blaming you for the bullet holes."

Disco joined us. "I didn't do the shooting, but I guess I was the only one on board, so, maybe I'm guilty as charged." He turned to me. "You're not going to dock my pay, are you?"

"We'll have to see how heavy Cotton's bill is before we make that decision."

He led us to the Skylane and pointed to the repairs. "Fortunately, other than the oil cooler, there was no major damage. The prop is fine, and he didn't hit the gas tanks or landing gear. I'd say you got off pretty lucky this time. It's nothing like the last time with the Mustang."

Disco eyed the flawless, sixty-year-old P-51 Mustang. "You got *that* shot up?"

Cotton scoffed. "Shot up don't cover it. He barely dragged that old girl back to the airport. She wasn't recognizable by the time he got all the pieces stopped out there on the runway. A few months of my life and a few pounds out of Chase's checkbook made her better than new."

Disco ran to the Mustang and embraced the wingtip as if it were his long-lost love. "Don't you worry, baby. I'll never hurt you."

I snatched the rag from Cotton, wadded it into a ball, and nailed our new chief pilot squarely between the eyes. "If you don't get your grubby hands off my airplane, you'll be flying a lawnmower for the rest of your career . . . Colonel."

Cotton shot a thumb toward Disco. "I like the new guy. He's gonna fit right in on your little island of misfit toys."

"Okay, that's enough messing around for one day," I said. "We need an airplane for some aerial surveillance. Is anything other than the Citation airworthy?"

Cotton scanned the hangar. "Well, technically, no, except for the Mustang, and that's not exactly what you need for surveillance. That guy from Hilton Head brought his R-Forty-Four down here for me to recertify the floats. I'm sure he wouldn't mind if you used it for a couple of hours."

I shook my head. "Have you ever seen me fly a helicopter? It's not pretty."

Hunter held up his hands in surrender. "Don't look at me. I can't fly it."

All eyes turned to Cotton, and he took a step back. "Oh, no. If somebody else will do the takeoff and landing, I can fly it in cruise, but that's it."

Disco cleared his throat. "Hello . . . chief pilot here. If it's got a stick, pedals, and a throttle, I can fly it."

I held up an open palm, and Cotton dropped a keyring into my hand. "Don't break the guy's helicopter. He needs it to make a living."

After a preflight inspection, Disco and I climbed into the front seats, and Hunter strapped into the back. A minute later, the blades were spinning over our heads.

Disco said, "Okay, Chase, you have the controls. I'll stay with you, but I want you to show me what you can do. We'll correct anything you do wrong. Just don't hit the hangar."

"All right, but you're going to regret this. I'm the world's worst helicopter pilot." I set the throttle and added collective, and the muscles in my forearms tensed. As Clark had taught me, I picked a point in the tree line across the airport as my visual reference. The chopper got light on the skids and started a nasty turn.

To Disco's credit, he waited as long as he could before speaking up. "I have the controls. You're going to hit the hangar."

"You have the controls," I said, lifting my sweaty palms from the cyclic and collective.

He righted the aircraft, lowered the nose, and flew us east over the taxiway. "I thought it would be worth a look around Bonaventure, just in case there was an abandoned vehicle."

"It can't hurt," I said, "but I don't think we're going to find anything."

I was right. There were no vehicles anywhere on or near the property that didn't seem to belong there. We followed the four-lane highway until we crossed the interstate.

"This is where Saint Marys Road becomes Scrubby Bluff," I said as the four-lane shrank into a two-lane.

"Right," Disco said, "and just beyond that pond is Lindy. How low do you want to go?"

"Unless taking off or maneuvering to land, you may fly no closer than five hundred feet from any person, vessel, vehicle, or structure. Come on, chief pilot, you're supposed to know this stuff."

He shot me a look. "I didn't ask how low we could legally fly. I asked how low *you* wanted me to fly. If I get closer than five hundred feet to anything, I'll be maneuvering to land, as far as the FAA knows."

Hunter said, "I think Cotton may have been right. He is going to fit in nicely on the island of misfit toys."

We focused our attention outside the helicopter, and Disco flew us down the road more slowly than most people drive. We scoured the tree line for any areas a vehicle may have been staged.

"I don't see anything. How about you?"

Hunter said, "Nothing on the right side."

"Take us down that creek, and show us where you lost the Jet Ski," I said.

Disco picked up a little speed and headed southwest. "I didn't lose it. I chose to break off the chase and save your airplane. Engines tend to run a little low on oil with a bullet hole in the oil cooler."

"Thank you for saving my airplane. Now, show us where you last saw the Jet Ski."

With the skids barely above the treetops, we followed every bend of May Branch for a half mile, and Disco pointed to an area of the creek with a round cove about thirty feet across. "That's the last place I saw him . . . or her. The oil pressure was falling faster than I was comfortable with, so I bugged out and headed for base."

I pointed to a clearing on the west side of the creek. "Can you put us down there?"

His answer came as a perfect landing with the blades missing the trees by only a few feet.

We walked the western bank of the creek, looking for any spot that someone would've been able to climb from a Jet Ski.

After ten minutes of nothing more than muddy muck, Hunter waved us over. "Guess what I found."

Disco and I made our way to where Hunter was standing beneath an outcropping of trees that almost touched the creek. When we were less than ten feet away, Hunter yanked a filthy green tarp from the ground, sending evergreen boughs, dirt, and pine straw in every direction. Beneath the tarp was a red-and-white Jet Ski with a 30-caliber bullet hole in the bow and two 9mm holes in the left footwell.

Hunter stuck his finger in the hole in the bow. "Would you look at that? I guess Singer didn't miss after all."

Disco took a knee in the mud beside the Ski and examined the two holes he'd put on the port side footwell. "Check this out."

I saw the only thing better than the arsonist's signature on the white fiberglass of the Ski.

"Is that blood?" Hunter asked.

"I do believe it is, my friend. You don't happen to have an evidence bag handy, do you?"

Hunter cocked his head. "Do I look like a forensics tech?"

"Let's see if it'll start. If it will, one of us can drive it back to Bonaventure and collect the sample there. If it won't, we'll go find some Q-tips and plastic bags."

The Jet Ski slid effortlessly on the slippery mud. It immediately began to take on water through the holes in the footwell, so Disco plugged the holes with a couple of sticks he cut from a fallen branch. There was no key, so I crushed the plastic around the ignition switch and hotwired the watercraft. At the touch of the starter button, the engine spun but made no effort to start.

"Wait a minute," Hunter said. "It's the kill switch."

He pulled out his pocketknife, sliced a piece of pine, and wedged it beneath the kill switch to take the place of the plastic disc that would normally be attached to the rider by an elastic cord. If the rider fell off, the plastic disc would pull free of the kill switch, and the engine would die, preventing the Ski from motoring away and leaving the rider stranded in the water.

I touched the starter again, and the engine coughed to life.

Disco hopped aboard the watercraft. "I'll see you guys back at Bonaventure."

Hunter reached for his pistol. "If you make me fly back to the airport with this hack at the controls of that helicopter, I think I'll just shoot you right here."

Disco dismounted the Ski. "I'm having a heck of a first day on the job. First, Chase tries to fly me into the side of the hangar, and now you're threatening to shoot me. I can see this job is really going to suck."

Hunter climbed aboard and disappeared down May Branch toward the Saint Marys River.

Disco flew us out of the tight quarters of the creek bank and then surrendered the helicopter to me. "Take us back to the airport, and fly your approach to the runway, just like you'd fly the One-Eighty-Two."

After a couple of minutes on the controls and enough forward airspeed to make the R-44 feel like a real airplane, I started building some confidence.

At a quarter mile from the landing threshold, Disco said, "Keep your hands on the controls, and follow me through the motions. Don't overpower me. I want you to feel what I do."

As we grew closer to the threshold, he raised the nose and gently eased the collective upward, bringing the helicopter to a hover just above the runway numbers. "Now, keep the airplane pointed straight down the runway with your feet, and hold us an inch off the ground. I'll stay on the controls with you."

I gripped the cyclic and collective, and suddenly, the helicopter flew backward and started a turn to the right. I overcorrected and sent us flying sideways toward the fence.

Disco gently urged the controls back into position and helped me fly back to the runway. "Remember, keep the nose pointed down the runway with your feet. Practice that. I have the cyclic and collective."

After a minute or so, I could keep the chopper generally pointed down the runway as we hovered over the numbers.

"Good. Now I have the pedals and cyclic. You have the stick. Try to hold us still with tiny inputs on the stick. I'll keep us pointed in the right direction and well off the concrete."

I chased the helicopter all over the sky but finally got it under control enough to keep it over the numbers.

"Good," he said. "Now you have the pedals and collective."

We continued the drill until I had full control of the helicopter and could keep it within fifty feet of our starting position.

"You're doing fine. Now, ease the collective and let the skids touch the ground, but just barely. We're not going to put all the weight on the skids. I just want them to kiss the ground."

Apparently, I don't kiss gently in a helicopter, but after thirty minutes, I was flying a helicopter more safely than I'd ever done before. Disco was already earning his keep.

Even with our hovering lessons, we arrived back at the Bonaventure dock only minutes after Hunter. He and Penny were dabbing at the bloodstain with a Q-tip as we walked up.

"How's it going?" I asked.

Penny looked up with frustration on her face. "Not great. If this is blood, it's really dried on there. Do you want to give it a try?"

"No, I've got a better idea," I said. "I'll be right back."

I climbed aboard *Aegis* and hopped down the stairs to the workshop. Finding the tool I needed, I returned to the dock and plunged the blade of the jigsaw into the fiberglass of the Jet Ski. A few seconds later, I had a section of the bloodstained fiberglass cut from the hull and deposited into a plastic bag.

"All that's left is to have Clark arrange for a lab to determine who belongs to this blood, and we'll likely have found our arsonist."

Penny screwed up her face. "How long will that take?"

"Maybe a week or so," I said.

Hunter lifted the bag from my hand. "There's an NCIS lab at Mayport, and I know a guy."

# Chapter 25
## *Strike While the Iron is Hot*

With Hunter and our blood sample bound for the NCIS lab at Mayport Naval Station, I was left to decide which piece of iron would land on my anvil next. I had so many irons in my fire that I was certain I'd soon need to build more fires.

I found Penny standing under the shower in the master head, eyes closed, and water pouring over her hair and cascading down her back in sheets. She wasn't washing her hair. She was merely letting the water separate her from the rest of the world. Clearly, she had no shortage of irons, as well. I chose not to interrupt. For the sake of our sanity, we all need an escape from the real world from time to time.

When she climbed the stairs to the main salon wearing one of my T-shirts and her hair still wet, I handed her a glass of wine and motioned for the settee.

She took the glass from my hand, cocked her head to the side, and smiled. "You always know exactly how to make me feel better."

"Not always," I said, "but I always *want* to make you feel better."

She kissed my cheek. "I'm just a little overwhelmed right now. They're making my movie without me. Our house is a pile of burnt rubble. You're getting secret calls on the presidential bat-phone. Government architects are waiting for me to pick countertops and paint colors. We're scraping blood off a Jet Ski. You just came out of a two-week coma, and you're not going to stop working so your brain can heal. We just bought a five-million-dollar airplane. My mother is a federal fugitive. And Skipper needs a ride. Did I miss anything?"

I had a lot of questions, but taking five minutes for my wife to drink her wine and breathe wouldn't bring the world to an end.

How would it feel, I wondered, to go to work at nine, come home at five, and always know what tomorrow would hold? It would drive me to irreversible, unmitigated insanity. That's exactly how it would feel. I'd never be happy without a hundred irons in a dozen fires and a blacksmith's hammer in my sweaty hand.

Penny was not the same. She loved hours, and sometimes days, of nothingness—absolute Zen. She preferred her Zen on the trampoline at *Aegis*'s bow with a pod of dolphins playing in our bow wake. I couldn't give her the bow time she so desperately needed, but I could do the next best thing. I could hire a few more blacksmiths.

I kissed her on the forehead. "I'll be right back."

After twenty minutes on the upper deck, I pocketed my phone and headed back for the main salon. Penny had poured another glass of pinot grigio and unrolled a stack of blueprints on the chart table.

I stepped behind her and pulled her long, wet hair into a ponytail, then landed a gentle kiss just beneath her left ear. "I just got off the phone with a designer and an interior decorator from Savannah. They'll be here tomorrow morning."

She spun around on the chart table stool and looked up at me. "Sometimes, a girl just wants somebody to listen and not try to fix things, but sometimes, the perfect guy does both. And I love my perfect guy. Thank you."

I returned her kiss and held her in my arms. "I'm far from perfect, but I'll always do everything I can to make your life better than you could've ever dreamed."

She took my head in her hands and turned me so she could examine my surgical scar. "It looks surprisingly good."

"It itches," I said, "but it doesn't hurt. I feel good, but I promise I'll take it easy. No wrestling matches with bad guys for at least another forty-eight hours."

She patted my Makarov pistol beneath my shirt. "Why would anyone with a gun let himself get into a wrestling match?"

I kissed the tip of her nose. "You make an excellent point. Now, your gun-toting wrestler has work to do."

I've loved my boat from the first second I stepped foot aboard her, just off Fowey Rocks Lighthouse, southeast of Miami. That was a day I'll never forget. Anya—the former Russian SVR officer whose high cheekbones and hypnotic blue-gray eyes could turn any man into putty—and I had just killed Dmitri Barkov—the Russian billionaire oligarch—and sent his body to the bottom of the Straits of Florida. I concocted a deal with my former handler, who happened to be Clark's father, to trade Barkov's yacht for something less conspicuous. I christened that less-conspicuous boat *Aegis II*, and she became my home. *Aegis I* rested at the bottom of the Straits, not far from Barkov's remains. I'd since dropped the *II* and spent more nights aboard the beautiful sailing catamaran than anywhere else in my twenty-nine years on the planet.

As much as I loved our boat, I chose the hangar at the Saint Marys Airport as my ops center. In the hangar, I'd be less likely to get distracted by the beautiful, wet-haired woman in my T-shirt, and more likely to hammer some iron into a blade. I'm not the kind of blacksmith who makes horseshoes.

I pulled out my phone and started hammering. "Hey, Skipper. I hear you're looking for a southbound train."

"Oh, hey, Chase. Where have you been? I've been trying to call you all day."

"I've been a little busy."

"Too busy to take a call from the analyst who found your missing sniper?"

She suddenly had my full attention. "I'm sending Disco to pick you up. He'll be there in two hours."

Our chief pilot looked like an infectious disease doctor when I found him and Cotton in hazmat suits, masks, and gloves, spraying anti-corrosion solution into every cavity of the Caravan.

"I hate to interrupt your little dress-up party, but I need to get Skipper home from Silver Spring, ASAP."

Disco was out of his beekeeper outfit in thirty seconds. "Let me grab a quick shower, and I'll be airborne in fifteen minutes."

"Perfect," I said. "I'll text you her contact information so you can give her a call when you land."

He shook me off. "No need. I have everyone's numbers in my head and in my phone. You get what you pay for, boss."

From analyst all the way to sniper and everyone in between, I had assembled the best team of operators and support personnel that existed outside SEAL Team Six, and we were almost as well-equipped.

With Skipper's transportation handled, I moved on to the second iron in my fire. There are two things in abundance in Saint Marys, Georgia: rock shrimp and men who own dump trucks and bulldozers. I didn't need any shrimp, but Kenny LePine, a Cajun from Dulac, Louisiana, answered the phone when I dialed the number for Terrebonne Construction.

"Dis Kenny."

"Kenny, this is Chase Fulton. I'm—"

"Yeah, I know who you is, you. You be the one wid dat big fine house out on the bayou somebody done burnt to da groun', you."

Kenny had been in Camden County, Georgia, long enough to lose the Cajun drawl and learn we have rivers instead of bayous, but nobody in the county moved as much dirt as Terrebonne Construction.

"That's me, Kenny. I need somebody to—"

"Yeah, I know what you be needin', you. I been lookin' for da phone to ring from you since I knowed 'bout dat fire. I be dehr to clean up dat mess here in a day or two, maybe tree day, me, but I get to it, sir. Yes, me do."

"I don't have a clue what you just said, but if it involves cleaning up my property so we can rebuild, that's exactly what I need."

"Dat's 'zactly what I said, me. Two tousand, maybe no mo dan tree tousand dollars, yeah? Take 'bout a day, maybe two, yeah."

I suddenly wanted to eat crawfish and gator tail at Kenny's house.

"That all sounds fine, Kenny. Start as soon as you can. I'll be on my boat at the dock behind the property if you need me."

"Two tree days. Bye-bye, you"

I believed Kenny had just agreed to clean up the mess the fire had left for three thousand dollars or less, and would get to it in two or three days, but I couldn't be sure. Maybe I should've added Cajun creole to the list of languages I wanted to learn.

When my phone chirped, I was relieved to see it was someone who spoke English.

"What's up, Hunter? Did you get the sample to your buddy at the lab?"

"I did, but I'm not smart enough to understand what he's telling me. Do you mind if I put you on the phone with him?"

"Sure, why not? I just got off the phone with Kenny LePine at Terrebonne Construction. I've got no idea what he was saying, so we'll just add a lab tech to the list of people we can't understand."

Hunter handed the phone to the lab tech.

"Mr. Fulton, I'm Anthony Granger. There's a problem with your sample. You see, our DNA lab is set up primarily for restriction fragment length polymorphism analysis. This process requires a relatively high molecular weight DNA, and your sample has been degraded by elemental exposure. I would theorize eighteen to twenty-one days of exposure since the sample accumulated on the fiberglass surface."

He nailed the timeline, so that bought the tech some credibility, but nothing else that came out of his mouth made any sense at all. He didn't slow down, though.

"Adequate analysis of your sample is going to require implementation of the multiplex polymerase chain reaction. MPCR analysis essentially magnifies the tiny particle of DNA left in degraded samples like yours. Under strict protocols, it is sometimes possible to analyze as little as one nanogram of DNA. Isn't that exciting?"

I squinted in a wasted effort to ward off the coming headache. "Mr. Granger, I don't even know what a nanogram is."

"It's simply one billionth of a gram. Can you imagine that?"

"No, I'm afraid I can't. Forgive my forensic ignorance, but can you determine whose blood that is?"

He made a soft gagging sound. "Oh, no, not remotely. That's not what DNA analysis does, Mr. Fulton."

The headache continued to build. "Again, forgive me, but what can you do with that blood to help me find its rightful owner? And please formulate your answer in a language I can understand. I'd even settle for Cajun."

"Cajun?" Granger said. "I don't understand."

*Oh, look, the headache just made a three-point landing on my frontal lobe.*

"Never mind," I said. "Just tell me what you can do, and keep it as simple as possible."

"Oh, sure. I can do that. Our lab cannot perform the MPCR protocol, but the lab in Norfolk can do it. It will take a few days, but we will be able to produce a DNA analysis for comparison to a known sample. Essentially, if you have a suspect, and if you have a sample of that suspect's DNA—that could be blood, urine, saliva, hair, bone marrow, semen, vaginal secretion, etc.— we can compare the known sample with the sample you provided and determine if the two samples came from the same person."

The headache pulled at least one of its claws out of my gray matter. "See? I'm smart enough to understand that, but what about comparing the sample we provided against DNA databases to find a match? Can that be done?"

Granger grunted. "That's not as easy as television makes it look, and it takes a long time. But if there's a match in the databases, it is theoretically possible, but not guaranteed."

"Do it," I said. The line went deathly silent for several seconds. "Mr. Granger, are you still there?"

"Uh, yeah, I'm still here, but it's not as simple as just doing it. MPCR is expensive and time consuming. It's not exactly the sort of thing that can be done without authorization from, well, someone pretty high up."

"In that case, how long will the sample last and still be usable?"

He said, "I'll preserve the sample by implementing a process known as—"

"Stop!" I said. "Don't explain it. Just tell me how long it will last."

He stammered, obviously anxious to explain his preservation process, but finally said, "Years."

"Perfect. Put it on ice, or whatever you do, and I'll get you the authorization you need."

Hunter came back on the line. "That sounded painful. Did you get it all?"

I laughed. "I got enough of it to know it's over my head. Your guy said he needed some high-level authorization for the testing in Norfolk. I'm confident I can get that done. Leave the sample with him if you trust him, and we'll go from there."

"I trust him with my blood, so I don't have a problem leaving somebody else's with him. I'll be home in a couple of hours. Do you need anything from Jacksonville?"

"Sure," I said. "Pick up one of those new Nine-Eleven convertibles from the Porsche dealership. I could always use one of those."

"What color?"

I laughed. "Black, blue, or red, of course."

"Ha! Bruises or blood, huh? I guess those are our official colors these days. I'll see you in a couple of hours."

The next iron out of the fire was what Penny called the bat-phone. There was no voicemail function, but the screen showed a brief text message that disappeared ten seconds after being read.

The two messages were identical: EXPECT CONTACT 1530.

My watch said 3:18. That meant I had twelve minutes to pre-pare for a conversation with the president of the United States.

## Chapter 26
### *Eavesdropping*

Waiting for the president to call is worse than sitting outside the principal's office, waiting to be called inside. There's something about speaking with the leader of the free world that is like no other experience on Earth. My palms were sweaty. My mouth was dry, despite the quart of water I drank in the twelve minutes of waiting. But most disconcerting of all was the fact that I feared he was going to ask for my help when I had no idea what I could do to come to the aid of my president.

At precisely 1530, the batphone vibrated without a sound, and I pressed the green button. "Chase here."

The president cleared his throat. "Chase. Thank you for taking my call."

I shook my head. "You're the president of the United States, sir. Does anyone *not* take your calls?"

"You'd be surprised," he said. "But that's not why I'm calling. I have a private meeting with Conrad Fairchild in exactly . . ."— he paused, presumably to check his watch—". . . twenty-seven minutes."

I pored through my mental Rolodex, but I couldn't place the name. "I'm afraid I don't know who that is, Mr. President."

"Mr. Fairchild is the director of the Secret Service. He reports to the director of the newly formed Department of Homeland Security, but serves at the pleasure of, well, me. When I appoint a new director, there is no requirement for Senate confirmation. Now that our civics lesson is finished for the day, let's get down to the reason I called."

"I'm listening," I said.

"As you know, especially now that you're a Constitutional scholar on the Twenty-Fifth Amendment, the appointment of a vice president isn't an easy thing to accomplish, especially when the House majority is held by the opposite party as the new sitting president. None of that is your problem, Chase. However, this is two thousand three. That means next year is an election year. If the House drags its feet—and it is likely to do exactly that—it is possible, even probable, that we may have no vice president until the inauguration in January of two thousand five. Are you following me?"

The headache I had while talking with the lab tech invited some of its friends over for a party. My brain had begun circling the proverbial drain. "I think I understand all of that, sir, but I'm not a political mind. I'm a . . ."

"You're a warrior, Chase, plain and simple. A warrior just like I was before I moved inside the Washington Beltway. It's a battlefield of a different kind, my friend. We don't wear uniforms, so it's not easy to decide who to shoot."

"I don't envy your position," I said.

"Sometimes, neither do I, but I've sworn an oath to the people of the greatest nation on the planet, and I plan to hold true to my oath and serve the people of this country just as bravely as I did when I wore the SEAL trident on my chest."

"I have no doubt you will do just that, Mr. President."

My palms were still sweaty, but my heart had stopped pounding like a jungle drum in my chest.

"Chase, here's what I fear is afoot. I believe there is a conspiracy inside the Secret Service, for the first time in history, to allow a sitting president to be assassinated."

The thought of what the president was suggesting was, in my mind, beyond the realm of possibility. How could an entire

agency devoted to the physical protection of the president become so corrupted that it would become an active participant in
an assassination attempt?

"Mr. President, I don't know what to say, and more terrifying
than that, I can't imagine that I have any power to do anything
to help you. I'm just one man. . . ."

"No, Chase, you are not just one man. You are a team of men
and women who've proven to be loyal to my predecessor. All of
you have risked your lives to do things most people would never
have one percent of the courage to attempt. For you and your
team, those things have become routine. It's men like you who
keep this great country afloat, and it's a thankless and lonely job,
but there's no endeavor more noble than what you do, Chase.
None."

"Thank you, sir, but what exactly do you want me to do?"

"I thought you'd never ask. The first thing I want you to do is
find someplace secure and silent in . . ."—another pause to check
his watch—". . . nineteen minutes. When I meet privately with
Director Fairchild, I plan to have this phone connected to the
one in your hand, and I want you to listen to every word he and
I have to say. There will be no other record of the meeting.
Should I be correct in my paranoia, you'll be the only other living soul to have heard the one-on-one conversation between the
director of the Secret Service and the president of the United
States. Will you do that for me, Chase?"

"Of course, Mr. President."

"Thank you, Chase, and I'm sure you know when I'm in a
man's debt, there is no hesitance on my part to repay that debt."

"I agree to help you because you're my president. I don't expect favors in return."

"You may not expect them, but you're a soldier, and all good
soldiers know when to pull out the big guns. There's no bigger
gun than the Oval Office, Chase. Remember that."

"Is there anything else, Mr. President?"

"No, not for now. Find a quiet, secure place, keep the phone in your hand, and listen to every word. I'll call you back when Mr. Fairchild arrives, but I will not respond when you say hello."

The line went dead, and a chill ran down my spine. I was about to be privy to one of the most potentially critical conversations in modern presidential history. I was in so deeply over my head I couldn't even see the surface. I was left in awe and staring down at the phone in my hand. The simple-looking, rectangular device looked so benign, so much like an object one would find in the back of a drawer of forgotten gadgets. The tiny, black-and-white screen could've been from the seventies. The port for the charging cable was nothing more than a round hole in a plastic case marked "CHRG." As I rolled the device over in my palm, I noticed a second hole, slightly smaller in diameter than the charging port. It was labeled "AUD-OUT."

My hangar office was little more than a plywood box with one plexiglass window overlooking the hangar floor. An air conditioner filled the space where an exterior window had been in years past. The other feature of the office was a wooden desk that must've weighed a thousand pounds. Five drawers rested inside the old, worn desk, and one of those drawers held a collection of things I'd been too lazy to throw away.

I slid the drawer open and rummaged through remote controls, batteries, telephone cables, rubber bands, and thirty pounds of other miscellaneous junk until I found what I sought: a handheld tape recorder with a tiny cable leading from the side. The probe on the end of the cable fit perfectly inside the AUD-OUT hole on the batphone. A microcassette tape rested inside the device, but nothing happened when I pressed the play button.

I thumbed the battery cover off the recorder and shoved a fresh pair of double-As into the spring-loaded compartment. At the touch of the button, the pegs inside the tape turned, and the low-quality speaker behind slits in the plastic crackled to life. The heavily Russian-accented voice of Anya Burinkova escaped in tinny tones.

"My Chasechka. I believe day will come and you will find—I do not know English word for device—is *rekorder* in Russian. Maybe is same for English. I will be gone from your life when this finding happens, but is for you only to listen."

My heart had stopped beating inside my chest, and goosebumps rose on my skin. I had loved Anya once, and I had foolishly believed she loved me. Love without trust is little more than lust, and I had come to believe that's what my time with her had been. There was no way to know when she'd recorded the message, but I knew deep inside that I would follow her instructions when she said, "Is for you only to listen." As much as I wanted to hear every word she left, my watch reported 1558, and the president would be calling in less than two minutes.

I popped open the recorder and flipped over the microcassette tape. Thirty seconds later, the tape had rewound to its starting position. I played it, making sure I wasn't recording over another message from Anya, and only white noise came from the speaker. I plugged the cord into the batphone and waited for the vibration.

A watched pot never boils, and a watched phone never rings. As the minutes and seconds ticked off, I never took my eyes off the phone. There was no vibration, no lights, and no indication of an incoming call from anyone, especially not the president.

In a near panic, I yanked the cord from the AUD-OUT port, believing I'd done something to prevent the phone from working. The instant I pulled the plug, the phone vibrated, causing me to jump in anxious excitement.

I checked my watch—1609—and pressed the button to accept the call, then stuck the phone to my ear. I heard shuffling and muted voices, but I didn't speak. The noises continued, so I carefully slid the probe from the recorder cable back into the phone. There was an audible click, and the sounds continued coming from the phone.

Relieved I hadn't screwed up the call, I pressed the button to begin recording the coming conversation.

A few seconds later, the sounds coming from the phone changed dramatically.

"Director Fairchild, it's a pleasure. Won't you please have a seat?"

"Mr. President, an honor. Thank you for having me. I know a meeting like this is highly unorthodox, but you'll soon understand the necessity of the privacy. Forgive me, sir, but I'm going to need your assurances that we're not being recorded."

"If we are," the president said, "it's not by my doing. That's your department, Conrad. May I call you Conrad?"

"Of course you can, Mr. President, and I assure you we are not recording this conversation."

"Now that we have that out of the way," the president said, "what is it the director of the Secret Service has come to tell me that is such a secret we have to meet in utter privacy?"

Conrad Fairchild hesitated before saying, "Mr. President, the Secret Service has been keeping a piece of information from you, and I cannot, in good conscience, continue to keep you out of the loop."

The president lowered his tone. "Director Fairchild, I recommend you choose the next words out of your mouth more carefully than any you've ever spoken in your life. If the Secret Service has been keeping information from me that is pertinent to my safety, and I find out you were behind the cover-up, at the very least, your career is over. And I'd like to remind you that I made a living for half of my adult life as one of the most elite warriors on the planet. I'm not the kind of man who lives his life in fear, regardless of me being on the battlefield or inside the People's House, right here in this cesspool called Washington, D.C. Am I making myself clear, Director Fairchild?"

"Crystal clear, Mr. President. That's precisely why I'm here, sir. It's necessary that I brief you on some of the details of the assassination last month."

"Before you go any further, I think you should know something. I've watched every video from every angle of every camera from that day. I've been to the Army's Sniper School at Fort Benning. I've pulled more triggers on live targets in one day than you will in your entire career, so I know exactly what happened that day in Columbia, South Carolina, Conrad. I know every detail, so whatever it is you're about to tell me, it better be consistent with exactly what I know. If it's not, you're going to prison . . . if I let you live long enough to get out of this room. Are we still clear, Mr. Director?"

"Yes, sir. We're perfectly clear, and I assure you I am here for no reason other than full disclosure."

"Okay, then. Let's hear it."

I couldn't believe my ears. The president of the United States just threatened to kill the director of the Secret Service, and he was more than capable of doing so.

Director Fairchild continued. "Mr. President. The man who killed the president, Landon Edgar Barrier, was killed by a countersniper one point nine two seconds after he pulled the trigger, sending the round that ultimately killed your predecessor." Fairchild paused before continuing. "Mr. President. You're a sniper. The three hundred Winchester Magnum round leaves the muzzle at just over three thousand feet per second. You can do the math without my help."

The president sighed. "Whoever killed Landon Edgar Barrier pulled the trigger before Barrier did."

"That's correct, sir, but the countersniper was not one of ours."

"And exactly why has it taken you nearly a month to bring your ass into my office and tell me the truth?"

"Sir, that decision was made on the day of the assassination, by individuals above my head who did not consult me."

The president roared, "You work for me, Conrad. You answer to me."

"Sir, with all due respect, I do serve at the pleasure of the president, but you were not the president that day. And even though I do serve at the pleasure of the president, as of March of this year, I report directly to the Department of Homeland Security."

"Are you telling me this cover-up is the creation of the Department of Homeland Security?"

"I don't believe it is necessarily a cover-up, sir. I believe the truth has been kept from the media and the American people to protect the reputation and trust of the Secret Service to protect the president."

"Well, you dropped the ball on that one, didn't you, Conrad?"

Fairchild's tone became weak and almost delicate. "Yes, sir, we did. That's part of the reason I'm here today, Mr. President."

I could hear movement, as if one of the men was pulling something from a pocket.

"This is my letter of resignation, Mr. President."

Suddenly, sounds of paper being yanked from a hand and torn to shreds poured through the phone.

"I'm not interested in your resignation, Conrad. I'm interested in finding the sniper who killed Barrier. Now, get back to work. Form a task force including SEALs, Delta, and anybody else you need to find the truth, and from this second forward, you report directly to me. I don't care what Homeland Security has to say. At only nine months old, that place is already a bureaucratic web of bullshit, and I'm going to clean house before it gets any worse. You're dismissed, Conrad."

I continued listening in awe as doors were slammed and the president's chief of staff was summoned.

"Yes, sir. Is everything all right?"

"No, Charlie, everything is not all right. I want the secretary of Homeland Security in that chair in ten minutes."

"Uh, Mr. President, the secretary is in Puerto Rico."

"He'll be in that chair when the sun comes up tomorrow morning, or Federal Marshals will escort him back to D.C. in handcuffs."

# Chapter 27
## *Team Players*

"Did you get that, Chase?"

The president's voice in my ear sounded like yelling after listening to muffled, muted voices for fifteen minutes.

"Yes, sir, I got it. In fact, I have it recorded."

"That's why you're one of the few men left on Earth I can rely on. Back on the Teams, I knew exactly what every man around me would do in every situation. I put my life in their hands, and they willingly put theirs in mine. That's how real teams work, and you understand that."

"Forgive me, but if you wanted me to record the meeting, why didn't you come out and say that?"

"Because, my friend, if I'd asked you to record it, I wouldn't have been able to look into Fairchild's eyes and tell him it wasn't being recorded by my doing."

"Once an operator, always an operator," I said.

"Damn right, Chase. You'll secure that recording."

It wasn't a question.

I said, "Yes, sir."

"Politicians and soldiers hate being wrong, but I'm man enough to admit that I'm glad I had this one wrong this time. I didn't want to believe there was a conspiracy by the other side to claim the White House by nefarious means, but everything I saw pointed to exactly that. I think Fairchild is a good man."

"I hope you're right, sir. I hope he's not a pawn."

"Paranoia is a deadly illness, Chase."

"Just because I'm paranoid doesn't mean they're not out to get me, Mr. President."

He laughed. "You guard that tape with your life, son. We may need it someday."

I swallowed hard. "I know this may not be the best time to ask, but . . ."

"Name it, Chase. Don't be shy. What do you want?"

"I have a DNA sample I need the NCIS lab in Norfolk to run, and they need what they call higher authorization to—"

"Say no more. Consider it done."

My irons in my fire were diminishing, and I was exhausted.

* * *

Penny and I were having tuna nachos on the upper deck when Disco landed and delivered Skipper to the boat.

She came bouncing up the ladder. "Ooh, that looks yummy. Is there more?"

I kicked a chair toward her. "Sit down. There's plenty. You too, Disco."

He waved me off. "Thanks, but I'm beat. Unless you need me for something else, I'm going to get some sleep."

"I'd offer you a bunk on the boat, but with Skipper back, you'd have to take the pullout."

"Thanks," he said, "but I have a nice room at the Spencer House for now. I've been looking for a place, but I need to sell my house in Tennessee before I can really afford to buy anything else. Good night, guys. Oh, and Skipper, nice job in the right seat. We'll find a light twin and get your multi-engine ticket out of the way so we can check you out in the Citation."

"Thanks, Disco. That'd be awesome. Good night."

I wiped my mouth with a paper napkin and eyed Skipper. "Right seat, huh? What did you think?"

"Stuff happens a lot faster in the jet than in the One-Eighty-Two, but I like it a lot. I think I can learn to do it."

"I'm sure you can," I said. "Help yourself. Penny made more than we'll eat."

She dug in and briefed between bites. "Okay, so out of the eight names on the list Singer gave us, we found and alibied seven."

She shoveled nachos into her mouth as if she hadn't eaten in days. "These are amazing."

I tossed a napkin at her. "So, tell me about the one you didn't find."

She wiped her mouth and fingers. "He's a guy named Ricco Vasquez. He was born in Mallorca, Spain, adopted a few months later by a Jewish family. He served six years with the Tzahal and then vanished."

Penny swallowed a mouthful of nachos. "What's Tzahal?"

"It's the Hebrew acronym for the Israel Defense Force," I said.

Skipper continued. "Rumor has it that he went to work for the French Foreign Legion, but that's impossible to verify. We know for sure he worked for Corps of Gendarmerie as a sniper for almost two years."

"But his family is Jewish," I said.

Skipper nabbed my tea glass and washed down another mouthful. "Yeah, his adopted family is Jewish, but he was baptized Catholic shortly after he was born."

Penny held up a hand. "Forgive me for being so far behind, but what does his religion have to do with who he works for?"

"Skipper, go ahead. Lay it out for her. I'm getting more nachos before you eat them all."

Skipper said, "The Corps of Gendarmerie is essentially the police force for the Vatican. Every member has to be confirmed Catholic, but that's where the requirements end. Unlike the Swiss Guard that is directly responsible for protecting the pope, kind of like the Secret Service, the Corps of Gendarmerie have a much wider range of responsibilities."

Penny nodded. "Okay, I think I'm caught up now. Sorry for interrupting."

I pushed the platter of remaining chips toward Skipper. "So, where is he now?"

"I already told you, we don't know. He may be in Argentina hunting Nazis."

"Hunting Nazis?" I said. "What takes a guy from the Vatican police to Nazi-hunting halfway around the world?"

"It's all a guess, but there've been three suspected former Nazi officers killed from really long range—like, way over a mile—in the last year. They were all killed in Buenos Aires."

Penny said, "There's Nazis in South America?"

"Unfortunately," I said, "that's where a bunch of them ran after the war."

"Wouldn't most of them be dead of old age by now?"

"Most of them, but a few are still hanging around. They'd be in their early to mid-eighties, at the youngest."

"So, what good does it do to kill an eighty-year-old man who's going to die soon anyway?" Penny asked.

I said, "If that eighty-year-old man had sent your parents or grandparents to the ovens at Auschwitz and got away with it for over half a century, it would make perfect sense."

Penny scratched her temple. "So, is this guy some kind of avenging angel or something? He joins the IDF to learn to fight and shoot, then he goes off to the French Foreign Legion, and then the Vatican. Now he's killing Nazis in South America and maybe shooting presidential assassins in South Carolina?"

Skipper shrugged. "I'm not making any judgments. I'm just telling you what the research found. He's the only name on the list who can't be accounted for."

Penny turned to me, and I said, "I don't know. There's a lot of psychology jumbled up inside the head of a Spanish kid adopted by a Jewish family. He's obviously got the Bushido mindset and a collection of skills that make him deadly anywhere in the world.

Figuring out what makes him tick wouldn't be easy face-to-face, and it's impossible from here."

Penny raised her eyebrows. "So, what are you going to do?"

"I'm going to talk to Singer about angels . . . avenging and otherwise."

\* \* \*

I met Singer the next morning at the small house he used near the stables at Bonaventure. I liked calling it a *hermitage*, but Singer wasn't a fan of being called a *hermit*.

"Good morning, Chase. You're on the go early this morning. Have you seen the news?"

I wiped my feet on the mat and stepped inside. "No, I've not heard any news this morning. I just came by to talk about a couple of things. What's going on?"

He motioned toward the television in the corner of the front room. The scene showed a high-rise building with the ocean in the background, and the scrolling text across the bottom of the screen read, "U.S. secretary of Homeland Security dead after fall from one of San Juan's tallest buildings."

I felt a lump in my throat the size of Miami. "Get your shoes. I have to show you something."

I pulled the microcassette recorder from my pocket and handed it to Singer. "Give that a listen."

Ten seconds in, he clicked off the recorder. "Where did you get this?"

"I recorded it yesterday afternoon. It's a long story, but I need you to keep listening."

He clicked the recorder back on and listened intently. When he heard the president say, "He'll be in that chair when the sun comes up tomorrow morning, or Federal Marshals will escort him back to D.C. in handcuffs," his face washed pale, and his jaw fell open.

"Exactly," I said. "There's more to this story than meets the eye."

He held up the recorder. "Is this what you came to my house to talk about?"

"No, but it may have just rocketed to the top of the list."

He laid the recorder on his thigh. "There's nothing we can do about this right now, so let's hear what *was* on your mind when you showed up at the buttcrack of dawn this morning."

"I wanted to talk about Ricco Vasquez."

He formed a wide circle with his mouth. "Oh, him."

"Yes, him," I said. "Skipper and Ginger narrowed down the list of eight names you gave her, and they ruled out everybody except Vasquez. What do you know about him?"

Singer spent ten minutes telling me a nearly identical story as Skipper. He had a few more details about Vasquez's training and some of the missions he'd worked. "He's as good as me, or maybe better. He's one of the best natural long-range shooters on Earth. Couple his natural talent with his training and zeal, and he's hard to outshoot."

"Why would he be in the States shooting a presidential assassin, though?"

"I just told you he's a zealot. If he believes a wrong is occurring, he wants to make it right. Most of us shoot for the money and the high of pulling off shots nobody else could make, but not Ricco. He's different. He shoots as if God Himself commanded it."

I tried digesting his words, but they weren't easy to swallow. "So, does this guy have some sort of god complex?"

Singer shook his head. "No, nothing like that. In fact, quite the opposite. He sees himself as the ultimate servant, not an authority of any kind."

"He sounds strange to me."

"We're all strange, Chase. That's part of what makes us snipers. Normal people don't do what we do. Psychologically healthy individuals don't lie on the side of a mountain for a week in their own feces and urine just so they can pull a trigger one time and erase another life from the planet. That's not normal behavior. Trying to rationalize what we do isn't possible. You've got to stop thinking like a psychologist on this one."

"We have to find him, Singer. We don't have any choice."

"I was afraid you were going to say that, but where do you start looking for a guy like that? It'd be like searching for one specific great white shark. You know he's somewhere in the ocean, but that's a lot of water."

"The difference is, great whites don't leave dead bodies in their wake. They eat what they kill. Ricco may be a vegetarian."

Singer tried not to smile. "You know I'm in if you ask me to help you find him, but if you think we're going to sneak up on him, you're crazier than Vasquez. He can hear a gnat a mile away, and he can see the flag we planted on the moon in sixty-nine. If we find him, it'll be because he lets us find him."

# Chapter 28
## *My Fight*

"There's one more thing I want to talk about before we go Ricco-hunting."

Singer poured two cups of coffee and handed one to me. "I'm all ears."

"I don't want you to be a passive listener for this one. I need to know what you think, so don't hold back."

I told the story of the warrior angels who protected me in my dream while I was in a coma, and he seemed to be hanging on every word. When I finished the story by explaining how Penny's face was the first thing I saw when I woke up, but that each of the angels looked just like her, he couldn't hold back the smile.

"So, what do you think? Was it all a figment of my imagination, a dream, what?"

He took a long drink of his coffee and placed his mug on the table beside a second-hand, worn-out La-Z-Boy recliner, the most expensive piece of furniture in his house. "Do you know what the Bible says about angels?"

"I know the story of Jacob wrestling with an angel and dislocating his hip. And Revelations has a few ominous stories about angels with swords coming out of their mouths, but I'm not the scholar, here. That's your role."

He chuckled. "I don't really think Jacob won the wrestling match. It's much more likely that the angel let him *think* he won.

You know, it's like playing cards with your sister's kids. You want to let them think they're doing well. It was like that. And Revelation may not be the best place to get a healthy picture of what angels are and what they do."

I waited, hoping he was going to spring some all-encompassing Bible verse on me that would be an Angels for Dummies primer.

"The Bible never gives us a good description of how angels look or exactly what their role is. There are clearly different kinds of angels with varying roles. A third of the angels fell with Lucifer when he rebelled, so not all angels are good. Did those fallen angels become demons? I don't know, maybe, but that doesn't have anything to do with what you experienced."

I took a sip while I waited for his words of wisdom.

"Here's what I believe," he said. "God sends us comfort in more ways than we'll ever realize. He gave me the ability to sing. Not everybody can do that. I didn't learn to sing. I've just always been able to do it. Singing lets my mind forget about the horrible things happening around me. That's one of God's gifts of comfort for me."

"What do you think is His gift of comfort for me?" I asked.

He shrugged. "Maybe He sent me to you."

I couldn't resist smiling. "Maybe He did."

"I believe with all my heart that He sent Penny to you. She loves you even when you're being a jerk, and that's real love. That's the kind of love God sends us. Your brain was a mess, and you were drifting back and forth between worlds for two weeks. Chase, your body died twice in those two weeks, but those angels beat back that death that was trying to take you. From our perspective in that room with you, the doctors and nurses were doing the fighting, but from where you sat, it was the angels with swords and fire beneath their robes. The truth is, it doesn't matter what kept you here. What matters is that you're still here, and you've still got work to do."

Singer could make the most complex spiritual scenarios so simple that a child could understand, and that was most certainly a gift.

He grinned again. "So, what difference does it make if the angels were real or imagined? Who's to say they weren't both? They brought you comfort and made you think about God's love. People like you and me need goodness to remind us that the world isn't all bad. We live in dark corners of humanity and see the worst people doing the most unthinkable things, but that's not the limit of the world, and thanks to things like Penny loving you and me being able to sing at the worst possible moments, we get to remember that our souls are well protected behind those swords and wings, whether we get to see them or not. Maybe you're one of the lucky ones—one of the blessed ones—who's been given a glimpse behind the veil that separates the living from the eternal."

I sat, silently pondering Singer's sermon, lesson, briefing, or whatever it was. I'd never have his faith or understanding, but every time he opened up and poured out his wisdom of things beyond this world, I grew a little closer to becoming the man who could believe without question and live without doubt.

The chirp of my phone yanked me from my thoughts.

"Hello, this is Chase."

"Why do you always answer the phone like that? Why can't you just say hello like the rest of the world?"

"Good morning, Hunter. And just so you'll know, most of the world doesn't speak English, so saying hello is not how the rest of the world answers the phone."

"Where are you?" he said.

"I'm at Singer's, and we've got a mission."

"A mission? From Clark?"

"No, not exactly. We'll go get some breakfast, and I'll tell you all about it. Have you seen the news this morning?"

"About the Homeland Security guy taking a leap? Yeah, I saw it. Why?"

"I'll explain in the car. Meet us at the boat, and we'll go from there."

Singer and I found Hunter waiting beside the VW Microbus, whittling on a stick and watching Kenny LePine's crew unloading bulldozers, backhoes, and various other implements of destruction.

"What's all that about?" Hunter asked.

"They're going to clean up the mess the fire made so we can start building," I said.

"Is that those Cajuns everybody talks about?"

"It sure is," I said. "Have you ever heard anything bad about them?"

Hunter shook his head. "No, not a single thing, except that you can't understand a word that comes out of their mouths. Other than that, they've got a good reputation."

We sat in the van and listened to the recording of the president's conversation with Fairchild and his chief of staff about the DHS Secretary.

Hunter let out a low whistle. "That doesn't sound good at all."

Singer was abnormally quiet.

"Are you all right?" I asked.

He sucked on his teeth. "Yeah, I'm just trying to piece together the timeline of the shots. Fairchild was right. Whoever the sniper was on the antenna, he was the first to pull the trigger. The bullet that killed Landon Edgar Barrier was already in flight when he pulled the trigger. That means one incredibly significant thing."

Hunter and I turned, waiting for Singer's revelation.

"The sniper on the antenna was trying to prevent the assassination, not retaliating for it."

I watched the thoughts pouring through Singer's eyes and asked, "Does that sound like something Ricco Vasquez would do?"

He nodded slowly. "Yes, but it also means Vasquez knew the assassination attempt was going to happen. How could he have known?"

Hunter's phone chirped, breaking the mood in the van. He stuck it to his ear and listened for thirty seconds. When the call ended, he stared me down. "You're never going to believe this. Your blood sample is in the back seat of an F-Eighteen Hornet on its way to Norfolk. I guess that means you came through on that higher-authorization promise of yours."

"It's nice to have friends in high places, sometimes. Let's get some breakfast. I have an appointment with the neurosurgeon at ten thirty."

Singer and I briefed Hunter on Ricco Vasquez.

"I think we have to go after him," I said, "but Singer doesn't think we can find him if he doesn't want to be found. What do you think?"

Hunter shoveled a forkful of hash browns into his mouth and washed it down with a long swallow of coffee. "I think we shouldn't do anything without talking to Clark. He's still the boss, right?"

I said, "You're right. I guess we need to brief him up."

Back in the van, I dialed Clark's number and waited for an answer.

"Hey, Chase. How're you feeling?"

"I feel great. I have to go back to the doctor later this morning for a checkup, but I'm almost back to full strength, and I'm sleeping better than ever."

"That's good to hear. Are you just checking in, or do you need something?"

"Both. How's your calendar look for the rest of the day?"

"I'm free after one o'clock. Why?"

"We're going to hop down and see you for a couple of hours. We hired Disco. Thanks for vetting him. He's a good addition. We'll close on the Citation by the end of the week, but we're treating it like it's already ours. All the money is in escrow, and Cotton says she's as fit as a fiddle."

"That's good to hear. What time will you be here, and how many?"

"Around two, and I'll bring Penny, Skipper, Singer, and Hunter. Of course, Disco will have to tag along."

"Great. I'll pick you up at Opa-Locka at two."

\* \* \*

The fifty-minute flight to Miami's Opa-Locka Executive Airport was perfect. Disco never touched the controls except for radios, flaps, and landing gear. I was falling deeper in love with the Citation with every minute I spent in the cockpit.

When we stepped out of the van and onto the circular drive of Clark's South Beach home, Skipper froze and reached for my hand. The last time she'd seen the house, it was no home. It was the set of a porn production, and she was an unwilling participant. Anya and I rescued her and left a significant body count in our wake, but the trauma of the memory had her momentarily frozen.

"Are you okay?" I whispered.

"I will be. Just hold my hand for a minute. It's all a little over-whelming right now, but I'll be okay."

I slipped my microcassette recorder into Singer's palm. "You and Hunter brief Clark. Skipper and I are going for a walk."

Singer frowned. "Is everything okay?"

"It will be," I said. "Just go ahead and get started. We'll be inside in a few minutes. I'll explain later."

Skipper laced her arm through mine, and we walked the six blocks to South Beach. Roller skaters, bicyclists, and even a guy on an ancient giant-wheeled bike rolled by. Perfect specimens of physical fitness played beach volleyball, and gentle waves lapped at the beach.

"Is there any place else like this in the world?" she asked.

"I doubt it. It's pretty unique, kind of like you."

She smiled and laid her head on my shoulder. "It's not easy for me, you know."

"Yeah, I know, but you won. The people who hurt you are never going to hurt another soul."

"Thanks to you," she said.

"I couldn't have done it without Anya."

She looked up at me. "Where do you think she is?"

"I wish I knew."

"It's weird. I can find almost anybody with a few keystrokes, but it's like she just vanished into thin air."

She squeezed my arm. "You loved her, didn't you?"

I watched kites dancing on the afternoon breeze and a cruise ship steaming toward the Bahamas. "I thought I did, but I was just a young, dumb kid back then. Until I met Penny, I had no idea what love was. I hope Anya's safe and happy, but I've made my peace with her being gone."

"What if she's the one who started the fire at Bonaventure?"

"If she was, I'll find her one day, and I'll make her tell me why."

She whispered, "You're not going to kill her, are you?"

"No. Penny might kill her, but I'm not going to."

Skipper laughed and pulled me back toward Clark's house. "Let's go back. I'm going to be okay. Thanks for walking with me and for . . . everything else."

"You never have to thank me for anything. We're family by choice."

"Does it ever end?" she said.

"Does *what* ever end?"

"All of this. The cloak and dagger stuff, chasing bad guys, saving the world."

We crossed Ocean Drive as a bright red Lamborghini plowed into the back of a garbage truck. "Everything ends sooner or later. But like Singer said, we've still got work to do."

Skipper climbed the steps to the palatial house and bounded through the door as if she were at Disney World. There wasn't a hint of hesitation, anxiety, or fear on her face. She'd come to terms with her past, just like I'd done with Anya, and we both moved on, never forgetting, but smart enough to never make the same mistake twice.

We found the rest of the team sitting around the outdoor fireplace in the rear courtyard.

Clark looked up as we came through the French doors. "Good, you're back. Come have a seat with us."

We joined the rest of the team and watched the flames dance in the massive fireplace.

Clark raised a whiskey tumbler. "I'd offer you one, but Disco says you have another lesson in the Citation on the ride home."

"Thanks anyway, but I'll just enjoy watching you enjoy yours. I assume the guys briefed you on the sniper situation."

Clark took a sip. "They did, and I need to be the voice of reason on this one."

I interrupted. "Listen, Clark. This is something that has to be done."

He held up one finger. "Let me finish. I agree with you that Vasquez needs to be found, but I want you to do one thing first."

"What's that?"

"Ask the president what he wants you to do before you jet off to Buenos Aires, chasing one of the deadliest men alive, even if he is a good guy."

I took the tumbler from his hand. "Skipper can ride up front. I'll take one of the cheap seats in the back."

Clark stood, poured himself another cocktail, and tilted his glass toward mine. "Cheers."

"Maybe you're right," I said. "I was ready to jump into the fire. Maybe I'll tell the president what we know and let him make the call. It doesn't always have to be my fight."

"No, Chase. It doesn't always have to be your fight."

## Chapter 29
### *Our First Step*

Two days later, Kenny LePine stood on the dock, knocking on the starboard hull of my boat.

"Hello in dehr. Anybody be home, no?"

I stepped through the companionway. "Good morning, Kenny. Have your guys finished up?"

"Yeah, day finish lass night, dem, but it be too late to come on down. You come look, you. If you ain't satisfy, I bring dem boys on back, me."

I walked the property with Kenny, even though I still had no idea what he was saying. Not only was Kenny's crew gone, but so was every bit of evidence that a fire had ever happened. I'd expected bulldozer tracks and mud puddles when they were finished, but they'd raked out every track they left and made the yard look like it was ready for grass.

"It looks great, Kenny. Your guys do good work. How much do I owe you?"

"What we say on da phone, we? Two tousan, yeah?"

"I think we said two thousand and no more than three thousand."

I pulled thirty one-hundred-dollar bills from my pocket and laid them in Kenny's hand. "Thank you for everything."

Never glancing at the money, he shoved it into his pocket and pointed toward the bare spot where our new home would soon stand. "Sometime, it be good luck to have sometin' from da old to put in da new, yeah, so I foun' dis in the mess we done cleant up."

He handed me a charred piece of an oak plank with one bent, rusty, square-head nail sticking from one end.

I took it from his hand. "What is this?"

"Dis be one of dem back steps dat be burnt up, but dis one didn't burn like dem others. Me thinks dis one don wan' die like dem others ones, me."

I turned the charred, two-hundred-year old plank in my hand and could barely hold back the tears. "Thank you, Kenny. I really appreciate what you did, and especially this piece. It means a lot to me, and my wife is going to love it."

He stuck his meaty hand in mine, and we shook. "Now you happy, me happy, and dat good business. When you needs more scrapin' and scratchin' at da groun' out here, you don't call no-body else, no?"

"Next time we need some scraping or scratching, you're my man, Kenny."

He drove away and left me standing in the yard, staring down at the priceless gift he left me.

I climbed back aboard *Aegis* and found Penny cooking break-fast in the galley. I handed her the artifact, and she held it at arm's length with two fingers.

"What is this? It's filthy."

"It's what's left of the steps where we stood and vowed forever together. Kenny found it in the debris and saved it for us. He says it's good luck to put something from the old into the new. Or at least I think that's what he said."

Suddenly the filthy, charred lump of wood became a priceless treasure, and Penny held it against her chest like a child holds her teddy bear. "I can't believe it survived. Can you?"

"Sometimes I can't believe *we* survived, but maybe it's a sign or something. Maybe it's telling us that when the world is burn-ing down around us, if we'll just remember how we felt that day we took our first step together, we'll make it. We might come out a little dirty and beaten up, but we can always survive."

She threw her arms around me as the eggs burned on the stove behind her.

Just after noon, my phone chirped, and I glanced at the screen. I didn't recognize the number or the area code. "Hello, this is Chase."

"Mr. Fulton, I'm Special Agent Brownley with NCIS in Norfolk."

"Hello, Agent Brownley. Should I assume this has something to do with the sample your lab is working for me?"

"You may assume that, but I'm not with the lab. I'm a criminal investigations agent. The results of the DNA analysis came to me because of the nature of the report. I need to ask you something, Mr. Fulton."

"Go ahead," I said.

"This packet is coded with presidential authority. Are you with the federal government, sir?"

"I carry Secret Service credentials."

It wasn't a lie, but I could almost hear his wheels turning through the phone.

"I see. If this is a Secret Service matter, why did this sample come to NCIS instead of going to the FBI lab?"

"Do you have a pen, Agent Brownley?"

"I do."

"Good. Write down this number. Two-zero-two, five-five-five, one-zero-zero-one. That's the number to the Whitehouse switchboard. Give the president a call and ask him."

"A-a-agent Fulton, I'm not making accusations here. I simply don't like when my agency gets thrown into somebody else's investigation so we can do the dirty work while somebody else—like the Secret Service—gets all the credit for making the bust."

"I understand your concern," I said, "but you have the wrong impression on this one. There's not going to be a bust. There will never be any fallout, and nobody is getting credit for anything. We're not working on a criminal case, and I'm afraid that's all I can tell you."

He sighed. "Not a criminal case, you say?"

"That's right. We simply need to know who that blood belongs to. Have you found a match?"

"No, Agent Fulton, we didn't exactly find a match."

"What does that mean?"

It was getting harder and harder to keep my cool. I needed answers, and Brownley had them if I could just pull them out of him.

"That means your sample was so badly degraded that it was impossible to find an exact match. I can have one of the lab techs explain the science if you'd like, but it's over my head."

"No, that's unnecessary. I'm not smart enough to understand it, either. Those guys don't even speak English, as far as I'm concerned."

He laughed. "At least we have that in common, Agent Fulton."

"Then it looks like we may have found some common ground. Can you at least tell me if the sample came from a male or female?"

"I can tell you it came from a human, but that's about as far as I go." He shuffled some paper. "Well, let's see. It does say Anglo-European descent, but it's really vague after that."

"So, we're dealing with a Caucasian?"

He laughed again. "Yeah, that should really narrow it down for you. The software is still running, but so far, the computer has spit out, let's see, about four hundred possible matches in the DNA databases we have access to."

"How long has it been running?"

"About thirty-six hours."

"And how much longer do you expect it to run?"

"To be honest," he said, "I've never seen it run this long, so I would imagine it's close to being finished. But you have to keep in mind that our databases are far from complete. The only names we're going to have are people who voluntarily submitted a DNA sample, served in the military since around eighty-six, or ever served time in a federal prison. There are a few other reasons somebody would be in the database, but those are the biggies."

I tried to imagine what value a list of four hundred veterans and parolees could possibly have. "When the software finishes regurgitating names, how long will it take for me to get a copy of the results?"

"If you have authorization. . . ."

"Remember the phone number?" I said.

He sighed again. "You can pick up the list as soon as the computer. . . ." He paused and then returned. "It looks like it's your lucky day, Agent Fulton. The initial results list is complete. Five hundred thirty-four names. Protocol says we run the list three times. The second and third times through the machine usually go faster because the software throws out the blatant non-matches. Do you want the refined list after two more runs or the one I have now?"

"Will there be more names on the second and third list?"

"Usually, there's fewer names, but occasionally, a couple more show up."

"Send me what you have, and as soon as I see the president, I'll make sure he knows how thorough NCIS Special Agent Brownley is."

He grumbled. "Oh, hell no, you won't. I don't need my name in the president's ear. I'm going to retire in eighteen months. You can forget you ever heard of me, Fulton."

I couldn't hold back the laughter. "Whatever you say. Email me those results, and I'll forget we ever talked."

"No, sir," he said. "Whatever this is, I don't want my fingerprints on any part of it. You can have a hard copy printed on plain white paper, but I'm not emailing, post-office-mailing, or carrier-pigeon-mailing this list on letterhead or in any other way that will trace it back to my office. You can pick it up, or I can shred it. Those are your presidential options."

"What time do you leave your office, Brownley?"

"Five o'clock, sharp, but your package will be in the receptionist's safe. Don't ask for me. Don't mention me. Just show her your creds, and she'll hand you a sealed envelope. She leaves at four thirty."

The click made it clear our conversation was over.

I briefed Skipper on the conversation with Agent Brownley, and she grunted. "Ouch. Five hundred thirty-four names on paper? That sucks. Are you sure you can't get an electronic copy?"

"Oh, I'm sure. We're getting paper, and that's it."

"It's going to be a lot of work," she said, "but I think we have to do it. Let's go get that list."

Penny, Skipper, Disco, and I boarded the Citation and blasted off for Norfolk, Virginia. I got another ninety minutes of flight time in the right seat and made a flawless landing.

Disco said, "Does your world ever calm down enough for you to study some academics on the airplane?"

I tried to remember the last time my world was calm. "I guess I could slam into another shrimp boat and get a little time off."

He rolled his eyes. "If you want a type rating in this airplane, you'll have to learn the aircraft systems sometime."

"I'll make time," I said. "I promise. But not before we find out whose blood that is."

\* \* \*

My Secret Service credentials got me through the gate at Norfolk Navy Base and through the front door of the NCIS building.

The lady behind the reception desk was shutting down her computer when I stepped up.

"Hello, I'm Supervisory Special Agent Chase Fulton with the Secret Service."

She looked up without a sign of being impressed. "Well, Supervisory Special Agent whatever your name is, it's four thirty-one. That means I'm no longer here, and you'll have to come back tomorrow."

"I just need to pick up a package in your safe, and I'll be out of your hair."

She put her hands on her hips. "You're not listening. It's now four thirty-two, and me and my hair got off at four thirty, so unless you're paying my overtime—and the union agreement says a minute is the same as an hour—you'll have to come back tomorrow."

"It'll just take a minute for you to pull the package from the safe."

She scowled and shook her head. "Look, Agent. It's not my problem that you couldn't get here before closing, so I'm not jumping through any hoops because you're too lazy to—"

I didn't want to do what was coming next, but desperate times sometimes call for ridiculously desperate measures. "Ma'am, turn around and put your hands on the counter. You're under arrest for impeding a federal investigation. Your choices are leave in handcuffs with me, spend the night in jail, and spend most of the next week trying to find a lawyer who can convince a federal judge why it wasn't worth two minutes of your time to provide evidence in your possession to a Secret Service agent, or you can open the safe, give me the package, and sleep in your bed tonight without an orange jumpsuit and handcuff bruises on your wrists. It's your call."

"What the hell is going on out here!"

A tall, lean man in his late fifties came through a door, pulling on his sport coat over a shoulder holster.

The receptionist said, "Oh, thank God. Clarence, this jackass thinks he's arresting me because I won't open the safe after hours. Will you get him out of here?"

The man slapped his forehead and groaned. "You must be Fulton."

I put on my smile. "It's nice to finally meet you, Special Agent Brownley. I'd like to pick up a package that someone—obviously not you—left for me in the receptionist's safe."

"Oh, for God's sake," he said. "Get out of here, Carolyn. I'll take care of this."

Carolyn snatched her purse from the counter and huffed her way to the door. Brownley took a knee behind the reception desk and typed the combination into the electronic keypad. The door to the safe swung open, and he pulled a pair of exam gloves from a pouch on his belt, slid them onto his hands, and lifted the package from the safe.

When he stood up, he laid the plain manila envelope on the counter, pulled off his gloves, and tossed them into the garbage.

I motioned toward the blue gloves. "You literally don't want your fingerprints on this thing, do you?"

He straightened his jacket. "You don't even have handcuffs, do you?"

I tucked the package beneath my arm, offered a mock salute, and turned for the door. "It was nice to never meet you, Agent Brownley. Enjoy your retirement."

# Chapter 30
## *You're a Genius*

By the time I made it back to the airport in Norfolk, the winter
storm that had been threatening throughout the day finally
pressed its way onto the Chesapeake Bay. Air traffic up and down
the eastern seaboard was being rerouted over the Atlantic. There's
nothing like a winter storm to remind me why living in the
South makes so much sense. On our climb out, we listened to air
traffic controllers issuing route amendments and broadcasting expected delays into Dulles, Reagan, and Baltimore.

When Norfolk Departure handed us off, Disco keyed up.
"Center, good evening. Citation five-six-zero-Charlie-Foxtrot
with you through seven point two for ten, heading one-four-zero
assigned."

The exhausted controller said, "Citation zero-Charlie-Fox,
Washington Center, thank God you're going south. Climb and
maintain flight level two-four-zero, and proceed direct Saint
Marys."

"Up to two-four-oh and direct destination. Thank you,
ma'am."

He set the altitude preselect and programmed the GPS for direct to Saint Marys. A second center controller cleared us up to
flight level three-eight-oh, and the Citation was right at home.
The ability to go high, fast, and far changed the size of my world
and made everything easier.

When we leveled off in cruise, Skipper stuck her head into the cockpit. "Chase, this is going to take forever. There's nothing here except names—hundreds and hundreds of names. Most of them don't even have dates of birth."

"Is there any way to tell who the parolees are?"

"No," she huffed. "It's just names in no apparent order."

"Are there any Russian names on the list?"

"A few, but I've only made it through a hundred names or so. If your real question is about Anya, the answer is not yet."

"I'm sorry to drag you into this, Skipper, but we'll divide the list up and get through it together."

She laid her hand on my shoulder. "Don't be sorry. We're family by choice, remember?"

My landing in the dark wasn't as good as the one in Norfolk, but I didn't break anything.

Disco said, "That was a lot better than your helicopter landing, but that's not saying much."

We put the airplane away and secured the hangar.

Disco eyed our paperwork. "Do you want help with the list?"

"I appreciate the offer, but I'm not sure you'd be much help. We'll be looking for names we recognize, and you've not been with us long enough to know who we've pissed off. Get some rest, and we'll see you tomorrow."

Back aboard *Aegis*, Skipper said, "I'm going to scan this list into my computer so we can at least sort the names alphabetically. My eyes are going to explode if I stare at this paper much longer."

She spent the next twenty minutes converting our hard copy into something she could manage. When the last page emerged from the scanner, she sighed. "Okay, how do you want them sorted?"

"Let's start with the obvious. I want to see every Russian-sounding name."

"That's not exactly a criteria I can tell the computer. Hey, computer, show me a list of everybody who sounds like they drink vodka."

"Sort by last names ending in -v, -va, or -vna."

"That, I can do. Give me just a minute."

She worked her magic, and we soon had nine pages of Russian-sounding names. She thumbed through the list and let out a disgusted groan.

"What's wrong?" I said.

She pounded on the keys as if she were playing Whac-A-Mole. "I'm an idiot. For some stupid reason, I included -no for a last name ending in the search results. Here, I'll take that out and run a new report."

"There's no need to run a new report. All of the names ending in -no will group together, and we can just ignore those."

We searched the pages, ignoring the -no endings, but Anastasia Burinkova wasn't on the list.

"Look for Fulton," I said. "Her driver's license and passport say Ana Fulton."

Skipper's fingers raced across the keys. "There are eight people on the list with Fulton as their last name, but no Ana."

"I guess it was just wishful thinking," I said.

Penny spoke up for the first time. "Remember, just because their name isn't on this list doesn't mean the blood isn't theirs. You said only veterans, parolees, and a few others would be in the database. The fact that Anya's name isn't on the list doesn't mean it's not her blood."

"I've got an idea," Skipper said. "Now that I have the list in the computer, I can run it against the VA database and the federal parolee databases. That'll give us one more way to sort the names. I can probably go even deeper and run known criminal associates for the parolees. That's going to make for even more names, but it might lead to something."

"Do it," I said. "How long will it take?"

"Overnight, at least."

"While it's running, we can divide the alphabetized list into three sections. I'll take A through G, Penny can do H through O, and you can search P through Z."

Skipper wrote a few lines of code and sent her computer on a quest for even more possibilities.

An hour into our grueling search through the hundreds of names on the list, I was having trouble staying awake. "Everything is running together, and they're all starting to look the same to me."

Skipper and Penny nodded. "Yeah, same here."

"Why don't we get some sleep and start on this again in the morning?"

Penny yawned and stretched. "That's the best idea you've had since you asked me to marry you."

* * *

When I climbed the stairs into the main salon the following morning, I found Singer sitting in the cockpit, watching a pair of dolphins chasing baitfish through the shallows.

"Good morning," I said. "I didn't expect to find you out here. Is everything all right?"

"I hope so. I've been lying awake all night thinking about what Clark said."

I replayed the conversation in South Beach, but I couldn't come up with anything that should be troubling Singer so badly.

He said, "Have you talked to the president since we got back from Miami?"

"Not yet. Why?"

"Clark said we should tell the president what we know and then wait for his orders, right?"

"Yeah, something like that."

Singer nervously rubbed his hands together. "I know Clark is the boss and all, but I just don't think that's the best idea right now."

"Why not?"

The pace of his hand rubbing increased. "If Vasquez is the second sniper, and we tell the president about him, what do you think will happen?"

I thought about his question. "Well, I don't really know, but I'm sure the Secret Service would want to talk to him."

Singer pointed at me. "Exactly. And if the Secret Service starts chasing Ricco Vasquez all over the world, he'll go into hiding, and nobody will ever find him. Even if they get extremely lucky and locate him, you know he's not a rational thinker. I don't know what he might do if he thought he was cornered. People like him react badly in situations like that."

"So, what are you saying? Do you think I shouldn't tell the president what we know?"

"We don't know anything, Chase. I gave you a list of eight people on Earth who I believed could make that shot. Skipper found all of them except for one—Ricco Vasquez. If you asked two dozen snipers who could make that shot, they'd all have a different list. Some of the names would be the same, sure, but you'd end up with a lot more than eight names on the back of an envelope."

"You're right, but. . . ."

"No buts," he said. "Let me have this one, okay? Just this one. Maybe I can find Vasquez. Maybe he'll talk to me."

I'd never seen Singer so emotionally invested in anything outside of his church.

"Okay, I'll tell you what I can do, or more correctly, I'll tell you what I won't do. I won't volunteer what we know about the eight names on that envelope, but if the president asks me directly, I won't lie to him. Is that good enough?"

"I couldn't ask for anything more. Thank you. I owe you one."

"You'll never owe me anything, but if you want to help with the names from the DNA analysis, we could use another pair of eyes."

He stood from the settee. "I'll help, but only if there's coffee."

Skipper staggered up the stairs and went immediately to her computer. I set a cup of coffee beside her, and she grabbed it like a toad catching a fly.

"Did your computer solve the world's problems overnight?"

She grumbled. "No, I think it just created more problems for us. The known-criminal-associates list came back with over eleven thousand names."

"That's unmanageable," I said, "but can you run that known-criminal-associates list against the Russian-sounding-name filter you created last night?"

"Sure, I can do that. Give me a second."

The printer started spitting out pages.

Skipper threw her head back. "Crap! I did it again! I forgot to take out the names ending in -no. Those definitely aren't Russian."

"It's okay," I said. "Just like last night, we'll ignore those."

I pulled the stack of paper from the printer and ran my finger down the first page. When I came to the block of names ending in -no, I quickly flipped through those pages until the -ova names appeared. I flipped back one page to make sure I hadn't missed any, and the last name on the list ending in -no leapt off the page like a catapult.

I sat back in my chair, closed my eyes, and silently thanked God for Skipper's mistake with the search filter. I crossed the deck in two strides, grabbed Skipper's head, and planted a huge kiss squarely on her forehead. "You're a genius, even when you're screwing up, and I love you!"

Like an idiot, I held the sheet of paper with Giordano's name near the bottom and danced in circles.

Penny came up the stairs in the middle of my happy-puppy dance and froze on the top step. "Uh, what's going on?"

"Skipper's a genius!" I yelled as I shoved the paper toward my wife.

Penny flinched but finally took the sheet from my hand. She stared at the page for several seconds with no reaction, so I jabbed at the list with my index finger. "That's the guy. Right there!"

She pulled the list closer to her face. "Who is Loui Alphonso Giordano?"

I grabbed her hand. "Come with me. All of you."

I led Penny, Singer, and Skipper from *Aegis* and onto the yard. "In nineteen seventy-eight, a man killed the Judge's wife. See that cannon in the gazebo? Well, when I delivered it to the Judge, I'd also handcuffed his wife's murderer to it. His name was Loui Alphonso Giordano."

Singer said, "Then he's either dead or in prison, right?"

I shook my head. "You'd think so, but that's not what happened. I never knew what the Judge did to Giordano after I left him cuffed to the cannon that morning, but I was always curious. I always assumed he put a bullet in Giordano's head and buried him beneath the cannon, but I was wrong."

I paused, remembering the day I'd taken the Judge flying in the Mustang. His great-granddaughter, Maebelle, told me it was one of the best days of his life, and I'd never forget the conversation we had in the cockpit over the Atlantic.

"The day before he died, the Judge told me what he did to the man who murdered his wife. He'd said, 'I looked him in the eye, pressed the barrel of my old forty-five to his cheek, and told him I forgave him. Then, I cut off his handcuffs with a pair of bolt cutters, and I spent the rest of the day talking to God and Mildred.'"

# Chapter 31
## *Find Him*

I turned to Skipper. "Forget the rest of the list. Find Giordano. No matter what it takes, find him."

She looked up at me but didn't move. A smile consumed her face, and her eyes lit up like stars.

"What are you so happy about?" I said.

She never stopped smiling. "Because this means Anya didn't start the fire."

"You're probably right, but we've still got a lot of unanswered questions, like the Russian tree resin in the accelerant."

She said, "When all of this is over, I'm taking a really long vacation."

"Me, too," I said. "Now, get to work."

I called Clark to break the news and confess that I wasn't going to tell the president everything I knew.

"That's up to you," he said. "I just don't want you going off and chasing some sniper all over the world."

"I'll wait until the president puts me on a mission," I said. "Right now, I've got enough to do finding Giordano. I'm going after him, though, even if I have to go alone."

Clark said, "Something tells me you won't be able to keep Hunter and Singer away from this one, no matter how hard you try."

After I hung up, I took a moment to sit in the gazebo beside the eighteenth-century cannon I'd pulled from the mud and muck on the bottom of Cumberland Sound. The history of my family ran deep in the black water, pecan trees, and marsh grass of the coastal Georgia low country. Maebelle and I were the last remaining descendants of the Huntsinger line. The injuries I'd sustained on the Khyber Pass, ten thousand miles from home, left me incapable of fathering a child, and Maebelle's career as the hottest chef in South Beach didn't lend itself to motherhood. The future is a gift left always unopened. No matter how hard we shake the box, we'll never know what's inside. I've come to believe there is no *now*. There's only what has been and what will be. Everything we've experienced and everything we know has already happened. Everything else has yet to arrive. Perhaps that precipice between yesterday and tomorrow is the only real definition of life. If the Huntsinger bloodline stops the day I leave this Earth, I pray that I will have left a better, safer, and freer future for all the box-shakers who come after me.

I found Skipper locked into the screen of her computer, and I could almost see smoke pouring from the keys.

"Any luck?" I asked.

"Oh, yeah," she said, "and you're never going to believe it."

She turned her computer screen so I could see. "Check this out. I searched for hits on Giordano's passport for the last six months, and I came up empty. He's not gone anywhere for over a year. In fact, his passport is expired."

"How's that lucky for us?"

"Just wait," she said. "I searched for known aliases for Giordano and got four hits. Three of the aliases were dead ends, but the fourth one, Nicholas Fortano, not only has a passport, but he used it to fly from Buenos Aires to Jacksonville two days before the fire at Bonaventure."

"What's he doing in Buenos Aires?"

"I don't know. Even I'm not that good. But look. Here's where he flew out of Atlanta and back to Argentina the day of the fire."

246 · CAP DANIELS

"Okay, so that puts Giordano in the area during the time of the fire, but who is on our original list that has Giordano as a known criminal associate?"

"That part is good, too," she said.

With a few keystrokes, the screen morphed into a photograph and criminal record for one Anthony DeStefano. I read through the list of his greatest hits: armed robbery, grand theft auto, aggravated assault, and the list went on.

"Where can we find Mr. DeStefano?"

"I thought you'd never ask. The poor guy died in a car wreck on Interstate Ninety-Five the same day you played chicken with an anchored shrimp boat and lost."

"Where was the wreck?"

"According to the Highway Patrol, it was at the intersection of Interstate Ninety-Five and Highway Three-Oh-One in Santee, South Carolina. DeStefano died at the scene, and the coroner's report says he had two wounds in his left thigh and calf consistent with a nine-millimeter bullet."

"Bring his picture up again."

She clicked her mouse, and the face of an Italian man in his late twenties filled the screen. His sharp nose, high cheekbones, and narrow-set eyes would have made him a beautiful woman if he'd been born a girl.

"I have to call Disco. Keep working on Giordano's whereabouts. We're getting close."

Disco answered on the first ring. "Hello, you've reached Crazy Train Airways. How may I direct your call?"

"Oh, you're funny. Get your butt to the boat, sharpshooter. You're never going to believe what Skipper found."

"What's with the sharpshoot moniker?" he asked.

"Just get over here. You'll see."

He arrived five minutes later, and I motioned toward Skipper's monitor. "Bring up that picture of DeStefano again. I want Disco to see it."

The picture filled the screen.

"Does he look familiar?" I asked.

Disco put on his glasses and leaned toward the monitor. "Not really. I can't say I recognize him, but he's got a bit of a feminine look about him. Don't you think?"

I said, "His name is, or more correctly, his name *was* Anthony DeStefano. He died in a car wreck on the interstate about two hundred miles north of here the day we chased Jet Ski boy."

"Okay, but what does that have to do with us?" he asked.

"According to the medical examiner, he had two nine-millimeter bullet holes in his left leg. That's not bad shooting for an old A-Ten driver hanging out the window of a crippled Cessna One-Eighty-Two."

Disco's eyes turned to saucers. "Are you serious? That's our boy?"

"It certainly appears to be."

He said, "How did you. . . ."

Skipper said, "It's what we do."

"So, do you think he was the arsonist?"

I shook my head. "No, I don't think so. I think it was a known associate of his named Loui Giordano, who just happens to be hiding out in, I'll give you three guesses, Buenos Aires."

Disco shot his eyes toward the ceiling. "That's probably a little over four thousand miles. It'll take at least two fuel stops, but we can be in Argentina in less than twelve hours. There's only two little problems."

"We're problem solvers," I said. "What is it?"

"First, it's an international flight, and a long one at that. We'll need two fully qualified pilots on board."

I held up one finger and dialed Clark's number. He answered on the second ring.

"Hey, Chase. How's it going?"

I didn't have time for pleasantries. "Are you type rated in the Citation?"

"Yes."

"Have you ever been to Buenos Aires?"

"No."

"Do you want to go?"

"What time are we leaving?"

"I'll call you back."

I loved the efficiency of communication with Clark Johnson.

I shoved my phone back into my pocket. "Clark's type rated. He's in. How soon can the jet be ready?"

"That brings us to problem number two. The airplane isn't legally yours yet. It's still in escrow, and we can't take it out of the country until it's yours."

Up went the finger, and out came the phone.

"Vinnie Castellano here."

"Vinnie, it's Chase Fulton. Are you ready to close on the Citation?"

"We're waiting for you, Chase. Are you ready?"

"I'll be in your office in ninety minutes."

"See you then."

I hung up. "If you can get me to Vinnie's office in ninety minutes, problem number two is solved."

\* \* \*

Closing went off without a hitch, and Vinnie Castellano made a nice little commission.

By the time we got back to Saint Marys, Skipper had a plan. "Here's what I have in mind. It's definitely going to take some fuel stops. The first, most reasonable stop after Miami is Panama City, Panama. I've already checked. They can accommodate the Citation, and fuel is actually pretty cheap. Are you guys okay with the plan so far?"

Disco shot a glance at me. "I'm good with Panama City."

I shrugged. "Sure, why not? Last time I was there, we sank a Chinese freighter in the Miraflores Locks in the canal, and I got blown up beneath the Bridge of the Americas and ended up in the recompression chamber on a research vessel skippered by a crusty old guy named Stinnett."

Disco rolled his eyes. "I really hope you're making that up."

"He's not," Skipper said. "Anyway, from Panama City, Lima, Peru, is just over fourteen hundred miles. You have the range for that, right?" Disco nodded, and Skipper continued. "Good, 'cause I've got you booked at the Westin in Lima for tomorrow night. From there, I think Santiago, Chile, then it's just seven hundred miles to Buenos Aires. What do you think?"

I turned to Disco, and the look on his face didn't instill confidence. "What is it?" I asked.

"That's a lot of flying and a lot of gas. There's a nonstop commercial flight out of Miami to Buenos Aires every day. That would save you a lot of money and time in the air, but hey, if you guys want to go bouncing around South America in the back of a Citation, I'm your huckleberry."

I met Skipper's eyes.

"He doesn't know," she said.

Disco glanced around the room. "I don't know what?"

"You don't know that we travel with our tool kits when we're going somewhere to start a fight. Delta Airlines frowns on automatic weapons in their cargo holds."

"Hey, wait a minute," he said. "We can't smuggle weapons into Argentina. They'll bury us underneath the prison if we get caught."

"That's just it," I said. "We won't get caught. Clark and I have diplomatic passports. They were a little gift from a friend of ours."

Disco scoffed. "Will I ever stop being surprised by you guys?"

"Probably not," Skipper said. "Are you leaving now, or in the morning?"

I called the team and had everyone meet at the hangar for a mission brief. Singer, Hunter, Skipper, and Disco piled up on the dilapidated couches, and I sat in what was left of the rolling chair.

"Here's the plan. We're going to Buenos Aires to find Loui Giordano." It took fifteen minutes to fill everyone in on the work Skipper had done to ID and locate the players. I said, "As you all know, this one is personal. If you don't want to go—"

Singer kicked a trash can toward me. "Cut it out. You know we're in."

"Okay, then. We're wheels up in one hour. We'll crash at Clark's place tonight and leave Miami bright and early tomorrow morning. Skipper, where do you want to be?"

"I'll stay on the boat with Penny," she said. "I can do pretty much everything from there."

I scanned the players, looking for questions, but none came. "I'll see everyone back here in forty-five minutes. It's time to sad-dle up, boys. We've got a firebug to stomp out."

# Chapter 32
## *Capisci?*

Disco was right. It was a long flight, and by the time we landed in Buenos Aires, we were already exhausted. Although our journey was over five thousand miles, it only took us one time zone to the east of Saint Marys, so we didn't have to deal with jetlag—just weariness.

Skipper booked a suite of rooms at the Four Seasons on the northeast edge of the city not far from the Atlantic Ocean. The hotel was spectacular, but I was disappointed by the ocean. Apparently, the abundance of rivers in the area dumped enormous volumes of mud into it, turning the blue water of the South Atlantic into brown muck you could almost walk on.

We arrived in time for dinner, and the Four Seasons chef put on a show. We ate for almost two hours and laughed and talked about everything except the mission. When dessert arrived, everyone ordered something different, and the table became the scene of almost constant plate passing. The fiasco seemed to concern Disco, but the rest of us felt right at home.

"Is this how deployments always go with you guys?" Disco asked.

"Oh, no," Clark said. "Most of the time, we stay somewhere nice. We don't usually rough it like this."

That brought a round of laughter from everyone except Disco. He hesitantly accepted a plate of something he couldn't identify and forked a bite into his mouth. "I'm keeping this one, whatever it is."

Hunter raised a knife. "You can't keep it if I cut your hands off, so pass it over."

By the time dessert was over and our coffee cups were empty, Disco looked like he was getting more comfortable with the group, but he obviously still had some concerns. He swallowed the last of his coffee, then said, "Do we have a plan of some kind?"

"A plan for what?" I said.

He froze, and that terrified look returned to his face until Singer laid his hand on the chief pilot's arm. "Take it easy. We're pretty good at this. It'll take a little time, but you'll catch on. We've got a plan. We just don't talk about it at dinner. Sharing food together is important. It's part of who we are. Clark and Chase will brief us back upstairs. For now, just relax and enjoy Buenos Aires."

I guess every team needs a momma bear, and Singer was ours. Perhaps it was part of his makeup as a sniper. He needed to know he was watching over the team and eliminating any threats we couldn't see. Or maybe he was one of God's gifts of comfort for all of us, not just me.

Back upstairs, Clark took the helm. "I've got a guy in the embassy. His business card says something like *cultural attaché* or some garbage. He's the assistant CIA station chief, and I'm meeting with him before the sun comes up tomorrow. You guys can sleep in, and I'll bring back the good news from the attaché."

I asked, "Can your guy help us find Giordano, or is this a courtesy visit to let him know we're carrying guns in his city?"

"Both, I hope. He knows the city as well as anyone, and for the most part, he's got the locals in his pocket. He may not know Giordano's address, but he'll know his neighborhood."

\* \* \*

It's hard for most people to believe, but operators usually sleep like babies the night before a mission. My team was no exception. We were all snoring like buffalo by ten o'clock.

Breakfast arrived just after seven, and we ate like a pack of wolves. Whatever the day held, we were going to need calories.

Clark came through the door a few minutes before eight with a bag hanging from a strap across his chest.

"Nice purse," I said. "Is that how we do it in South America?"

He struck a pose. "Yes, it is, and you're just jealous. Did you save any breakfast for me?"

"We assumed you'd eat with your CIA friends."

He held up a hand. "Cultural attaché. Get it right."

We cleared the dishes from the table, and Clark laid out a map of the city. He pegged his finger onto a section just south of us. "This is La Boca. That means *mouth* in Spanish, so I guess it has to do with the area being at the mouth of the Matanza River, but I don't know for sure. This is where we'll find Giordano. There's a sizable population of Italian mafia types who like to think they run the area. It's exactly the kind of environment Giordano loves. He'll feel safe because most of the muscle in the area probably know what he does for a living, and they don't want to wake up with him looming over their beds with a suppressed pistol in his hand."

"That's solid intel," I said. "Did your attaché give you any feel for the local police in the area?"

"He said they do a lot of hands-off policing in La Boca. Problems there tend to take care of themselves."

"Of course they do," I said. "Why wouldn't they?"

Hunter said, "I guess that means it's time for us to go scumbag-hunting. What are we going to do with Disco?"

I pulled the map in front of me and scanned the area. "Disco, I want you to move the airplane from San Fernando down to Jorge Newbery. If we get lucky and find this guy, we're going to do our business and run. Do you know any Spanish?"

"A little," he said.

"Can you speak enough to arrange for an APU to keep the Citation spooled up and ready to go?"

"Sure. I can manage that."

"Good. All of our cell phones are international, so keep yours on and well within reach. If any one of us calls and says it's show-time, I want you to pick up your clearance and be ready to roll the second we get there. We tend to mess up the place and leave in a hurry. Are you good with all of that?"

"I've got it. No problem."

The look on his face had morphed into confidence instead of disbelief and awe. I liked the transformation.

Clark surveyed the room. "Any questions?" None came, so he continued. "Skipper arranged for a pair of rental cars for us. We've got a blacked-out van and a Mercedes sedan. The Mercedes is yours, Disco. You'll take our bags and stow them on the plane. If we fail and end up back at the hotel tonight, you'll bring our gear with you. The rest of us are in the van, locked and loaded. Are we ready to rock?"

"Let's do it!" I said.

Hunter and I watched Disco drive off to the north in the rented Mercedes.

"Do you think we scared him off?" he asked.

"No, he's on board. I don't know if he's going to be a shooter yet, but he's got some serious skills in the cockpit."

Hunter laughed. "Ask the girly-man on the Jet Ski if he's a shooter."

Clark yanked open the door of the van. "Knock it off and get in. Let's go catch us a fire-starter."

The traffic in Buenos Aires was insane. It made Atlanta look like a leisurely Sunday drive. Cars were lined up six wide on a four-lane road. I'd never seen anything like it, but Clark took it in stride. Apparently, in Argentina, the horn is just as important as the steering wheel.

Traffic lights were just suggestions, it seemed, so we fell in line with everybody else and headed south toward La Boca. My Spanish was good, but the street names changed so often it was impossible to keep track of where we were.

Once away from the main highway, the roar of the horns and chaos of the traffic died away. It would've been easy to believe we were in a New York City neighborhood.

We drove for an hour, learning and memorizing every street, alley, and cut-through in La Boca. The map Clark scored from the embassy was excellent but didn't show construction, so I made note of every blocked street and torn-up sidewalk. The neighborhood was working class and a little rugged, but not disconcerting.

After we were confident we could find our way out of trouble if we fell into it, Clark backed the van against a pharmacy and paid the clerk to make sure nobody blocked us in. Apparently, Argentinian women aren't immune to Clark's charm, either, because the clerk was eating out of his hand seconds after the first flash of his crooked smile.

We found four wise guys who could've been picked up and dropped into little Italy without missing a beat.

"I guess it's time to try out my Italian, huh?"

"Why not?" Clark said.

I leaned closer to him. "Are we going hard or soft?"

He smiled. "Let's go hard. Hunter, you make the introductions."

"My pleasure. Do you think they're strapped?"

"Maybe," Clark said, "but let's not show ours unless they show theirs."

The four goons watched as we approached them. Hunter stepped toward the muscle of the group and threw a side kick to the leg of his chair, crushing the leg and sending the big man to the sidewalk. Before the man could scramble to his feet, Hunter pinned him to the ground with a knee and looked up at me. "You've got something to ask these guys, right?"

I leaned down. "*Stiamo cercando Loui Giordano. Capisci?*"

The oldest of the quartet snuffed out a cigar into a tin ashtray. "Yeah, we understand, asshole, and our English is a lot better than your Italian. We don't know nobody named Giordano, so keep moving before you end up in the river. *Capisci?*"

He held back the jacket of his nylon tracksuit, exposing the handle of a clunky pistol.

I leaned in, only inches from his face. "Yeah, I understand, but there's just one problem. There's only four of you, and it would take at least ten pieces of garbage like you to put any one of us in the river."

The man twisted and reached for his pistol, but I beat him to it. I drew his piece from his elastic waistband and fieldstripped it, sending springs, bullets, and barrel flying in all directions. The two remaining tough guys at the table went for their pistols in time with their elder, but Clark and Singer made them regret it. Based on the sounds it made, the first man's hand probably broke in at least four places when Clark twisted the pistol from his grip. The second guy's nose and lips exploded as Singer's palm drove his head into the metal table.

After disarming and humiliating the guy in front of me, I shoved a knee into his crotch. "I think I'll ask one more time before I lose my temper. Where is Loui Giordano?"

He reached up to grab me, but I caught his wrist and drove it into the brick wall above his head. I heard the tendons tearing as I stretched his arm farther than it should've gone. "How about Nikki Fortano? Ever heard of him?"

At the mention of Fortano's name, the expression on the man's face changed from agony to humor. Through the biting pain of his twisted arm and battered crotch, the man actually laughed. "You clowns think you're here to score Nikki Fortano? Get outta here with that. You can do whatever you want to us, but when Nikki Fortano gets ahold of you, there won't be enough left of you to bury."

I refreshed my encouragement with another knee shot. "Where can we find Fortano?"

"You don't need to worry about that. He'll find you."

We unburdened the four men of their sidearms and deposited the pieces all over the street as we walked backward away from the scene.

"How's that for going hard?" Hunter said.

Clark straightened his shirt. "Not exactly what I had in mind, but I think we announced our presence."

I said, "They know Giordano as Nikki Fortano down here. At least we learned one thing already."

We stepped around a corner into an alley full of garbage and kept an eye on the foursome at the table. The muscle pulled out a cellphone and made a ten-second call.

"That call could've only been one of two things," Clark said. "Either he warned Giordano to get out of town, or he invited him to come play. I'm hoping for the latter."

When the show was over, we left the alley and walked up an incline toward a bakery and meat market on opposite corners. Before we made it to the corner, seven guys who looked a lot like the four from the table stepped from a doorway and onto the sidewalk in front of us.

"Oh, look," I said. "They sent out a welcoming party."

I was not looking forward to seven-on-four fisticuffs with the scar on my head still not fully healed, but it looked like we were about to dance.

The seven guys were reduced to five in less than a second when Hunter and Clark sent crashing blows to the first two would-be assailants. They melted like butter, but their buddies weren't yet intimidated.

Hands went for waistbands, and to my surprise and delight, they came out with batons and slapjacks instead of pistols. The first man with a baton stepped into me and planted his left foot solidly in front of mine. The next thing he *planned* to do was bring the baton down on my head, but I had another plan. I pivoted on my left foot and sent a crushing right kick to the man's knee. It folded backward, and suddenly, I had his baton.

I didn't hesitate to watch knee boy go down. I raised the baton into the air and destroyed the collar bone of the next closest aggressor. His will to fight faded with his ability to stay on his feet.

Singer threw a nasty head-butt into the next guy's face, and blood flew in every direction. Our sniper took a step back, shook off the blow, and reached up to wipe his brow. When he pulled his hand down, he held one of the man's teeth between his thumb and index finger, then tossed the tooth to the man as he squirmed in pain on his back. "Here, put that under your pillow. Maybe the tooth fairy will bring you some brains."

Clark and Hunter made short work of the two remaining losers, and we thundered through the door they'd exited. What awaited us on the other side of the door was nothing like we'd faced in the street.

## Chapter 33
### *Remember Me?*

We moved through the door and into the dark interior of the building, where streams of light filtered in through holes in the roof and broken windows. Our eyes slowly adjusted, and objects began to take shape.

"What is this place?" Hunter whispered.

"It's some kind of warehouse," I said. "Have you got a light?"

"Yeah, but lights make awfully good targets. Let's keep moving."

We continued our progression into the building and listened for movement as we went. Other than traffic sounds coming from the street, the space was silent. The longer we stayed in the darkness, the more our eyes adjusted, giving us depth perception and relieving our disorientation.

The four of us moved almost silently and far enough apart that we'd not only be difficult to detect, but almost impossible to take down with one attack.

A narrow ribbon of light shone from beneath a door near the back of the space, and we all noticed it simultaneously. We moved toward the door with Clark and me leading the advance while Hunter and Singer watched our six. An iron ladder led up the wall to our left and onto a loft above. The ladder was covered with fine dust but no tracks, so the loft likely offered no threat. We continued beneath the overhang and approached the door.

Clark whispered, "I'll breach. You cover."

I drew my pistol and gave Clark room to work. He lunged forward and landed the heel of his boot just below the doorknob, and the flimsy structure collapsed under his force. Splinters of wood exploded inward, and I stepped into the light with my pistol at the ready. Hunter and Singer turned to make entry behind me, and that's when it happened.

Four men armed with light machine guns landed behind us, even with the ledge of the loft. Four seasoned, battle-hardened, covert operatives walked into the most obvious ambush imaginable.

Clark had drilled into our heads his combat mantra: Violence of action . . . speed of response.

We didn't waste a second. Clark and Singer went left, while Hunter and I dived to the right with fire belching from the muzzles of our pistols as we went. The air was full of lead, both outgoing and incoming. Hunter and I landed side by side on the concrete floor and scampered behind a wall of wooden crates. If the crates were empty, there was little hope of them stopping any incoming fire, but if our luck was good, they'd be full of something dense and hard.

Automatic machinegun fire rattled through the warehouse, punctuated by sporadic pistol fire from my team. A brief pause came in the pattern of fire, and I took the opportunity to sneak a look at our adversaries. Two were down, two more were reloading, and a fifth man was moving slowly away from the fight. Our time had come to make our move.

I yelled, "Hit 'em!"

Pistol fire poured down on the two men reloading their machine guns, and we stepped over their wilting bodies in pursuit of the fifth man. He made the door before any of my team, so we picked up the pace.

I strained through the darkness to find my team. "Is anybody hurt?"

Three shouts of "Negative!" came in return, and the chase was on. As we burst through the door and back onto the street, our eyes were murdered by the mid-morning sun, but we didn't slow down. Hunter and I went right, while Singer and Clark turned left.

"We've got him!" I roared as the man's silhouette shot around a corner in front of us.

We gave chase, accelerating with every stride, and I could hear footfalls behind us keeping pace. Hunter was faster than me, but my strides were longer, so we stayed side by side for the first half mile of the chase. The man we were chasing was fast, but we were gaining with every block. We made a turn to the south toward the river and started down the slope.

As we neared the bridge across the river, our prey knocked a man off a motorized bike and straddled the machine. If we didn't find something faster than the bike, the pursuit was over. Two more motorized bikes, considerably larger than the one our target had commandeered, came down the slope from behind us.

Hunter and I shared a knowing glance and drew our pistols. We sighted on the innocent riders, and they slid to a halt, sending their bikes tumbling toward us.

I grimaced. "We're really sorry, but we need your bikes."

Hunter and I mounted the bikes and opened the throttles. We weren't going to break any land speed records, but we were gaining on our runner. I shot a glance over my shoulder to see Clark and Singer helping the two downed bikers back to their feet.

We raced across the four-lane intersection and hit the bridge across the Matanza River. We hadn't studied anything outside the La Boca area, so I didn't know where we were heading, but as long as it wasn't into another ambush, I didn't care.

As we drew closer to our target, the man turned to check our progress. There was no mistaking his face. He was the same man I'd handcuffed to the cannon—the man who'd burned my house to the ground—and I was about to make him pay.

He turned left into a container yard where a series of gantry cranes were unloading a pair of cargo ships. We followed him through every turn, even though his bike was smaller and nimbler. The power of our bikes made up for his maneuverability.

He turned down the long alley beneath the cranes and opened the throttle hard. If he didn't make another turn, we'd catch him before he reached the end of the dock. Every few seconds, he looked over his shoulder as we grew ever closer. I took the gamble and drew my pistol left-handed. I held the throttle full open with my right, and sent a pair of shots toward Giordano. The first shot missed wide left, but the second caught his back tire, sending his bike into an out of control dance.

The bike squirmed and twisted beneath him, but he didn't go down. The edge of the dock loomed only feet ahead of him as he fought desperately to get the bike under control. I watched as his front tire left the dock, and I hit the brakes to avoid following him into the filthy water.

At the last possible second, Giordano leapt from the bike and grabbed the rigging of the gantry crane overhead. He swung himself violently through the air and landed against the steel framework of the crane.

Hunter and I slid our bikes to a stop and took aim on Giordano as he climbed the structure of the crane. My first shot clanged off the steel just beside his head, and the slide of my pistol locked to the rear. I plunged my thumb into the magazine release and reached for my spare magazine on my left side. My hand found nothing where my spare mag should've been.

"I'm dry!" I yelled to my partner.

"Me, too!"

I threw my useless pistol into the water and started up the framework of the crane. Giordano was at least twenty years older than Hunter and me, but he moved like a cat as we chased him up the crane.

My head pounded with every stride, and my breath came harder as my body grew weary in the climb.

"You okay?" Hunter shouted from beneath me.

"Yeah, I'm just running low on juice."

"I'm coming around you," he said as he picked up his pace and passed me on his way up the structure.

Giordano was on the upper deck of the crane, his hands on his knees, and his chest heaving. Hunter topped the crane and sprinted toward him. The instant before Hunter's shoulder would've collided with the hit man, Giordano stepped off the platform and let his body fall six feet, then caught the railing of the platform with his fingertips. Hunter's momentum was too much to overcome, and he left the platform a hundred feet above the Matanza River.

I watched my partner fall and prayed he'd enter the water feetfirst. Anything else would mean certain death.

Giordano grunted as he struggled to climb back to the platform, but I was on him before he could get a foot over the rail. I didn't see Hunter hit the water, but I heard the sound. It wasn't the sound of boots hitting the water, but I couldn't focus on that until I dealt with Giordano hanging beneath me by his fingertips.

I sent the heel of my right boot into the knuckles of his left hand, and his grip failed as blood and flesh peeled from bone. He was left hanging by one hand, and I knelt on the platform directly above him.

I looked into the face of evil and saw fear. I lay down on the platform and hung my shoulder across the rail, taking his wrist in my hands. "Remember me? The last time I saw you, I was handcuffing you to a British cannon."

His eyes closed as realization overtook him.

"You burned my house to the ground, and you killed the Judge's wife. He showed you mercy, but I'm all out of that particular kindness."

His hand trembled under the weight of his two hundred pounds, and he began to negotiate. "I know who killed your president."

He suddenly had my attention. "Talk now," I ordered.

"They came to me. They needed a dummy sniper. I wouldn't take the hit, but I gave them some names. They found Landon Barrier, and he took the money."

"Who are *they*?" I demanded. "Give me a name, or you're going down the hard way."

His grip on the railing failed, and he was left suspended by the wrist, dependent entirely on the strength in my hands. His weight was more than I could bear for more than a few more seconds.

My arms trembled, and I gritted my teeth. "Give me a name."

"It was an Arab. Jameel Bin Hitari. Now, pull me up."

I stared into his soulless eyes and whispered, "I'm sorry, Loui, but I'm going to have to let you down."

The climb back down the framework of the crane felt as if it took a lifetime. I didn't watch Giordano's body collide with the deck of the freighter below, but the report was unmistakable.

At the base of the crane, Singer waited beside the open door of the van, and Clark sat impatiently behind the wheel.

I met Singer's eyes and asked, "Hunter?"

Singer pressed his lips into a thin line and motioned for me to get in the van. The sickening feeling in my stomach was almost too much to bear as I stepped into the vehicle.

A pair of dripping wet arms flew around my neck, and Stone W. Hunter cried out, "Did you see that? It had to be a nine point seven, at least. I never made a splash, man."

\* \* \*

When we landed back at Saint Marys, Penny, Skipper, Maebelle, and Mongo, our gentle giant whose heart had been crushed by Anya's departure, stood in the doorway of the hangar with arms open wide.

We shut down the Citation and descended the stairs into the arms of the best welcome-home party I'd ever seen.

Mongo laid his island-sized hand on my shoulder. "I can't believe you went on a mission without me."

I squeezed his huge arm. "You had enough on your mind. I wasn't willing to shovel another load into your lap."

The strongest man I'd ever known stood with his eyes cast between the toes of his boots and his broken heart evident in the lines of his weary face. "I think I know where Anya is."

# About the Author

**Cap Daniels**

Cap Daniels is a former sailing charter captain, scuba and sailing instructor, pilot, Air Force combat veteran, and civil servant of the U.S. Department of Defense. Raised far from the ocean in rural East Tennessee, his early infatuation with salt water was sparked by the fascinating, and sometimes true, sea stories told by his father, a retired Navy Chief Petty Officer. Those stories of adventure on the high seas sent Cap in search of adventure of his own, which eventually landed him on Florida's Gulf Coast where he spends as much time as possible on, in, and under the waters of the Emerald Coast.

With a headful of larger-than-life characters and their thrilling exploits, Cap pours his love of adventure and passion for the ocean onto the pages of The Chase Fulton Novels series.

Visit www.CapDaniels.com to join the mailing list to receive newsletter and release updates.

Connect with Cap Daniels

Facebook: www.Facebook.com/WriterCapDaniels
Instagram: https://www.instagram.com/authorcapdaniels/
BookBub: https://www.bookbub.com/profile/cap-daniels

Made in the USA
Coppell, TX
14 March 2024